I0726661

As Far As We Knew

Award-Winning Author
Alyssa Milani

This is a work of fiction. All of the characters, organizations, and events portrayed in this novel are either products of the author's imagination or are used fictiously.

Content Warning: **As Far As We Knew is intended for ADULT readers only.** There are mature themes/subject matter and sexual content not intended for readers under the age of 18. Thank you.

Copyright © 2024 by Alyssa Milani

All rights reserved

No part of this book may be reproduced, or stored in a retrieval system, or transmitted in any form or by any means, electronic, mechanical, photocopying, recording, or otherwise, without express written permission of the author. Not for AI use or study.

ISBN: 978-1-7388834-6-2

Edited by Christine Wheary

Cover by Juniper Hartmann

My Jordan.

PROLOGUE

It didn't take more than an instant for the two sets of green eyes to find each other in the dimly lit bar. Loud Irish music blared through the crowd, overtaking the conversations. Smoke floated listlessly in the air, even though in a nonsmoking environment, people always seemed to light up when drinking a pint or two when the terrasse doors were open.

Without skipping a beat, he made his way to her and sat down, resting his forearms on the bartop. With a smile, he inhaled her floral scent. Aspects were uniquely familiar with it. Hints of roses and cinnamon, something he'd remember come morning.

"Hey," he said, shifting his beer so the label pointed toward him before looking over at her. Blush formed on his cheeks at the way her lips curled into a grin, her long lashes batted twice before settling on lips, then meeting his gaze for the night. "I've never met anyone with green eyes before."

"Is that your pickup line?" she asked with a chuckle, sipping her tequila sunrise.

He shook his head, a nervous laugh left him and he dropped his head. "No, not at all. Just pointing out the one thing we have in common."

She took the orange slice off her glass and bit into it; a single drop of juice rolling down her chin. "We green-eyed people have a secret club, you mustn't have gotten the memo," she teased, wiping the juice from her chin.

"Always late for the party." He drained his beer,

waving over the bartender and ordering two tequila sunrises.

Brushing her long brown hair off her shoulder, she leaned an elbow on the bar and she turned on her seat to face him, her chin resting on her hand after that. Breathtaking was an understatement when describing her. The way the black dress hugged her curves and accentuated her breasts, how her pouty lips curled into a grin whenever they locked eyes, and how her cat-like eyes thinned slightly when scanning him — he was a goner and he didn't even know her name.

"Tell me something about yourself, green eyes." He turned to face her as well, a tattooed arm resting on the bartop and his hand hung off the edge. Their legs brushed together, igniting a rose tint in their cheeks.

She didn't hesitate when she crossed her legs, moving her foot slightly on the back of his calf. "Like what?"

Your name for starters, but he didn't say that out loud and he couldn't understand why. He needed to know everything about this girl, yet his nerves were getting the better of him.

Their drinks were placed on the bartop and the bartender added extra orange and lime slices to hers. Her shoulders shimmied slightly, taking another orange slice, biting into it before stirring her drink, and returning her attention to him.

"What's your favorite color?" he asked, clinking their drinks together.

Gulping half of it, he watched as she studied him, taking on the sharpness of his jawline, the slant in his eyes, and the way his Adam's apple bobbed as he drank.

Her foot grazed the back of his calf again and she smiled, leaning forward. "Gray."

Arching an eyebrow, he leaned in, too, inhaling that scent. "That's your favorite color? Gray?"

She nodded, sipping her drink and leaning in again. "Black is devoid of anything. White absorbs everything. And well, all those vibrant colors never truly did it for me. But gray, it's like the middle man. A little bit of everything for everyone."

He nodded, staring at her mouth as she spoke. Her beautiful supple lips and the way her tongue licked them at the end of her explanation. "Never thought of it like that."

She *tsked*, clinking his drink. "That's because you look at what's in front of you instead of all the things the world has to offer, my good man."

"Yeah? Like what?"

Stabbing a maraschino cherry in her glass, she bit down on it and slowly chewed as she thought of an answer. He did the same, pulling the stem off the cherry and tossing it on the bartop, watching that tongue dart out of her mouth once more.

"Lemme ask you," she started, finishing off her drink and flagging down the bartender for two more. "Do you believe in an afterlife?"

Finishing off his drink, he took the orange slice and smirked, holding it out to her. That smile was killing him slowly. She was stunning with a rawness and natural beauty to her. Even the way her eyes were painted in a dark shadow, and how her long brown hair fell in waves. Something about this woman was like a dream.

Taking his hand, she leaned forward and bit down on the slice, holding his gaze as she did it. All he thought about was what she'd look like when she woke up in the morning. Would that makeup be smeared? Would her long hair be wild and crazy? Would she wake up with the smell of him all over her?

That was the important question.

Because as she stared at him with her eyebrows raised, the sight of her gaze like this as she blew him—he knew she was coming home with him tonight. There was no stopping that.

He cleared his throat, wiping juice from the corner of her mouth. "Define afterlife."

"The place we go after we die. What other afterlife would I be talking about?" She laughed, leaning her head on her hand. "But then again, it depends on what you believe in. Some would say we all go to heaven, right? Then others believe in reincarnation. And then…well, there's the darker side of people who believe once our cognitive mind shuts off, everything is done. Just, finished."

He soaked in her words, nodding as she spoke and letting his mind wander to the parts of his brain he rarely used. "Never thought about it like that."

She hummed, dropping her hand and resting it on his forearm still leaning on the bartop. The feel of her hand on his sent a shiver down his spine, and goosebumps rose on his exposed skin shortly after. "And then there's the doofuses like me who believe in ghosts." She laughed at herself. "Like when we die, our souls roam around the world, watching our loved ones grow until they join us. And when we're finally ready, we just shut off, too."

"That's morbid," he said, turning his arm so he could run his fingers along the back of her upper arm as her elbow rested gently in his palm.

"Maybe." She tilted the glass at him, then sipped it. "But death is scary, y'know. It would be cool if we could be aliens and when our time on this planet is done, we're just shot out to another planet or dimension, or what have you, and are born again. Living a new life with new people. They say, when you die you see a flash of light, and when you're born that same flash of light comes to you. What if that flash of light isn't all the nerves and brain activity shutting down, but beams of light taking you somewhere new?"

They were two drinks down together, not including the ones they drank before noticing each other. She felt alive and light for the first time in months, and he wanted to stop drinking so he could remember every detail of her face and the way she spoke her words—but another two drinks were placed on the bartop and she smiled, clinking his glass again.

"Think you're onto something, green eyes."

She giggled, leaning closer to him as her heart pounded in her ears. He felt it, too, swallowing slowly. "I'm kinda a conspiracy nerd," she admitted, scrunching her nose.

He smirked, leaning closer as well. "Wouldja look at that, I'm kinda into conspiracy nerds."

Raking her teeth on her bottom lip, her left hand propped nicely on his thigh, inching closer to him. At this point, his heart was blanching at the tip of his tongue. He needed on those lips. It was his life's purpose to consume them.

Which he did.

His fingers brushed the back of her arm and his other hand curled at the back of her neck, pulling her forward. "I wonder if you taste as good as you smell."

That perfect smile shone brighter on her face. "Fuck around and find out."

As soon as their lips touched, the universe itself shifted, causing the noise around them to stop. Nothing mattered but this moment, everything else in life could wait until they united.

His fingers splayed, getting lost in her hair. The way her tongue felt against his sent a moan to seep from her lips. This was it for him. This connection the experienced. This once-in-a-lifetime moment where they would be in the same bar at the same time, matching green eyes finding each other out of the herd. Fate called to them and they answered.

The longer they kissed, the more they realized they weren't going home alone tonight. No, they would wake up in the morning together. Hungover and ready to go again.

She pulled away first, licking saliva from her lips. "It's funny, I don't even know your name."

"Likewise, green eyes."

She chuckled, tilting her head. "Tell me, what's your favorite color?"

A laugh escaped him, making her smile grow again. Those perfectly straight teeth were hard for him to look away from. And the way her almond-shaped eyes squinted when she laughed, made him want to make her laugh all the time. Her eyes were magnificent.

"Green, I guess. I never really thought of it. But I always liked the color green."

She nodded, nodding her head at his jacket draped on his lap. "Is that why your bomber jacket is green? And your shoes?" A cackle escaped her. "Your Converse are marker green."

He frowned, staring at her in confusion. "Marker green?"

"Yeah, you know the green. The ones that come in a box of Crayola markers for school."

He hadn't thought about it like that, but as he looked down at his shoes, they truly did look like the green from those broad tip markers. "I'm sure there's a better name for that shade."

She nodded as a fourth drink was placed in front of them. "Probably, but you knew the color as soon as I said it."

"That I did."

She did her routine; ate the orange slice and took a sip of her drink before tilting her head to look at him. "Tell me, what's something interesting about you?"

He chuckled, wondering where the heck he could begin. There was a whirlwind of interesting facts about his life, but he didn't want to scare her away or make her want to run for the hills if he revealed any of them. At least not tonight.

"I'm secretly obsessed with aliens, so the fact that you

brought them up—"

"Gave you an instant boner, didn't it?" She laughed, leaning forward to kiss his cheek. "It's okay, I—"

"Hey," a curly-headed woman yanked on her arm. "C'mon, I think it's time you head home."

His green-eyed beauty pouted, taking her things, then stopped and winked at him. "You coming with me?"

He didn't hesitate and dropped a few bills on the bartop, lacing his fingers with hers as they headed to an Uber waiting out front. He wasn't buckled in yet before her lips found his and they made out all the way to an apartment complex. He'd never been to this part of town before—owning a penthouse downtown and all—but he liked the quaint pale blue building with white metal stairs on either side to gain access to the second floor.

Her friend scowled at him when they climbed out of the Uber and she remained, rolling her eyes at his green-eyed beauty.

"Your friend seems upset," he said, following her up the stairs to the first apartment on the second floor.

His green-eyed beauty unlocked the door and turned around, biting her bottom lip. "Her fiance owns the bar and she hates going home without him. That's just jealousy because I get to bring you home and show you what a bad little girl I can be."

He growled, slamming his lips on hers before he lifted her and stumbled into a very dark apartment.

Things clattered from her purse and she pulled her phone out, laughing as they stood in the middle of her apartment. "Keep walking straight until you find my bedroom."

"What happened to your lights?" His lips met her neck as he staggered in a semi-straight line toward the open bedroom door.

She licked from his neck to his lips, sending a shiver through him. "You picked me up before I could turn them on."

The bedroom had a faint blue glow to it from the lava lamp in the corner. A large queen-sized bed lay in the middle with pale gray sheets neatly tucked. He dropped her on the bed, standing tall, watching her. The way she kicked off her high heels and slowly peeled out of her thong, he knew he was going to destroy this woman tonight. Ravish her until they lay there, out of breath and satisfied.

He stripped off his clothes faster than that slinky black dress left her and separated her legs around him. "You're so fucking beautiful."

Biting his bottom lip and pulling it toward her, she purred. "Right back attacha."

Shoving his head between her legs, he lapped her clit a few times until a moan bounced off the walls. Its sound trumped her laughter and now he needed inside her, badly.

He gripped his cock, and slid it into her moistened entrance, groaning as he did. She felt like paradise, he felt like heaven. It was a match made and they didn't even realize.

The room span, slick bodies rubbed against each other, and moans danced in the quiet.

This wasn't an unexpected encounter for her, nothing

something she'd blush about in the morning. But for him, one-night stands weren't something he necessarily enjoyed. Yet there he was, riding a queen he knew he'd never forget.

Biting her breast, he thumped, harder, deeper, and grunted with every thrust. Her nails dung into his back, scratching down his muscular frame and gripping his ass. He moaned loudly and slowed his movements as her fingers tickled his hole. This was new to him and something struck. A lust he never imagined. A bond he'd never experienced. An infatuation with someone so breathtaking. And he smiled, licking up the side of her neck, then biting down on her jaw.

"Fuck, baby," he breathed, his hot breath fanning her neck. "Do that again and I'll come."

She moaned, slithering her hand between them. "Wait for me."

Gripping her wrist, he smirked, tossing her legs over his shoulder. "I *need* to do that, let me do that."

His thumb pressed to her clit, diddling it rapidly. They way she pulsated around his cock made it hard for him to hold back. But he'd do it. He'd hold it in until she came undone.

And she did.

Her back arched, and a cry of pure pleasure escaped her. He was right there, right behind her, milking every last drop of his cum deep inside this wonderful woman.

There was no stopping after that first go. She straddled him for the second, her tits bouncing against her ribcage, and then he got her on her knees for the third go, playing with her clit as he slipped a finger inside her tight, pink ass and finished inside her for the third time that night.

And yet, when they lay there out of breath and satisfied, hand gripped tightly between them, he knew he couldn't stay the night.

Life would get in the way in the morning and he couldn't let that happen. Not to her. She deserved only the best.

She kicked her lips, her bare chest rising and falling before she gasped. "It's almost four o'clock in the morning."

He laughed, bringing their twined hands to his lips. "I had fun tonight."

She smiled back, swallowing nervously. "Me too."

Kissing her pillowy lips once more, he got out of the bed and changed, smirking whenever he caught her checking him out.

But who was he kidding? This gorgeous woman was all his eyes could feast upon.

When his last shoe was tied tightly, she got out of bed, slid into a pair of underwear, and pulled a tank top over her head. Bite marks lined her ass, scratch marks decorated her back. He couldn't wait to do it again, and again, and again…

"What's your address?" he asked, clearing his throat.

She made her way to him, long hair in disarray on her head as she took his phone and typed in her address, grinning when she handed it back. "Lemme walk you to the door."

With hesitation in his step, he breathed slowly, following her through her apartment. Books scattered the dining room table, coffee mugs lined the kitchen sink, and a flannel shirt hung off the back of the couch in the living room.

He didn't want to leave, but he knew if he stayed, they'd be doing nothing but fucking for the rest of the weekend.

He stepped out into the cool morning, rubbing his eyes. "Can I see you again?"

She chuckled, rising on the tips of her toes to kiss him, tapping his chest. "Your Uber is here," she said against his lips, kissing him delicately once more.

He licked the taste of her from his lips, smiling down at her and nodding. This sensation burst brought him, a longing to come home to her. Something he's never experienced before.

And yet, he walked away. Jogging down the steps to the Uber out front, he left with so much as a glance back at her and a wave, blowing her a kiss before the door shut and he got into the car filled with wonderment of if he'd ever see the woman of his dreams again.

As Far As We Knew

CHAPTER ONE - ALORA ASHTON

My best friend, Annie Green, is having her gender reveal today—kind of doubling as a Jack and Jill baby shower. Usually, I'd mind since I'm the only single one left in our friend group. I'm constantly on the sidelines keeping score for her board game nights. She's been my ride-or-die since we were kids, but ever since she got married, then pregnant, she hasn't been the best friend I've known for years. Our lives have changed, I knew it would happen when life took hold. It's been less partying, and more birthday parties or gender reveals. It's loads of fun.

Insert eye roll here.

It's awkward at board game nights being the third wheel, and even more embarrassing when I want to go out and everyone is in bed by nine or can't go out because they can't find a sitter.

But that's what I get—the reputation I ooze as the slutty friend. And once upon a time, they were, too, before they met their person.

My person just doesn't exist.

I blow a breath through my lips and hold my head high with my shoulders back. I'm great at acting like nothing's wrong. Been doing it for years and no one has noticed. What's another party that's not my style where everyone pokes fun at me because I like to sleep around and completely ignores the fact that I'm a medical student?

You can do this.

Walking right into Annie's house, I flip my long brown hair over my shoulder. I've let it grow out to the middle of my back. Sometimes it gets in my way, and strands of hair are everywhere all the time. But it's pretty. Truthfully, the way I've been feeling lately, my brains and looks are all I have going for me.

"Alora," Annie squeals, doing a little two-step jog toward me. Her deep brown eyes are teary-eyed, and it could only mean one thing—Kelvin gave her flowers. Pink roses, I'd put money on it. "You're early." She embraces me and I leave a kiss on her cheek. "You can help me set up." She claps her thin manicured hands as her thick blonde curls bounce on her shoulders. "I'm so excited to play some games."

Gosh, just the thought of playing another "guess-the-shit" game is literally making me nauseated. But I laugh, pretending I'm all for it, and hold up the gift bag. Walking into a baby store was horrendous. Everything is overpriced, tacky, and *so* not for me. But I'd do anything for her. She's like my sister and the only person in my life I trust.

"I'm raiding your liquor cabinet first, then I'll help. *If* I'm feeling up for it." I stick my tongue out and she rolls her eyes with a grin.

Kelvin snorts from the kitchen, arranging pink roses in a vase on the marble island. *Called it.* "Whose bed did you stumble out of his morning to need a drink at 10 A.M.?"

Been here for less than five minutes, and I'm already

accused of my adventurous adultery. It's something I'm used to, so I roll my eyes and jab him in the ribs.

I'd say I blame them, that they're disrespectful pricks. But they aren't. I do end up in someone's bed most Friday nights. It's usually the same guys, but sometimes it's a fresh face. Like last night. A night I desperately wanted to forget — and not because the sex wasn't good. What he and I shared was incredible, beyond words and reality. I've never connected to someone on an emotional level or a physical one. Which is why I'd do anything to shake him from my thoughts.

Guys like him don't exist.

Guys like him don't want to settle down — I don't want to settle down.

Love doesn't exist and I will prove it to anyone who says otherwise.

***

It was a typical night out.

Leila and I got wasted at a local Irish pub her fiancé owns. Drinks were flowing and the music was thumping. The vibe was in check and I planned on getting hammered, knowing I wouldn't be able to let loose for a little with finals coming up. It was my last hurrah for a minute.

After my second tequila sunrise, I felt eyes on me, and when I scanned the crowd and found my culprit, my body reacted to his stare. My cheeks heated up, and goosebumps spread along my skin like wildfire. His short messy brown hair, devilishly green eyes, and toned body I couldn't wait to undress. I spotted him staring at me from the end of the bar. Smug little smirk I needed to taste.

Those big green eyes matched mine, and I couldn't say no. Especially when he came over and offered to buy me a drink.

He bought me one.

Then another.

And after the third we kissed.

When he ordered a fourth, Leila pulled me away and said we should get going.

So, I invited him over.

He downed the fourth drink and followed us to an Uber. We made out the entire way to my apartment, swapping saliva like the sky was falling. Maybe it was. It didn't matter. Being with this mysterious stranger I couldn't get enough of was new to me. Taking a stranger home, however, was not.

But there was something different about him.

Something unique that my heart thumped for wildly.

I've never had a conversation with someone I was interested in more than riding their face. It scared the living daylights out of me but I was too drunk to overthink it. Yet the way my stomach ached with curiosity, I knew I'd be fucked.

Leila stayed in the Uber when it dropped me off, sighing heavily. She constantly told me to change my ways, that med students shouldn't be this loose.

But I still waved goodbye to her as my mystery man and I stumbled to my front door.

We were a mess of kisses when we walked into my apartment, knocking over my favorite Venetian glass vase I purchased over my summer in Italy a few years ago. Although, it didn't bother me until I woke up this morning.

He scanned my apartment quickly before we went to my room. He tossed me on the bed, arching an eyebrow as I slowly took off my thong and threw it at him. The way he ran his fingers through his brown hair, styled in this messy way, had me shivering.

As soon as we were naked, he crawled on top of me and took me raw. I don't usually go for this—no, I never went for this—but I was too fucked-up to notice until I woke up with his semen all over my thighs.

We tore up my bed three times before calling it a night.

He left, thankfully, on his own around four in the morning.

We kissed goodbye.

And that was that.

***

"No one, unfortunately," I lie, putting a strawberry in my mouth.

Annie's mom waggles her finger at me. "One day, all that promiscuity will catch up with you."

I chuckle, taking orange juice from the fridge. "How? I'll go dry? They have lube for that." Finding vodka in the cupboard, I make a screwdriver to get through this hangover.

She rolls her eyes, her cheeks growing red. She's never liked me. From the moment Annie brought me over, her mother has had it out for me.

Alora's a bad influence, she'd say.

But what she doesn't know is my promiscuity caused

Annie to come out one night and meet Kelvin in all his glory. I urged her to talk to him, only to find out he's a defensive player for a professional hockey team. They met a year ago, were married within three months, bought a home two months after that, and now they have a baby on the way.

You're welcome.

Annie squeezes my shoulders, bringing her mouth to my ear and whispering her usual warning when I'm around her mother. "Be nice."

I'm always nice; her bitchy mother doesn't realize what a snob she can be. But for the sake of my best friend, I'll keep my snarky comments to myself and pretend this day is the best.

CHAPTER TWO – SCOTT WESLEY

Guzzling back an energy drink, I pull up to Kelvin's. I don't know why he invited some of the team to attend a gender reveal. That's something girls do. But he's one of my best friends. I'd do anything for him. Even sit through a gender reveal/baby shower.

Pinching the bridge of my nose, I try to wake the hell up. I only got to bed at a quarter past five after leaving this bombshell's apartment around four this morning. I wasn't planning on going out last night. I'm kind of getting tired of it. Always the same women gushing over us because we're pro hockey players. I try to keep it casual and let them flirt a little, but I never kiss them and I never take them home. I try to be respectful like that.

But last night when Brett and Marshall wanted to go out, I figured what the heck. We've had a great undefeated week, might as well celebrate.

Well, that celebration was brought to a standstill when I spotted her sipping a tequila sunrise at the other end of the bar. I was hooked and I didn't even know her name.

Shit, I still don't.

I bought her a couple of drinks, and she was interested in what I had to say. I don't think she realized who I was. I don't think it mattered to her. She wanted to know me, not my status. And we talked for at least two hours about life and the universe. The most eye-opening conversation I've ever had.

Well, after four drinks with her, she invited me over…more like I was leaving with her whether she invited me or not. I couldn't let her go, not yet.

We made out in the Uber the whole way to her apartment, all the while her friend kept giving me death glares when I came up for air. Don't think she approved, but I don't care. I got to spend the night with an angel, and no one can take that away from me.

When I tossed her on the bed, I stared at her, imagining myself doing this often. Living with her, sleeping with her, starting a life.

And that's not like me.

I snapped out of it as soon as her thong hit my chest and that sexy little black dress was pulled over her head. I focused and got back into the headspace of what I was going to do with her.

I flirt with women and never see them again. Sometimes I'll sleep with them, but only when we have an out-of-town game. I don't like the reputation some of the guys have. The scandals and maybe-babies that are brought their way. Not happening. So, whoever I hook up with, I make sure to wrap it double-time, and like I said, always out of town.

But last night I slept with her, and as luck would have it, I never got her number.

We had the best conversation that trumped any lay,

and I don't even know her name.

And I don't think I'll ever see her again.

When she kissed me goodbye this morning, a tired smile touched her face and it felt like I was heading off to practice and I'd be home for dinner to kiss those lips again.

I wonder if she felt it, too.

What if it was all a dream? *Please, God, no.*

Fixing the collar of my bomber jacket, I crack the bones in my neck and exhaled. "All right, let's do this."

Kelvin and I go way back. We started on the farm team and made our way to the big leagues. We were on separate teams, at first. But after bitching to our managers and barking at our agents—throwing a little money at something—I got what I wanted. Kelvin and I are finally on the same team. I'm forward and he's defense. If the two of us are in play, people better move out of the way.

I gave it my all for three years at a team that ranked one of the highest in the league, but the second Kelvin and I started playing together, we've been undefeated for three months and counting. That bodes well for me; the playoffs are at our fingertips.

When Kelvin met Annie last year, he got hitched almost immediately. *Got me a little blonde,* he told me. *This little blonde will be my forever.* And now they're having a baby.

I care for the guy like a brother, but lately, I feel like we lost that connection. He bails on hanging out a lot. And I get it, he has a wife and a baby on the way. But I don't have any of that, and sometimes, I need my friend.

Maybe he's right. Maybe settling down is the right

thing to do. We're nearing thirty, it's about time we grow some roots in this town.

Who am I kidding? I'm not laying any roots down. My soulmate doesn't exist.

Ringing the doorbell, Kelvin opens the door, chuckling. "Sorry, I'm late, dude," I say, clapping his back.

"Ah, no biggie." He smiles, the guy's happier than a pig in shit. "Come on in, the guys are in the kitchen and the girls are playing games in the living room."

I nod, handing him a gift bag and turning the corner to avoid Annie trying to get me to play a game. If she gets one of the guys in on it, we'd all have to join. She's too innocent and sweet. Half of us feel bad saying no to her.

Think that's what Kelvin likes about her, too.

Saluting at the guys in the kitchen, my heart swells knowing these men are like brothers to me. We're lucky, we get along on the ice and outside of that chaos. When we're skating, sticks on the ice, heartbeats rising, adrenaline pumping, we're focused. We know where we're supposed to go. We know each other. How we think. What our plays are.

And it's similar in the real world.

But being at a party like this, they fit in. They understand this and love this type of shit. They're all in relationships and some of them have kids.

I don't. Neither do Brett and Marshall, it's probably why they aren't here. Maybe they weren't even invited. Kelvin isn't a fan of Brett, details unknown.

When I see the baby in Corey's arms and hear the kids screaming and laughing in the other room, an unsettling feeling churns my stomach. I'm not like these guys. I'm out of place and I need a drink—stat.

Gregory shakes my shoulder as I sit down beside him. He's six feet, six inches tall with a light blonde mane of hair and beard that's all muscles and legs. A shit skater, but put him on the ice, and he's a brick wall no one can get through. "How's it going, Scotty?"

I lean my arms on the glass table that's covered in plastic baby bottles and baby blue napkins. "Exhausted."

"Had a rough night?" Kelvin asks, cracking open a beer for me.

I bring the bottle to my lips and pause. "Went out with Brett and Marshall."

Corey laughs, then shushes quietly as the baby strapped to his chest fusses, his brown locks dangling against his forehead. "Get laid?" he whispers.

The cold bubbles rush down my throat, and the ensuing smirk turns into a smile. "You know I don't pick up random chicks." But I can't help it, I'm smiling wider than I've ever smiled before. "But I made an exception last night and this one was a dream, dude."

"Oh, yeah? Do tell," Corey says, a boyish grin on his face.

Rising, I lift my shirt and show the bite marks and scratches on my chest like I was attacked by a wild cat. And truthfully, that's exactly what she was. "It was fucking crazy, dude."

Gregory sucks his teeth as his daughter, Clara, runs into the kitchen. "Watch the swearing."

I have to sensor myself for interviews and the press.

Sensor myself because my manager says I swear too damn much.

Now I have to sensor myself at get-togethers.

This kind of thing isn't for me, but what do these people know? They think all I do is drink, workout, and party. It's not true. Yes, okay, I tend to go out a couple of times a month, I get laid once in a blue moon, and I work out like it's going out of style.

But that doesn't define me.

I'm a nice person.

Caring.

Giving.

I'd give the shirt off my back to anyone in need. Yet, these people act as if my lifestyle defines me but they have no idea who I am. Kelvin knows me and still, he treats me as such. Maybe if I had this life, they'd see me and understand I'm not a player like the rest of the uninvited guys.

A wake-up call is coming. When I can't take it anymore, I'll remind them of the person I truly am that they're too blind to see.

"What's up, baby girl?" Gregory asks, moving his daughter's hair behind her ears.

"Auntie Alora said I can wear her lipstick, but only if you and Mommy say yes," she replies, big brown eyes like her dad, a pouty little mouth like her mother.

Gregory chuckles, looking at the hallway to the living room, then back at his daughter. "What did Mommy say?"

He married Sophia two years after they graduated

from high school and they now have two kids. They've been together since they were fourteen. Says Sophia's the love of his life and no puck bunny can change that.

The truth is, the fans haven't. Sure, he'll flirt with one or two, take pictures with them like all of us. When they offer him sex, he's like me and turns it down. He's one faithful bastard, I'll give him that.

"Ask Daddy," Clara says, taking a cookie off the table. "It's pink lipstick."

Before he can even answer, the bombshell from last night strides into the kitchen, holding dirty napkins in her hands. Liquid is dripping from them. She doesn't look up at first, but fuck, she's even more alluring in the daylight. I thought I'd never see her again. Thought our night was short-lived. But she's here. In the flesh.

Fuck, who is she dating? Which one of these bastards brought her here?

The real question is, why the fuck am I so jealous?

No, why the fuck do I have this urge to beat the living daylights out of them for not keeping her happy?

"What happened?" Kelvin asks, taking the dirty napkins from her.

She shrugs, rinsing off her hands. "Sammy kicked my cup over. I got most of it, but your carpet is wet."

Then she turns, eyes wide when they fall on me. I bring the bottle of beer to my lips and wink, making her smile and chuckle.

I wonder if she'll keep our night a secret. Why don't I want her to? Why is there this burning in my stomach that demands she come over and plant a kiss on me, occupy my lap, and tell these fuckers she's mine?

But fuck, what if she belongs to someone else?

Kelvin takes the dishrag from her to dry his hands. "There's more vodka, just make another drink."

"That's the plan, big man," she says, breaking eye contact with me.

Gregory looks up, scanning her backside as she bends over, looking for something in the fridge. Shit, I give her ass a glance, too.

She's less made-up today. Not as heavy on the eye makeup and a touch of pink on her lips. She's wearing a soft pink dress that hides all her curves instead of that strapless black one from last night that hugged her body.

She's breathtaking and my dick has a mind of it's own, growing by the second.

Shit.

"Can you ask my daddy, Auntie Alora? Can I wear your lipstick?" Clara says, her voice going up an octave.

Alora. Unique name for a unique woman.

I wonder if she feels this spark like I do. No, she doesn't. She's probably already in a relationship, too. *We're at a fucking gender reveal, get it together, Scotty.*

Alora reaches into the pocket of her dress and pulls out a tube of subtle pink lipstick. "See, it's sparkly. "

Clara bobs in place. "Please, Daddy."

Alora smirks, side-glancing at me. "Yeah, please, Daddy."

Gregory laughs, nodding his head as Kelvin comes to

sit back down. "Have to say, kinda hot hearing you call me daddy."

She forces a laugh and rolls her eyes. "Fuck off."

Kelvin drops a hand on the table. "Couldn't hold off on the swearing for one afternoon? There are kids here."

She crouches down and applies the lipstick on Clara's lips. "Nope." Then arches an eyebrow at him. "I'm sure they've heard way worse than *fuck off.*"

Clara snickers, wrinkling her nose as she does. Have to say, she's a cute one compared to her parents. Took only the best of both their genes.

I chuckle at Alora's comment, making Kelvin, Gregory, and Corey glance at me. She glances, too, and scrunches her nose. Fuck, why do I find that sexy?

"Alora, this is Scotty. Don't know if you met him yet. The team just signed him a few months ago." Kelvin takes his beer off the table. "Scotty, Alora. Alora, Scotty."

Rising a little, I put my hand out. "Nice to meet you, Alora."

She bites her lip and shakes my hand. "Likewise, Scotty."

As our hands meet, a warmth blooms between us. I know she feels it, too, because she looks down at my hand before releasing her grip. How could I have not recognized her from the wedding pictures? Was she there? Did I not pay attention? It was a tough time for me, but I would've noticed *her.*

When her big green eyes meet mine, I swallow hard. Just like that, I know I'm in trouble.

CHAPTER THREE - ALORA ASHTON

Well, I'll be.

The hot guy I brought home last night not only has a name but an occupation and a tie to my life.

This is not a good thing.

My flings are never brought into my home life.

They're left at bars, left in a cold bed, or invited to my apartment for one thing and one thing only.

Now, my latest conquest is sitting in my best friend's kitchen, watching me make a screwdriver.

And my hands are shaking.

Fuck.

Clara smiles, proud of the lipstick I put on her. I love making her up. Sophia lets me dress her whenever I babysit and it's like having a little doll. Babysitting Clara is my favorite thing, we're the same person with the same interests in movies and makeup. This scares me because when I look at her, I see myself as a child. Someone always in need of approval from people with the way I look and always desperate for a good time. If she grows up to become like me, then life will have done her wrong.

She pokes Gregory on the shoulder. "Don't I look pretty?"

He smiles, chuckling softly and brushing back her hair

with hands as big as her head. He's the only one of Kelvin's friends who hasn't hit on me. And that's okay because as soon as Annie started dating Kelvin, they warned me that I wasn't allowed to get with his friends. Like I'm some sort of pit bull on the verge of attacking any male with a pulse.

I'm not. They paint me in this light, looking at me surface deep instead of knowing who I truly am.

I'm picky with who I hook up with and usually stick with the same handful of guys I always sleep with. Except for last night. And I have a funny feeling it will bite me in the ass.

"The prettiest, baby girl," Gregory says, pushing her along to go back with the other kids.

She runs around the island to hug me, smiling as she does. "Don't ever let anyone tell you otherwise, my love," I add, blowing kisses at her as she runs off.

As soon as I straighten up, that same sensation from last night washes over me. That unbridled lust, that longing I didn't notice was missing. And when I look at Scotty, he's staring right at me. Those beautiful green eyes rake over my body like they did last night.

I can't lose control.

I won't lose control.

He licks his lips slowly, smirking as he brings the bottle of beer to his lips again.

Goddammit, I'm going to lose control.

Corey leans over, nudging Scotty's side. "So, tell me, how do you go from telling us you're done fooling around and the next woman you sleep with will be your wife—" He chuckles. "—to taking a woman home last night."

"Was she good?" Gregory asks.

Corey taps the table, arching an eyebrow. "Did you not see his chest? All those scratches and bite marks. You damn well know it was amazing."

Kelvin leans forward, lowering his voice. "She hot?"

Scotty's face turns red and he chuckles awkwardly, shifting in his seat. "She was…uh…she was…" He sighs, smiling at his beer as he picks the corner label. "Best sex I ever had, dude. Shit you not."

Okay, so my ego is inflated.

Although, I think he just said that because I'm in the room. But I'm still flattered.

Flustered is more like it.

"Alora?" Annie says, shaking my arm. "You didn't hear me calling?"

I stammer as the men lower their conversation. "N-no, sorry."

She whines and pouts, tugging on my arm. "I need you in there. I had no idea these things were so boring."

I cackle, sipping my drink. "What the hell am I supposed to do to make it better?"

"Take off your dress," Corey says, snickering.

I narrow my eyes at him. He's such a douchebag. I don't know how this guy is married and has a newborn. The only thing he has going for him is his money. Other than that, he's an all-around prick. But the funny part is, we get along so well. And I hate it. "You can suck a dick, Corey," I say, flipping him off.

Kelvin laughs, looking over his shoulder at me. That

cinnamon skin crinkles around his eyes. Scotty laughs, too. Something about the deepness of it makes me want to hurl.

I can't tell if it's a good thing or not, yet.

"I love you, too, Alora," Corey says, sticking his tongue out as he sips his beer.

Some day soon, these people will respect me. I guaran-*fucking*-tee it.

Annie smiles, opening her arms as she walks toward Scotty. "When did you get here?"

He stands and gives her a one-armed hug, his shirt and jacket rising. "'Bout thirty minutes ago or so."

She taps his chest and takes a cookie from the table. "Food's in the dining room if you want to eat."

He tips his beer to her and drains the rest of it, eyes on me long enough for her to notice. She takes my hand and tugs me toward the living room. "Come, come. Don't need you drinking with the boys."

I roll my eyes and groan, following her even though I'd like to sit with Scotty and pick his brain a bit more. We had the most interesting night last night. Both intellectually and physically. "Probably more fun than eating baby food."

"Oh, stop," Annie says, threading our fingers together.

"Betcha had worse in your mouth." Gregory cackles, making everyone else at the table laugh. All except for Scotty.

I don't laugh. Why would I? It's embarrassing. It's wrong, and it's hurtful.

But they don't know that. They think it's funny because I flaunt this *I don't care* attitude.

But I do care.

I don't want Scotty to think of me as these men do because I'm so much more than that.

I'm a med student, for chrissake!

But that doesn't matter to them. What matters to them are all the people I open my legs to. For once, a normal conversation would be nice. Like the one Scotty and I shared when we met.

Our conversation yesterday was the most intriguing one I've had in a while. We spoke about life and the things we want to do before we kick the bucket. We spoke about places we traveled to, our favorite food, and movies we like. We didn't introduce ourselves or discuss our jobs. We spoke about everything but that.

He didn't know me and I didn't know him.

That's probably what intrigued me the most. The unknown.

I'm dragged to the living room, and I toss a glance over my shoulder at him. He smiles when we lock eyes. An innocent smile.

Shit, I'm in trouble.

***

Not even forty minutes go by before I sneak off again. I'm all for supporting my bestie, but this gender reveal/baby shower event is not my cup of tea. The girls are talking about their experiences during pregnancy and delivery, and how it was afterward…something I can't relate to.

Slipping away, I tiptoe quickly toward Corey. He's bobbing his son, Seth, in his arms and grins at me as I approach. "Scooch over," I say nudging my hips on his shoulder, standing between him and Scotty.

Gregory points out the empty seat beside him. "Just sit here."

"You have cooties." Sticking my tongue out, Corey moves over enough for me to sit on the chair with him. "No, I want to hide between these giants so I don't have to join the ladies. If I have to hear one more story about giving birth, I might hurl."

Corey snickers, kissing Seth's head. He's cute with a head full of dark blonde hair compared to Corey's brown. Steph, his wife, is so blonde her hair is practically white. I wonder why she's not here, how did she get out of this one?

Seth reaches out to me and I scrunch my nose, taking him with a smile. "Hey, little one."

Corey leans his head on mine, draping his arm on the back of the chair. "Man, he's cute."

"Thank fuck he doesn't look like you," I tease, sticking my tongue out.

Corey flicks my ear, hissing. "Shut up, he's my twin."

Scotty laughs, his leg moving closer and grazing my knee. It's not like there's a surge of electricity coursing through me or anything. No, none of that causes my cheeks to heat up. *Holy hell, what is this feeling?*

"Kid's cute because of Steph, dude." He brings the bottle of beer to his lips, slowly licking them before taking a large gulp.

Fuck. Shit. Fucking shit I don't like the way my stomach feels right now. He was just a one-night stand, woman. Just. A. One-night stand.

Smirking, I look over at Corey. "See, even your friends think you have an ugly mug."

Corey sucks his teeth, draining the rest of his beer. "Screw all of you."

Chuckling, I scrunch my nose at the baby as he takes my hair, tugging on it with all his tiny might. "Slow your roll, little one."

Corey unfurls my hair from his grasp. "It's all good, she likes it when men do that."

Rolling my eyes so far back my sockets hurt. "You can go fuck yourself."

Again, Gregory and Kelvin laugh, but Scotty doesn't, frowning at them for being such assholes with me. I'm used to it. They look at me like one of the guys and treat me just as stupidly.

Corey wraps his arms around my shoulders, leaning his head on mine. "I'm sorry, I'm joking, I love you, don't hate me."

Elbowing him hard in the ribs, I smile down at his son who smiles largely after I do that. "Oh, you like it when I hurt Daddy, huh?"

"Ooh, don't call me daddy, I'll come." Corey snickers, shielding himself from my wrath as I hit him again. "Ahh, sorry, sorry. Don't hurt me."

Scotty's knee grazes mine again, bringing my attention to him. There's a twitch in his jaw, a wrinkle in his forehead. Is he jealous? No, maybe defensive over this little fuckface beside me. But Corey is one of the only ones I don't take his words to heart. He's an all-around prick, yes, but we look at each other like siblings and tease each other as such, too. When talking about him to people, I refer to Corey as my little brother. No harm no foul, but lately, his words are starting to sting.

"Daddy's an asshole," I say to the baby. "Can you say that? Ass-hole."

Gregory sucks his teeth. "Don't be teaching the kids to swear."

Grinning, I look up at him as Seth grabs my face. "Who do you think gets Cara to swear all the time? Hearing her say 'fuck you' is hilarious."

Reaching for the beer bottle in front of me, I take a swig of it thinking it's Corey's only for Scotty to look at me with his big green eyes and chuckle. "I know we just met and all, and I don't mind sharing, just let me know you want some first," he says.

Licking my lips, I put the beer down and my face heats up. "Sorry, I thought it was this loser's beer."

Scotty laughs, shaking his head as he holds my gaze. The way my heart palpates and sends wavelengths of excitement throughout my body is reason enough to look away and force him from my life. I don't do relationships. I most specifically don't do relationships with people my friends warned me to stay away from.

"I'm not a loser, bitch." Corey wraps his arm around my shoulders, pretending to get me in a headlock. "But if you wanted a drink, I can make you one. Beer or screwdriver?"

"Surprise me," I say, winking at the baby as I sit him down on the table with his back against my chest.

Immediately he reaches for anything in his grasp, taking the napkins and bringing them to his mouth. Scotty and I snatch the napkins away, our fingers touching and sending a shock between the both of us.

His smile falters, quickly looks away from me because he feels it, too. Fucking Christ, this is not good.

Getting up from the table, I rest the baby on my hip and join Corey in the kitchen. "Where's Steph?"

He sniffs the vodka and pours enough in two glasses. "She's still going through her postpartum. And today was a bad one, so I figured I'd give her a day to rest while I grace everyone with this masterpiece." He fans his arms out and smiles. "Perfection."

Giggling, I shake my head and drop a strawberry into my glass. "No wonder this party blows."

Gregory laughs, nearly spitting out his drink and Scotty chuckles, scanning me up and down with that smile that weakens my knees. It's the one thing about him I distinctly remember from last night. That gorgeous grin.

"You're in a fiesta mood today, I love it," Corey says, sticking his tongue out.

Taking my drink, I gulp from it and head back to the table. The pull and need to sit beside Scotty is swooping in full force, it's surprising even me.

"Mmm." Corey taps the top of my head as I sit in his spot, pulling up a chair beside mine. "Can you look at something? We noticed it this morning, and I'm not sure what the hell it is."

Putting my drink down, Corey lifts the baby's shirt to

show me his pale chunky belly I love nibbling on. But right under the baby's ribcage is a small red circle.

"What the hell is that?" Gregory asks, leaning forward.

Turning the baby onto his side for a better look, I blow a raspberry on his belly, causing a giggle to leave him. "It's nothing serious," I say, smoothing out the red mark with my fingertips. "He's got a hemangioma. I'll get you a referral for a dermatologist. He'll be fine."

"How the fuck did he get that?" Corey takes the baby from me, kissing his belly before holding him to his chest.

Lifting a shoulder, I move my dress off my shoulder to reveal something everyone believes is a scar. "I had one, see. Some cases are worse than others like mine and leave a mark, and others go away with simple medicated creams."

Corey smooths his thumb over the mark, nodding. "Will your dad take a look at it?"

It's all fun and games until they need me for something, isn't it?

Shaking my head, I gulp from my drink. "Probably not. It's fairly common." Scrunching my nose at the baby. "You'll be fine, little one."

"Sammy had one of those on the back of his neck. Doctor put him on beta blockers," Gregory says, taking a cookie to his mouth. "There's barely a mark on him anymore."

The men go into discussing how their kids give them heart attacks and how they have no idea how they're going to survive the teenage years.

All the while Scotty and I remain silent, our knees

touching under the table as if pulled together by a magnet.

And the one thing about magnets that can be dangerous is attracting the wrong things.

And this is the wrong fucking thing.

CHAPTER FOUR – SCOTT WESLEY

The gender reveal is dying down, and it feels like the time to get up and mingle.

But I can't find Alora anywhere. Annie pulled her back to the living room a second time and she never came back to the kitchen. Every so often, I'd check the hallway in hopes that those beautiful green eyes would appear. Instead, I got jabs in the ribs by Corey as he waggled his eyebrows at me.

Gregory and Sophia are sitting on the L-shaped couch in the living room, his arm draped on the back of it and she's leaning into him. It must be nice to have that closeness, that person to speak with whenever there's an issue.

I don't have that. Kelvin is the second person I call when there's a problem. Like my sister, he's on my speed dial.

Sophia snorts, tapping his leg. She's right for Gregory. Keeps him in check and holds his attention on hockey. He's happiest when she's around. "Heard you finally met your match last night."

I slide my hands in my pockets, looking down the hallway to the washroom. Quick escape if this gets too personal. "What do you mean?"

She smiles. "Best s-e-x of your life?"

Chuckling, I scratch the back of my head and nod.

"Too bad I never got her number." I scrunch my nose and shake my head. "Shit, or her name."

Corey laughs, holding his baby's legs in the air as he changes the diaper. "Best s-e-x of your life and you'll never see her again."

As if on cue, Alora opens the front door, wind blowing her dress and hair everywhere until she closes it. I found a strand of that long brown hair in my clothes when I showered this morning, something that made me smile.

She runs her fingers through that hair I tugged on last night, and flips it over her head. "Holy fuck, it's windy as shit outside."

Gregory drops his hand on his lap. "The swearing."

She sticks her tongue out and chuckles, continuing to the kitchen. I can't help it, my gaze follows her, so much so that my entire body turns as she walks away. Beauty on a pair of long legs.

Kelvin nudges my side, shaking his head. "Don't even think about it. We don't need the two of you hooking up and making it awkward."

"They already had the talk with her when you got here," Sophia adds, biting a gummy worm.

Like we're menaces to society; we need to have talks about what we do with our private lives.

I put my hands up, acting innocent. "Hey, I was just looking. Am I not allowed to look?"

"You can look, all right." Corey winks at me and stands up with Seth held against his chest. "Just remember to wear sunglasses when we have pool parties."

"Oof, the bathing suits she wears," Gregory comments, getting a punch in the chest from Sophia. "What? You're telling me you don't check her out?"

Sophia scoffs. "Well, I do. But it doesn't mean I wanna hear you gush about it."

"I'm not gushing—"

Alora makes herself known again, brushing past me and her arm grazes mine. "Gush over what?" she asks, plopping down beside Corey and reaching for a gummy worm from Sophia.

"How cute these kids are," Corey says, kissing the baby's nose.

Are they just going to lie as if they weren't talking about her like she's some piece of meat? Albeit, she's beautiful and deserves to be put on a pedestal, but she doesn't deserve to be spoken about like these pigs are doing.

Sophia taps Gregory's chest and pouts, looking at Seth. "Let's have another."

He chuckles, kissing her head. "Whatever you want, babe."

Catching Alora's gaze as she rolls her eyes. "Ugh, kill me now," she groans.

"Oh, stop." Sophia tosses some candy at her, setting the bowl on the couch. "You're just jealous." That gets another eye roll from Alora.

Kelvin taps the spot beside him on the loveseat for me to sit, leaving enough room for Annie if she wants to join us. "We're killing it, there's no doubt in my mind we're making it to the playoffs. Think we'll end up in Vancouver in two months?"

Corey groans. "Three days without my wife is going to kill me."

"Are you coming to that?" Sophia asks Alora. She looks up from her phone and frowns. "To Vancouver?"

Alora shrugs. "I don't go to the games, so why would I go to one out of the country?"

Sophia pouts again; have I mentioned how annoying she is? "Yeah, but what's a party weekend without you there?"

Alora laughs, but it's not genuine. Last night when she laughed, her smile lines would show. And she'd do this thing where she'd scrunch her nose when she thought something was funny. Now, her smile lines aren't showing. I don't think these people notice it. She fakes her smiles around them. This group has known her longer than I have, but they don't have a clue. They have this idea of who she is but have no idea what kind of woman she truly is.

I had one intimate and meaningful conversation with her and I betcha I know her better than they do.

Annie comes in with two water bottles in hand, tossing one at Alora. "What's so funny?" she asks, sitting beside me and leaning into Kelvin.

"I'm trying to convince Alora to join us in Vancouver," Sophia says, curling her legs on the couch and looking at her. "Their coach already said yes, when wives aren't usually allowed to these things. So, it's fate, Alora."

Annie gasps. "Oh, please, *please* come."

Alora stretches, arching her back and pushing out her

chest. My dick twitches, staring at her succulent breasts that were in my mouth just last night. But I force myself to look away. I have to look away before someone sees me staring.

"Hmm, I'll think about it," she says, looking at her wristwatch. "I do have to leave—"

"Booty call?" Corey snickers and she punches his knee. "Hey, we have a game tomorrow."

"And I got finals, jackass," she says snarkily.

Taking my phone from my pocket, I check the time as well; it's almost three thirty. I have nowhere to be, but leaving right now would mean I'd be able to walk her to her car.

No harm in that.

"I should head out, too. Get some sleep before tomorrow," I say through a yawn.

Annie taps my leg. "Late night?"

Rising, I zip up my jacket. "Didn't get home until five."

Kelvin whistles, rising with me and pulling me into an embrace. "Thanks for coming, man." He lowers his voice into a whisper. "Please don't do anything with Alora. For my wife's sake."

I nod, pushing my lips together. The less he knows about my time with his wife's friend, the better. No one but Alora and I will know. But it'll be super hard to keep this bombshell a secret.

We say our goodbyes, and she walks out first, leaving me like our night meant nothing. Maybe it didn't. Maybe I'm reading too much into it.

Maybe I want to read into it because I'd like something more. I wasn't lying when I said she was the best sex I ever had.

Unprotected, no less, so it felt that much better.

I'm not one to be careless. I rarely am. But I had to have her last night. We connected mentally and I needed her physically to know if it was right.

It was.

It is.

She's already at her car, searching through her purse for her keys when I walk out of the house. As if fate brought us together last night, it made us park next to each other, too.

I jog over, trying my hardest to hide my smile. But I can't. She's breathtaking. "Hey," I say, coming up to her. She lifts her eyes, smiling quickly. "Funny coincidence, isn't it?"

She nods, cold as ice compared to last night. Maybe she didn't want to remember me. I'm not easily forgettable, but the way the guys talk about her, maybe she doesn't want me to be remembered.

She sighs, looking up at me and licking her lips. "Did you get a million warnings like I did about not sleeping with you? Or are our friends so ashamed of me they have to only warn me of good-looking acquaintances?"

That comment hits me hard in the chest, taking my heart and crushing it. I was right. They don't know her at all.

"Kelvin warned me the second you walked into the kitchen," I say, leaning a hip on her car. "Then again when I said goodbye."

"Degenerates, the pair of us." She smirks, still searching through her massive purse.

I study her, the way she purses her lips, how she blinks

quickly as frustration takes hold because she can't find her keys. It's adorable.

I could get on board with adorable. I shouldn't, but I definitely could.

"It's funny how we spent an entire night together, spoke for hours, then fooled around for hours, and I only discovered your name today," I say, causing her to look up at me.

Those devilishly green eyes melt my heart.

What is this girl doing to me?

"Alora Ashton, at your service." She puts her hand out with a closed-mouth smile.

I take it, rubbing my thumb on the back of her hand. "Scott Wesley."

She chuckles but doesn't release my hand.

A beat passes and we're just staring at each other.

After another, she slowly licks her lips and nods. "Well, I guess I'll see you around."

"I guess so."

Still, we don't let go of each other's hands.

Her demeanor changes suddenly and she retracts her hand, going back to rummaging through her purse. A thought crossed her mind, something that probably crosses it every time she's in someone else's presence. I'd be self-conscious, too, if my friends thought so little of me.

"Ah-ha." She pulls her keys out and unlocks her door. "Good luck at your game tomorrow."

"Good luck with your, what did you say? Finals?" I need just a few more minutes with her. I may never get this chance again.

She nods, opening her door. "Those fucks may make fun of my partying, but I'm the most educated one in the bunch."

"What're you studying?"

She lifts a leg into her car, ready to leave like this conversation means nothing. Maybe it doesn't. Or maybe it does, but she thinks it means nothing to me. "I'm med student."

Wow. Color me impressed.

No wonder Corey asked her about the red spot on the baby's belly.

"Doctor Alora Ashton," I say, raking my eyes over her. "It would be my honor to take you to dinner sometime—"

She puts her hand up, stopping me. "Annie is my best friend, and if she warned me to stay away from you, it's either because I'm a whore and she's tired of it, or you're not a good guy. And for my self-esteem, I'll go with the latter." She gets in her car like that comment didn't sting. "So, if you'll excuse me, have a good life, Scotty."

Why does that make me want to scream and kiss her all at the same time?

Corey wasn't lying when he brought up what I said about being done fooling around. Three weeks ago, the guys were hassling me for never joining them for couples nights. And I told them I wanted to end my promiscuous ways and find a woman to love.

And by God, I found her. But she's stubborn and so misunderstood.

Yet, as I watch her taillights shrink down the road, I realize she'll be one hard nut to crack. The woman of my dreams just became a pain in my fucking ass.

CHAPTER FIVE - ALORA ASHTON

Maybe I left him a little harshly last week, but this is me, right? I open my legs to everyone and expect nothing in return.

I don't do relationships because committing to someone is chaotic. How can they love me and only me forever? It's not like I'm some prize anyone wants to win. I'm a prize they want to borrow for a night or two and return in the morning.

Scotty is no different. I'd put money on it.

Then again, if he were different, I wouldn't even care. I wouldn't try anything or let him in. My view of love is tainted. It's always been tainted because love doesn't exist. It's a false belief that people want so they won't end up alone.

Well, I hate to break it to you, but we all end up alone in the end.

My view toward love started when I was young. My parents split before I can remember, but that didn't stop my father from having a revolving door of women. No one was ever enough, but he was happy with the women who shared his bed. He and my mother never spoke, unless it was my birthday when they'd sing an off-tune "Happy Birthday" just for me. And my mother? Well, she was lonelier than the lone crumbs lodged in the corner of the room that are looked over every cleaning spree. She was forgotten, guarded, and never wanted to see another man again because of the love she had for my father.

I'd watch Mom cry most nights while looking at photos of her and Dad. They were in love once upon a time, but something fucked it up. That something was probably me.

Mom faked a smile and pretended to be happy when she was still madly in love with someone who had a new girlfriend every month.

She died when I was fourteen.

An aneurysm, the doctor's said.

Mom died of a broken heart. I'm sure of it.

I was eight years old when I officially moved in with Dad. His phone was never silent, he'd get calls and text messages nonstop. Sometimes the doorbell would ring and a pretty brunette would smile on the other side of it. Sometimes she was a blonde. Occasionally, he'd have a redhead.

I moved to the dorms after I graduated from high school, eventually moving into this apartment. At home, it was an endless revolving door of women who never seemed to satisfy him. It was like a job with the women coming and going. Punch in, punch out.

Maybe he was as depressed as Mom was. It would make sense. They married for a reason, didn't they? Or maybe they got married because of me. Did I ruin them?

Maybe they missed each other but didn't know how to express it. No, if he missed her, he'd have gone back. He didn't miss her. Why would he miss someone who cried at the thought of him kissing another woman?

I don't do relationships just like I don't do love because

it never existed in my life.

I never saw it.

Never witnessed my parents sharing a kiss under the mistletoe or a dance in the kitchen.

There was never a happy, loving moment when it came to them. All I got were falsities.

I won't get more lies from Scotty.

Staying with one person guarantees you unhappiness. *Be free, be happy, don't settle down.*

I go by that motto; I live by it. I guess I'm happy. I have my own apartment downtown, minutes from school. I'm studying for a successful career with a job lined up at my father's practice as soon as I start my residency. Life is simple. Life is good.

But maybe, just maybe, it can be a little better.

However, a man will not be the answer to that.

I finished one of my finals on Wednesday, taking all the energy out of me. I come from a long line of doctors. It would be a sin if I didn't become one, too. But holy crap, is it a handful. I've done my undergraduate degree, now I'm two years into medical school. It's a lot of work, but my father always said that with hard work, you'll sweat, you'll bleed, but the end results are incomparable to the horrors you endured to get there. *I'm trying, Dad, I really am.*

I'm on a cleaning spree, three espressos in, trying to tidy up this pigsty I call my apartment. I've been living off takeout and caffeine all week, and I haven't left this place since the gender reveal. It's well overdue.

I have nothing on but a flannel shirt that belonged to

someone I brought home a couple of years ago. He left it here and never tried to get it back. Now, it's become my lazy day shirt.

Music is blaring and I'm in the zone, twisting my hair into a messy topknot with a pencil I found under the coffee table when there are thundering bangs on my front door. I must've not heard the first set because of the music.

Putting my Swiffer down, I make for the door, tripping on the cord for the vacuum. "Motherfu—" Opening the door, I find Scotty smirking at me with two coffees in hand. "Uh…"

He raises his eyebrows curiously. "Hi?"

"What—" I swallow hard, forgetting how good he looks when he grins. His entire chiseled face lights up, and a dimple pokes out on his cheek. Holy Christ, I forgot how tall he is, too. Was I still drunk at the gender reveal or something? "Wh-what're you doing here?"

He looks behind him at the white Range Rover sitting in the parking lot outside my apartment, then back at me. "I couldn't really ask Kelvin for your number or speak to you more at the party since you shut me down—"

"And I'll do it again. I'm not dating material, shithead," I remind him, crossing my arms.

He holds out a coffee toward me, pushing his lips together in a smirk. "Yeah, I know. And before you say anything, this isn't that. I, uh." He scoffs with a chuckle. "I think I left my necklace here. Kelvin was talking to Gregory about you. Said your exams were done. Figured it was as good a time as any to come see you." He lifts a shoulder. "Got your address from the Uber I took when I left here after our night together." The nerves in his voice awaken the butterflies in my stomach.

"Necklace, huh?"

He nods, scratching his neck where a shadow of a beard seems to be sprouting. "It's a white gold chain with a moon hanging from it."

If I hadn't found that exact necklace on Sunday tucked between my headboard and my mattress, I'd think he was lying just to weasel his way into my place again.

"Yeah, come in."

I trip over the cord to the vacuum again and curse under my breath, going to my little lost and found in the kitchen. It consists of ID cards, watches, money, and jewelry. I could spend the money, but I wouldn't feel right if they asked me about it.

Yeah, I'm good-hearted like that.

I pull the chain from the bowl and dangle it in front of me. "You're lucky you came for it, I almost kept it for myself."

He puts the coffee on my counter and groans when he realizes the necklace is broken. "You didn't say anything to anyone about it, did you?"

Arching an eyebrow, I take a sip of the coffee—cappuccino without sugar. Gross. "And get an earful from Annie about sleeping with you after she warned me not to? Of course, I didn't say anything."

"In our defense, we slept together before we knew we had mutual friends," he says, putting the necklace in his pocket.

"About that." Taking my jar of sugar, I put two

spoonfuls into my coffee. "I didn't see you at their wedding, or any of the events they throw."

He nods, smiling. "I played for LA before moving out here, so coming to every event was kind of hard until Kelvin's team drafted me a few months ago." He sucks in a rush of air and looks down at the Venti in front of him, taking a slow sip before setting it down again. "Three days before they got married, my mom got sick, then died the morning of their wedding. I didn't wanna miss it, but I had other priorities."

My body reacts before my head does and I reach a hand out, placing it on top of his. I know what it's like to lose someone—a parent, no less. He's handling it a helluva lot better than I did.

I'm still a mess about it; I just hide it with studies and partying.

"Annie never said anything," I say, as if he needs an explanation. "All she said was Kelvin's best man couldn't make it."

He grins, staring at our hands. I retract mine quickly, like I just touched the hot element on a stove. The last thing I need is to feed into the thought that we could be more than I'm letting on. We can't. We won't. It was a one-time thing, our lives just happened to be mixed in with each other's.

Just a coincidence, right?

He looks around, seeing my place in disarray. "You expecting company?"

The way he says *company* is colored with a little teasing and a little jealousy. It's cute, I'll give him that.

"Nope. Been studying all week and haven't had the

chance to clean." I tuck a loose lock of hair behind my ear, realizing I probably look insane right now. My hair is wild and I'm wearing a fling's shirt with no bra. And I have on my fuzzy socks that no one has seen other than Annie—a cute little dinosaur pattern and they're all wearing Santa hats.

He shrugs out of his jacket, placing it on the counter beside his cappuccino. "What can I do to help?"

Shaking my head, I study the tattoos on his arms quickly. A traditional ship sailing through water, a swallow, a mermaid, I think maybe even an anchor. I can't tell. The colors are so vibrant, I'm surprised I didn't comment on them at the bar.

Oh, that's right, I was too busy shoving my tongue down his throat.

Or was he the one to make the first move?

"You really don't have to do that."

He smirks, lifting his drink and clinking it on mine. "I have nothing better to do."

Crossing my arms, I arch an eyebrow. "I'm not sleeping with you in exchange for maid services."

He pauses the drink at his lips. "Not expecting anything in return, sweetheart."

I waggle a finger at him. "Don't call me sweetheart."

Mirth and amusement paint his face, and shit, he looks good when he smirks. A single dimple pokes out the right side of his cheek which makes me weak in the knees.

Why does he have to be nice *and* good-looking? He's going to get me into trouble, I can feel it.

"You sure you want to clean? I mean, we don't even

know each other."

He nods, fixing the leather braided bracelet around his wrist. "We don't, but we will. I like getting to know the people I've been inside."

I roll my eyes and hand him a paper towel roll and a spray bottle, pointing at the table as I get back to Swiffering the floors. "There're four-day-old coffee stains you can try to get out, shithead."

He laughs, making his eyes squint. Gah, why do I find that adorable? *Stop!*

I trip on the cord of the vacuum *again* and curse, kicking it aside. "Fucking cock sucker."

Scotty glances up at me as I bend over and move the Swiffer under the couch. "I take it laundry was also on your to-do list?"

"If you're looking at my ass, you can rethink whatever thoughts are going through your head." I stand upright and fix the shirt, resting a fist on my hip. "I don't do relationships, *sweetheart.*"

He laughs, points the spray bottle at me, and squeezes the trigger. It's the cutest thing and it makes me want to hurl again. Why does he have to be adorable around me? Why does he have to act like a boyfriend? God, why do I fucking want to lick his face until he pins me down and shoves himself inside me again?

Oh, this isn't good.

He jerks his head at the floor, that smirk I want to sit on still present. "You missed a spot."

I narrow my eyes and get back to cleaning, knowing

full well if I spend another second with this guy, I'll either, rip his head off or shove it between my legs. It could go either way at this point.

He winks when I glance back at him and he sprays my table down, rubbing harder in one spot than the rest. I have to hand it to him, I don't think a guy has ever done this for me before. Shit, not even my father has offered to help clean my apartment. *Hire a maid*, he'd probably say. *Give her my number*, he'd probably add. Which, let's be honest, he's the reason I have this apartment in the first place.

Scotty doing this ignites a weird feeling in the pit of my stomach. No, it's not butterflies. It's nausea, I'd put money on it. I don't get butterflies over men.

At least eight songs go by and neither of us says anything to the other. We exchange glances, his eyes roam, then mine. I'm sure I flashed him at least sixty times. But I wasn't expecting company. I mean, gosh, look at me! My hair is in even more disarray and sweat is added to the mix. This poor guy has seen me at my best and now…this isn't my worst, but I look horrid.

He's breaking a sweat, too. He's wiped his brow twice with the back of his hand. Both times it lifted his shirt a smidge, giving me a sneak peek of that line of hair leading to that fortress between his legs.

This guy needs to stop before I'm the one who pins him to a wall.

I glance around and the place looks a helluva lot better than it did a couple of hours ago. Plopping down on the couch, I sigh. I haven't stopped since I woke up this morning.

I hate to admit it, but Scotty has been a real help. He cleaned my table, mopped the floors in the kitchen, and now he's doing my dishes. Where has he been all my life?

And that damn t-shirt is so tight I can see every contour of his taut back muscles. What a damn tease!

The water shuts off in the kitchen and he wipes his brow again, drying his hands on my pink dishcloth. "Taking a break?" he asks, looking over his shoulder.

Groaning, I drop onto my side on the couch. "I'm spent."

I close my eyes and take a deep breath, the fatigue taking over after the craziness of the last few days. I haven't stopped studying for my finals, and now that they're almost done, the tension headache has started, with the addition of teeth grinding. I grind my teeth so much that I broke two mouthguards in three months. Waking up beside me is not sunshine and rainbows.

He chuckles, coming to the couch and crouching beside me. "So..." He bops my nose. "Feeling up for something to eat?"

I open my eyes to his smirking face, his shoulder muscles flexed, and his forearms resting on his knees. "No."

"One date, what's the worst that can happen?" he says, eyeing my cleavage.

"You'd get attached and expect more than I can give you. I don't do relationships, no matter how hard you try, you're not getting one out of me, shithead."

His face changes, that grin slowly disappears, and his eyebrows rise, pinching together. "I'm not seeing anyone if that's what's stopping you?"

Sitting up, I sigh, shaking my head. "No, that's not what's stopping me. I just…don't…do relationships, okay?"

He's still crouched in front of me, staring at me like I just told him he's disgusting—he's far from that. The stare is intense; not one of us blinks for at least ten seconds before he lets out a nasal chuckle and taps my knee. I think I struck a nerve.

Did he come here on a mission to find his missing necklace and end up expecting a date out of it? Shit, did he help me clean my place and hope I'd say yes?

Now I feel bad.

No, I shouldn't. I owe him nothing. He chose to help me because that's who he is. I don't have to spend more time with him to know that he's kind. A heart of gold.

He rises, takes his jacket from the counter, and puts it on. Nothing else is said when he heads toward the door and stops, turning to look at me. "If you're ever swamped, don't hesitate to give me a call." He points at the tiny whiteboard on my fridge with his digits written on it. When did he do that? "I'm not a sleazebag like I'm sure the other guys you bring home are. And, just so you know, I see you for who you are, not for the guys you bring home." He grins. "I see *you*, Alora."

He opens the door, hesitating before he steps through it and shuts it behind him, leaving those words hanging in the air that mean more than anything anyone has ever said to me.

CHAPTER SIX – SCOTT WESLEY

Another week goes by and no word from Alora. I still think about how shocked she looked at my comment toward her. Maybe I came off too strong. I just wanted to spend more time with her. Offering to help clean her apartment seemed like a good thing, I think she appreciated it. I hope she did.

Who hurt her enough to not want to go out for a simple dinner? It didn't even have to be a date. We could've gone as friends…why didn't I suggest that?

I guess she really doesn't do relationships. I haven't gone out once, haven't flirted with a single girl, and haven't answered any of the ones that texted me. I went as far as deleting them from my phone. I'm not obsessed or anything, I just really like Alora. I like the thought of coming home to her, holding her, making love to her…starting a life. This isn't like me. This is…oh, man, I'm fucked.

Stepping out of the shower, I towel dry my hair as the guys in the locker room are boasting about our game. Still undefeated. *We're in the playoffs, baby!*

"Whatta game, Scotty." Gregory claps my back and sits on the bench in front of his locker. Right next to mine. "We're going out to celebrate, you coming?"

I shake my head, taking out a pair of boxers to jump

into. "Nah, I got a training in the morning." *I don't.* "I wanna rest up before I tear a muscle."

"Code for a booty call," Corey shouts, cackling.

Rolling my eyes, I finish getting dressed. I don't need this fucker getting me annoyed right now. He tends to do that a lot, razz us, or jokes with us at our expense. But we're all getting tired of it. He's the youngest, a ripe twenty-two-year-old with the biggest chip on his shoulder. He thinks everyone's out to get him. So, he acts like a tool in the hopes that we'll laugh and praise him. But there will come a day when we get tired of his shit. And that day is coming real fast.

My phone dings as I tuck it in my pocket, but I don't check it right away. I want out of this locker room and in my bed. It's been a heck of a few nights of games back-to-back, not including practices and training. I'm exhausted.

Kelvin follows me out, his bag on his shoulder, and sighs. "Annie is driving me crazy."

I chuckle, nudging his side. "Aren't pregnant women supposed to have this sexual phase? Or was *Friends* full of crap?"

That makes him laugh, hand on his stomach as he does. "Can't believe Frannie made you watch that show. I still haven't watched it and it's Annie's favorite."

I shrug, pushing the back door of the arena open and stepping out into the cool evening. "I'd do anything for my sister, dude, you know that." He readjusts the strap on his shoulder and I smirk, wishing my sister could be here right now. She'd be much happier with me than our dad. But she's stubborn as shit and likes California more than the state of

New York. "Tell me, why's Annie driving you crazy?"

Kelvin groans, shaking his head as he walks with me to my car. "Everything I do sets her off. And it's not like we argue, either. If I breathe too loudly, she sighs. If I chew with my mouth open, she shoots daggers at me. Fuck, I left a sock on the floor the other day. *A sock.* One single sock and she nearly tore my head off, saying she does everything around the house when we have fucking people who come clean our house and do our laundry." He scoffs and grumbles. "One fucking sock, man."

I can't help but chuckle, squeezing his shoulder as I toss my bag in the back seat. "A few more months and she'll be back to herself—just tired and cranky with a baby attached to her. But back to Annie, nonetheless."

Kelvin drops his head back and groans loudly. "I bet you anything she won't have sex with me for months after the baby's born. She hardly has sex with me now because she feels *icky*."

"Hey, she's growing a human inside her. Give her a break," I say, pulling him into a hug. "Go home and lie down next to your wife, knowing you have someone to go home to."

He narrows his eyes at me when I step away. "If you gave anyone the time of day, you'd be doing the same thing."

I shrug, putting my hands in my pockets as Alora's grin flashes through my mind. Her kiss goodbye on our first night together is engrained in my memories because that's exactly what I want. A kiss goodbye from the green-eyed goddess I can't stop thinking about. "Maybe one day."

"What's that look about?" He waggles his eyebrows at

me. "You're seeing someone, aren't you? Who're you seeing? She cute?"

I laugh, opening the door and getting in. "I'll see you soon."

"No, no, no. You can't get away from me that easily —"

"I already said goodnight," I interrupt him and start my car. "Go home and relax."

He chuckles, nodding slowly with a grin. He's going to pry it out of me, but I can't tell him who it is yet. I won't until I know where she stands with me when she's not even mine to begin with. But fuck, I can't get this woman out of my head.

Jetting out of the parking lot, I attempt to speed through the crowded streets. The arena was packed tonight given that it was our last game until playoffs. And once playoffs begin, the more the crowd gets riled up. Sometimes after press, I'll stay behind and sign some autographs, but I was in no mood tonight. I just want to get home and sleep. Maybe give my dick a jerk before crashing while scrolling through Alora's Instagram. She posts a lot of selfies.

I've tried to contact her twice. I followed her on Instagram and then sent her a DM. No response to either. Not even a follow back. Mind you, she hasn't posted anything since Annie's gender reveal. Maybe she hasn't been online because of school.

Parking in the underground parking garage, I drag myself to my condo that overlooks the city. It's nice and flashy, just the right amount of modern for my liking. But the place is empty, cold. It needs a woman's touch and Frannie always reminds me of that when she comes. So, I hang all her paintings in my place, to the point where the empty guest room looks like an exhibit.

Face-planting on my bed, I groan, exhausted from the back-to-back games we've had. I love hockey and wouldn't change a thing about my life. But sometimes, I ache for playoff season to end so I can relax a little during the summer.

My phone dings, reminding me to glance at it before I close my eyes for the night. Three missed texts from an unknown number.

UNKNOWN: *Hey, good game* 😊
UNKNOWN: *It's Alora*
UNKNOWN: *Alora Ashton, y'know, the chick you fucked two weeks ago only to realize all our close friends are the same people.*

I chuckle, turning onto my back with a smile. I haven't felt this obsessed over someone since high school. And even then, she used me.

ME: *I thought I'd never hear from you again!!!*
ME: *Wait, I thought you didn't watch the games?*
ALORA: *I don't…just happened to be on while making dinner and I decided to just finish watching it. That hit looked like it hurt, shithead.*

My heart's bouncing around like a jackrabbit. She watched my game! She saw me dominate the other team.

Unfortunately, she also saw me get slammed into the boards by their biggest guy. Anton Yemmin, six feet, eight inches of nothing but steel. He checked me and I lost my breath for a moment before Corey helped me up. I got Anton back, tripping him, which landed me three minutes in the penalty box. Fucking worth it now that I know she watched me do it.

> ME: *Did you see me get my revenge?*
> ALORA: *I did* 😊

Hockey doesn't impress her. She isn't the type of girl I'd swing my title in front of and she'd swoon. No, Alora's an intellectual and our conversations are deeper than body checks and tripping.

> ME: *How was your day?*
> ALORA: *Hectic* 😟
> ME: *Wanna talk about it?*
> ALORA: *I did, then I didn't. And I still don't.*
> ME: *And yet you texted me* 😊
> ALORA: *Shut up*
> ALORA: *Goodnight now! Forget I messaged*
> ME: *NO! Hold up, let's chat. Nothing harmful in having a conversation. One of the things we're great at together*

Three dots pop up and leave almost as quickly. She messaged me for a reason, but I think she's going back on her reason. I should've fucking answered sooner. Then I'd probably be lying beside her, out of breath and sweaty.

ME: *What's up, Alora? What's going through that head of yours?*

ALORA: *Why the crescent moon necklace? I saw you kiss it before getting on the ice.*

I sputter, blowing out a rush of air before staring at the screen. No one has ever asked me about it, so I'm not prepared to explain myself. Not like I *have* to explain myself, but there's a lot of meaning behind it. It was my mother's, something she wore constantly. Frannie used to call me "her moon" when I was a baby, sometimes she still calls me that. When my mother died, the last thing she said to me was *be brave, my little moon*. Then she gave me her necklace. She died fifteen minutes later, holding on to my hand with the necklace between our palms. The necklace means everything to me, and when I thought I lost it, I nearly tore my apartment apart to find it, and called the Uber company, then the bar, but nothing was reported. Alora was my last chance at finding it, even though I was sure it was gone. But as fate would have it, there it was with her all along.

ME: *It was my mother's*
ALORA: *Say no more*
ME: *Really?*
ALORA: *My mother died when I was fourteen, all I have to remember her by other than photos are the earrings I never take off. So, yeah, say no more.*
ME: *How'd she die?*

ALORA: *Aneurysm, yours?*

ME: *Cancer took a turn for the worst*

My thumbs hesitate over the keyboard, unsure of what to say to this. Such a downer of a conversation but speaking with Alora is so easy. I can open up and she won't judge me. I can tell her my darkest secrets and she'll understand. Alora is my new hockey.

ME: *Is her death what made you want to be a doctor?*

ALORA: *Negative.*

ALORA: *My dad's a doctor*

ME: *No way, so you have someone at your fingertips whenever you have a question*

ALORA: *Lol, not entirely. Love my dad and all, but he's a little full of himself and thinks he knows everything. I prefer speaking with my professors and the doctors at the hospital we intern for.*

ME: *You close with your dad?*

ALORA: *Next question.*

ME: *LOL, okay.*

ME: *Any siblings?*

ALORA: *Next question.*

ME: *Not going to ask if I have any?*

"Daddy issues" is a given, considering her promiscuous ways. But it's not something I said about her, that was the guys. They put her down so much that I'm going to snap one day from how hard I bite my tongue. She's an intelligent woman who likes to sleep around. Big whoop. If she were a man, no one would bat an eye, but because she's a woman, it's frowned upon. Double fucking standard, isn't it?

ALORA: *Well, do you?*

ME: *An older sister, Frannie. She's my world but lives on the other side of the country.*

ALORA: *What's she do for a living?*

ME: *She volunteers at an organization for kids with special needs.*

ALORA: *No way! I used to do that in high school. Lasted about six years before this doctor thing kind of took over my life* 😵

ALORA: *Frannie Wesley, I'm assuming? I'll just find her on your Instagram* 😊

It's radio silence for a second; I'm sure it's because she's creeping on my account and looking for my sister. Frannie has high-functioning Down Syndrome. But that's never stopped her. She's an incredible painter, having had three gallery showings last year alone. She's my biggest inspiration. The only constant in my life that I never grow tired of.

I glance at my phone and see Alora followed me and liked the DM I sent her. All I asked was, *hey, you wanna have another coffee while you're the one who helps clean my condo?* I thought it was a funny joke, but when she didn't respond, my second-guessing started taking hold. Now, I'm just happy she's talking to me.

ALORA: *She's amazing!*

ALORA: *I need one of her paintings for my living room. The sunflower one.*

ALORA: *Side note, can she be my best friend?*

ME: *In order for that to happen, you'd have to admit you like me and I'll introduce you both.*

ALORA: *Shut up, shithead.*

I chuckle, shaking my head and looking above me. The sunflower painting is my favorite, too. I actually have it in my bedroom, hanging above my bed. So, I send Alora a picture of me smirking at the camera with the painting above me.

ME: *This one?*

ALORA: *You're bringing this to my place ASAP*

ME: *Inviting me over?*

ALORA: *Inviting the painting over, you can leave afterward*

ME: *I'll win you over soon enough lol*

ALORA: *You can try*

ME: *What's your favorite flower?*

ALORA: *Nope.*

ME: *C'mon!*

ALORA: *Red roses.*

ME: *Noted* 😊

ME: *My sister is coming down three days after we get back from Vancouver.*

ALORA: *Then I guess you're taking us to dinner*

ME: *LOL*

ME: *It's a date!*

I'm smiling like a fucking child. But I can't help it. I'm infatuated with her. Most of my exes avoided my sister, never asked about her, or liked any of her paintings. *It's a little much,* one of them said. I broke up with her that second.

But Alora, she's everything I could have ever asked for. And then some. So, if she likes my favorite painting, then I guess I'll give her my favorite painting.

ME: *Are you coming to Vancouver with us????*
ALORA: *Haven't decided yet.*
ME: *I'd like you to come.*
ALORA: *Then I guess I'm not coming*
ME: *Oh, c'mon! Don't be like that*
ALORA: *I'll think about it.*
ME: *That's not a no!!*
ALORA: 😐
ME: 😄
ALORA: *It's funny, I've watched games every now and then, but this was the first time I actually paid attention*
ALORA: *Nope, ignore that last statement*
ME: *I'm not blushing, you are!*
ALORA: *Shut up!*

Laughter fills my bedroom, staring at the three dots popping up and disappearing. She wanted to watch the game and I'm letting myself believe it was because of me.

ALORA: *What's your drink of choice?*

ME: *I usually go for beer*

ALORA: *Boring!*

ME: *What's yours then?*

ALORA: *We threw back I don't know how many two weeks ago, shithead*

ME: *Tequila sunrise?*

ALORA: *Nailed it*

ALORA: *That paired with pizza or some Chinese food! Muah, chef's kiss.*

ME: *Those your favorite foods?*

ALORA: *Yes. What're yours?*

ME: *Truthfully? Same*

ME: *For someone who isn't interested, you sure are trying to get to know me a lot better.*

ALORA: *Shut up, shithead!!!!*

ME:

ALORA: *I'm going to go now!*

ME: *NO!!!*

ME: *Don't go!!!*

ME: *I'll stop teasing, promise*

ME: *What're you up to?*

ALORA: *Had a shower after the game and I should be reviewing, but my brain won't register anything I'm reading.*

ME: *I can come over and help you focus*

ALORA: *Scotty!*

ME: *What? I didn't say anything about sex. But if you're up for it, I won't say no*

ALORA: *I'm already in pajamas and in bed.*

ME: *Me too, let's lie down together. I'm an amazing cuddler*

ALORA: *Says who, your exes?*

ME: *Nope, none of them were big on cuddling. My pillows can confirm, though*

ALORA: *Lucky pillows, I guess*

ME: *Lucky indeed*

My heart is beating so fast that I don't think I'll be able to get a wink of sleep tonight without the thought of getting into my car and driving over to her place to hold her. That's all I'd want at this point. To hold my beauty and hope she'd hold me in return.

ME: *You busy tomorrow?*

ALORA: *I don't do relationships, Scotty.*

ME: *Just asking what your plans are, sweetheart*

ALORA: *Don't call me sweetheart!*

ME:

ALORA: *For real, get some sleep because I need some. Have an early meeting with my professor in the morning*

ME: *Okay, good luck and goodnight, Alora*

ALORA: *Night, shithead*

And that pain in my ass just became everything I ever wanted.

And then some.

CHAPTER SEVEN – ALORA ASHTON

I woke up around seven, readying myself for my meeting at 8:30 A.M. with my professor. It's the last meeting before summer break, and then I'll be working for my dad until the fall. I start two days before the Vancouver trip that Annie insists I attend. I don't see a reason to go. I'm not dating anyone on the team. I'll be left out whenever everyone hangs out. Sophia has Gregory, Annie has Kelvin. Not a single other spouse is attending. I don't understand why I should go.

Then again, there's Scotty. Texting with him last night reminded me of our conversation at the bar. Easy. Flowing. No pressure to act like someone else. Just us.

Discovering that his sister paints and whatever money she raises from her paintings goes to the organization she created for people of all ages just like her is so inspiring. As soon as I have a minute, I'm purchasing a couple of paintings. They'd look good in my place, maybe even brighten up my father's office.

I grab my bag and keys, opening the front door, when something clatters at my feet. I stop abruptly and see the painting of the sunflowers Scotty's sister created. The one that was hanging above him. We stopped speaking around midnight. Did he drive all the way over here and drop it off last night just for me?

Heart, don't you dare beat faster.

Traitor!

I shake my head to snap out of it and squeeze my eyes shut. Nope, not falling. *Not falling.*

There's a note taped on my door with my name on it, written in really crappy penmanship.

Alora,

I couldn't let this stay at my place knowing how much you liked it. Just promise me you'll take a picture and tag my sister in it. It'll make her happy.

See you soon,

Scotty 🖤

I was smiling until I saw the heart. Why the heart?! Now I feel trapped in a relationship.

Is this a relationship?

No, it's not. I made that perfectly clear. But he's trying to make it something.

Something I can never give him.

Groaning, I carry the painting into my apartment. "You're giving it back to him and that's final."

I grunt, letting myself stare at the painting. It's perfect. Two sunflowers are front and center, with a field in the background and a blue sky.

I have to give it back to him. If I keep this, it means I want something.

Yet here I am, taking down the bland picture of a seascape I bought at Walmart that hangs above my couch and replacing it with Frannie's painting.

Yep, now I'm taking a picture and sending a text to Scotty.

I can at least say thank you, right?

ME: *Well, now you're trying too hard. Even though I appreciate the gesture, I can't accept it.*

ME: *No, I will. I love this painting and look how pretty it looks in my living room.*

ME: *This does not mean anything, right?*

ME: *You're a pain in the ass, shithead.*

With one last glance at the painting, I lock my phone and skedaddle or else I'll be late. This heavy, heartwarming feeling swims through me. I hate it. All of it. I've never had a crush on a boy before. Well, I have, but never a crush that drove me mad and gave me this longing to be with him forever. My previous crushes were urges. And I've had my urges fulfilled by Scotty, but this is different.

This is a need for more.

Shit.

But fucking Christ, the painting looks amazing in my living room. As soon as I plop down in the driver's seat of my car, I open my Instagram and post the photo with the caption, *and just like that, my living room got a whole lot brighter thanks to my secret admirer* 😊.

When Scotty sees this, I can just picture his smile; that dimple popping out on his cheek.

No, Alora. Stop it.

Ugh, why is he so damn dreamy? And why am I so damn stubborn? No, broken.

It's going to be a long day of overthinking, isn't it?

CHAPTER EIGHT – SCOTT WESLEY

I'm overwhelmed with warmth by this woman. She's opened my eyes to things I never thought I'd want. Marriage. Kids.

I barely know her and she's consumed me.

How is this even possible?

I wish I could've seen her face when she opened the door and saw the painting. No one has ever taken an interest in my sister's art before. My exes just glossed over her pieces like they were nothing but a painting on a wall. They're so much more than that.

She's gifted, insanely talented, and I know she'll get somewhere soon with her work.

So, when Alora fell in love with the sunflower painting above my bed, I took it down and rushed over. I didn't have to be anywhere until two in the afternoon the next day, so I stayed up until one driving to her place to give her that painting, then went back home. I couldn't tell if her excitement was genuine through texts, but the fact that she followed my sister on Instagram and went on a liking spree had my heart skipping beats I didn't know it was able to do. This woman has me whipped.

I finish my training session at my condo, shower, and throw on a pair of shorts and an undershirt when my phone dings. There it goes again, my heart racing with anticipation that it'll be Alora.

It isn't. It's Frannie, the next best thing.

FRANNIE: *Baby bro, your girlfriend is harassing my Instagram account with likes.*

I'm laughing out loud, but I won't correct her. I like the thought of Alora with that title. And cringe at the fact that I knew she liked my sister's posts already. I may have done some creeping this morning when I saw the picture she posted.

ME: *I gave her the sunflower painting you made me.*

Sending Frannie the picture that Alora took of the painting hanging in her living room, I smile at it again. It's perfect there, front and center for everyone to see. And when she looks at it, she'll always be reminded of me. I wonder if she'll want more paintings. I'll gladly give all of them to her just to see that smile.

FRANNIE: *She must be the one, you never talk to your women about me*
ME: *That's not true, you're always the main topic of conversation* ☺
FRANNIE: *Yeah, yeah. Sure, I am* 🙄
ME: *LOL*
ME: *She has a good eye, sis. But I have yet to win over her*

heart

FRANNIE: *Make her dinner. Your spaghetti bolognese is the best. She'll love you forever once she tries it* 😊 😊

ME: *Love your optimism, Frannie.*

FRANNIE: *Love you the mostest!*

ME: *Same, kid, same.*

FRANNIE: *You can't call me kid, I'm three years older than you AND adopted!*

ME: 🖤

Chuckling, I fall back on my couch. Frannie may be adopted, but she's still my sister. Nothing will take that away from us.

I stare at our chat thread for a second, then do the one thing I shouldn't do—I stalk Alora's Instagram. She's been inactive for a couple of weeks because of finals, I can't wait to see what else she'll post.

The last post is the photo of her new painting with the caption, *and just like that, my living room got a whole lot brighter thanks to my secret admirer* 😊 . I tag my sister in the comments and let my fingers do the typing. *Yes, Alora, I am yours if you'll let me have you.* Nope, can't have that. I erase it and just leave a smiling face. The mushy-gushy stuff will come once she opens her eyes and sees we're perfect for each other.

Of course, I like the picture, and a second later, I accidentally like the fifth picture on her feed. But that's okay, Instagram is showing she's active. I feel like I'm in high school again, chasing after the popular chick. I won that one over, and I'm sure I can win over this bombshell, too.

A new DM comes in from the woman herself.

DrAloraAshton: *Stalker*

ScottyWesley: *Am not,* 😌

DrAloraAshton: *FYI, if your sister is interested, my dad's ex is a graphic designer. She can add bookmarks and postcards and what have you to her website with the paintings. Great way to get her work out there and raise more money for the organization*

ScottyWesley: *Have I told you how amazing you are?*

DrAloraAshton: *You may have belted it while balls deep inside me lol*

ScottyWesley: *Can't wait to do it again* 😌

DrAloraAshton: *Fat chance, Scotty.*

ScottyWesley: *Then gift me with something to relieve myself, sweetheart. I'm hard as rock*

DrAloraAshton: *Don't call me sweetheart.*

Ten seconds later, a new text comes in. A picture of Alora in a blue lace bra and a hot pink thong. Jesus fucking *fuck*! Her breasts are so perfectly supple, her waist thin, yet curvy, and the way that thong hangs low, teasing me with the goddess between her legs makes my dick shoot up like a flagpole.

ALORA: *Happy?*

ME: *Extremely* 😌

I whip myself out and stare at the photo, pumping my hand quickly. It won't take me long to unload, but holy shit, just the thought of her being here, watching me, it's making my body buck and surge with pleasure…*I see her, crawling toward me in that blue bra and that fucking thong that's see-through. She's biting her lower lip as her long, brown hair falls off her shoulder, slapping against her breasts.*

"Hey, baby," she says, kissing my chest. *"There's a better way to fix this. Maybe kiss it better?"*

I groan, rolling my head back. "Kiss it, baby. Oh, please kiss it."

Her plump lips wrap around the head of my cock, tongue teasing me before she forces the length of me into her mouth. She gags—I'm far too big for her pussy let alone her mouth—but goddamn, she takes it.

Moaning, I pump my hand faster. *I see her blowing me, holding my gaze, and swallowing me whole as I release.*

For you, baby. All for you.

Even after I finish and I'm drenched with my seed, I stare at the picture of her, that lip bite making me smile. Holy crap, this woman is driving me insane and she isn't even mine yet.

Quickly washing my hands and changing my shirt, I go back to the couch and smirk.

ME: *Keep sending me pictures like that and I'll praise the ground you walk on.*

ALORA: *You touched yourself, didn't you?*

ME: *I refuse to answer that question.*

ALORA: *Hot.*

ME: *Come over?*

ALORA: *In your dreams, shithead!*

ME: *Okay, so if you come over there will be two of you lol real you and dream you.*

ALORA: *I'm in the middle of prepping for a job I'm nowhere near prepared for. Nervous and stressed out of my mind about it. So, no, I will not come over.*

ALORA: *And I don't do relationships, remember!*

ME: *Then I'll come to you, I need ten minutes tops.*

ALORA: *That's ten too many.*

ME: *Thirty seconds, promise!*

ALORA: *We'll talk soon, shithead. Nothing more than friends.*

ME: *For now* 😊

ALORA: *You're relentless!*

ME: *You love it!*

ALORA: *Shut your mouth*

ME: *Make me* 😗

ALORA: *Argh, I hate your stupid, handsome face so much sometimes.*

ME: *Keep talking dirty and I'll come again* 😚

ALORA: *Ah-ha! So you did touch yourself!*

ME: *I refuse to answer that question.*

ALORA: *I just got this bra, too. It's cute, isn't it?*

ME: *I don't know, I might need another picture to compare*

ALORA: *Of it on or off?*

ME: *OFF!*

A new image comes in and the bra is definitely off, but it's a picture of it on the gray floor of her bedroom. A laugh booms out of me because it's something I would have done if I were in her position. She'll see it soon enough, Alora and I are two peas in a pod.

ME: *You're killing me, Alora!*
ALORA: *Thought you'd find that funny lol*
ME: *Send another with you in it? You know the shot, the one of what that bra was covering.*
ALORA: *Fat chance, Scotty*
ME: *Fine, then I'll send you one*

Biting my lower lip, I peel my shirt off and go to the stand-up mirror in the hallway. I've never sent pictures to anyone before, not even selfies. Sure, I take them and post them on my Instagram. But this is new to me, and I hope she likes it.

Lowering my shorts just enough to tease, I hook a thumb in the waistband and flex, taking a picture just for her eyes only.

ME: *And think, this is yours if you want it*

It's radio silent for a good two minutes, and I'm pacing my living room staring at the chat thread. The screen has tried to go black twice, but my thumb taps it again, hoping she'll reply. And she does, with a new picture. Her arms are covering her tits, pushing them up for ample cleavage, and there's that lip bite again. She's giving me just enough to tease.

ME: *Goddamn!*

ALORA: *Ditto, shithead.*

ME: *Like what you see?*

ALORA: *It doesn't take a genius to know how hot you are*

ME: *Not blushing or anything*

ALORA: *Shut up!*

ME: *Seriously, though, when can I see you again? We don't have to do anything but listen to music. I liked doing that with you while cleaning.*

ALORA: *Never, Scotty.*

ME: *That's what you say now, but when you're touching yourself to the thought of me, all you have to do is give me a call and my tongue will work wonders on that clean-shaven pussy, baby.*

ALORA: *I hate you*

ME: ♥

ALORA: *We'll talk later, I have studying to do* 😊

ME: *Studying, sure* 😏

ALORA: *I'm serious! We'll talk later, shithead.*

ME: *I'll be here* 😚

Maybe she'll come around and we can test this thing out. If it doesn't work, then at least we gave it a try. She already gave me a nickname. "Shithead" isn't the greatest, but it's ours.

I wonder what hurt her so badly she had to shut herself off from relationships completely. Vowing to keep a smile on her face, I wonder if it means losing myself in the process.

CHAPTER NINE – ALORA ASHTON

I got home about an hour ago, exhausted beyond belief. I haven't stopped in weeks and I just need to relieve this migraine.

Tossing my clothes on the washroom floor, I prepare to start a bath when there's a knock at my door. *Ugh, great.* Wrapping a towel around me, I head for the entryway. I'm not expecting anyone, maybe a few late-night orders on Amazon. I tend to add things to my cart throughout the day and hit order by the time my head hits the pillow. Half the time it's useless knickknacks, most of the time they're vibrators. This time around, I'm sure it's that Himalayan salt lamp I've had my eye on for months.

Running my fingers through my hair, I unlock the door, widening my eyes when I see Scotty standing there with Chinese takeout in hand. I haven't spoken to him in almost four days. I was becoming okay with that...wasn't I? "What're you doing here?"

He shrugs, licking his lips. "I was in the neighborhood."

"Oh, um, y-you live nearby?" I say, adjusting the towel and glancing at the crescent moon hanging from his neck.

He glances back and points to his left. "Thirty minutes by car that way."

My eyebrows pinch together. "You drove a half hour to bring me food? Are you nuts?"

"It would've been, but traffic, y'know," he says, smirking and revealing that dimple that has me swooning.

Stop it, heart, you're not allowed to beat this fast over a guy.

"You can't take no for an answer, can you?"

He shakes his head and pushes my door open, helping himself into my place. I want to be upset, but I'm still so shocked that he'd come all the way here to bring me dinner after I complained briefly about my hectic week a few nights ago.

He looks back at me as he sets down the food on the dining table. His taut back in those tight t-shirts is becoming too much of a tease, it's like he's doing it on purpose. "You gonna close the door?"

I'm still a little tongue-tied that he's here. That he's been nothing but kind and generous.

I don't like it.

Folding my arms across my chest, I pop out a hip. He needs to leave before I let this excitement between my legs take hold. And it's throbbing like a son of a bitch. "Scotty, I don't do relationships. So, whatever this is, has to stop—"

He laughs, pointing at my kitchen and helping himself to plates. "Can't bring a friend some grub?"

I close the door and grumble quietly. Why is he so damn adorable when he thinks I'm not being serious? "Who says we're friends?"

"I was inside you, Alora, I think we're a little more than acquaintances at this point," he replies, pulling a chair out for me and waiting behind it. "Now either go put clothes on or sit down and have a meal with me, you stubborn woman."

Narrowing my eyes at him, I strut over, plopping myself down in a different chair than the one he's standing behind. I don't need a man to wine and dine me. I don't need it.

But fuck, I think I like his company a little too much. He cares for me—something I sure as shit am not used to—and our banter is easy. Everything is easy with him. Effortless. All my worries evaporate. All my tension releases.

Usually, I have a rule of three. I don't sleep with a guy more than three times if I think I'll fall for him.

My regular fuck buddies are different, I know I'm only getting one thing from them.

But with Scotty, the second we lock eyes, I'm fucked.

He chuckles and goes back to my kitchen, getting two forks, then opening the fridge like he lives here. For a second, I imagine this is what he would do after a game. He'd come home, have a meal with me, then crash on the couch as we watched some cheesy rom-com over a bowl of popcorn. Maybe even a bag of M&M's, too.

I mean, is it so wrong to imagine him living here?

Yes, yes, it is.

When he sits down, he holds a fork out to me and smiles; that damn thing on his face deserves to be in a museum.

Damn him.

"Wipe that smile off your face, shithead," I say and snatch the fork from him.

"You hung up my sister's painting. Thought you were giving it back to me," he says, sliding the fried rice over to me.

"Yeah, well, I changed my mind. I do that a lot, get used to it." I dump a few scoops of rice on my plate and stop when I feel him still staring at me. "I didn't mean it like that and you know it."

He laughs, taking the box from me. "But you change your mind a lot, so who knows? Come next week. Next month. Hey, maybe even tomorrow…I might be able to call you my girl."

I roll my eyes and grab another container, forking a few General Tso's chicken bites from it. "You're relentless."

"I like what I like." He shrugs, his eyes meeting mine. "You'll come around, and in the meantime, we can settle on friends."

"Friends, huh?"

He drops a spring roll on my plate and smiles. "Yep, friends with benefits if you like. Friends who send each other pictures. But friends, nonetheless."

I take cherry sauce and spread it on my spring roll. If I shove food in my mouth, then I won't say anything stupid. With an inhale of his fucking cologne, I bring the spring roll to my mouth and crunch it between my teeth. "Annie asked me not to associate with you. She's my best friend and I'm already lying to her about us, I won't do it again."

He chuckles, taking the cherry sauce from me and adding it to his rice. "You won't have to do anything."

"Good." I lick my lips. "As soon as you're finished eating, you can leave, my friend."

That laugh. My insides twist and turn with so much adoration, it's killing me.

Stop it!

I toss chopsticks at him angrily. "Stop laughing."

"Why?" He leans forward. "You find me adorable, don't you?"

Narrowing my eyes, I take another bite of the spring roll. I refuse to satisfy him with an answer. But yes, I find him so adorable, everything I ever stood for is crumbling.

Guys don't make me crumble like this.

"Any change of thought about coming to Vancouver? As friends, of course," he asks, tonguing food from his cheek. "Coach never lets the girlfriends come, so this is a treat."

"I'm working for my dad. So no, I haven't decided because that's my priority," I reply, licking sweet sauce from my lips. Gosh, hearing *girlfriend* come from his lips is making me squirm in my seat and clench my thighs together. Am I seriously getting turned on at the thought of being his? "*Friends*, not girlfriend, shithead."

He holds my gaze for a moment, stealing my breath as he does. This isn't good.

Nope. Not good at all.

I release the hold he has on me, trailing my gaze to the tattoos on his arms. I didn't get a good look at them our first night together or when he came over to help me clean my apartment. But studying them now, I see they're art his sister drew. This man is melting my heart and I want to slap him for it.

"Your sister drew those?" I ask with my mouth full,

tilting my head to get a better look at his arms.

He nods, wiping his mouth on a napkin. "She drew the mermaid for our mom," he says, turning his arm to show me the mermaid with the green eyes and blonde hair. It's something out of a museum. The way she draws is so detailed, every fine line, every scale on the mermaid's tail. It's a beautiful tribute to their mother. He turns his arm to show me his bicep, flexing it no less. "And the sunflowers she did when I got drafted to the pros."

And he willingly gave that painting to me? Something his sister painted for him when a memorable moment happened in his life. Jeez, the walls are closing in on me, the air is thinning, and I swear the temperature went up by six degrees. He must like me a shitload.

Am I reading too much into this? Maybe.

No, no. I am. My heart isn't allowed to feel things.

Stop feeling things.

"She's crazy talented." My hand has a mind of its own and turns his arm, studying the ink and the artistry of his sister. "Are sunflowers your favorite?"

"They are." He chuckles, turning his arm over and catching my hand before I retract it. There it is, that damned spark, the same one like at the gender reveal. That instant connection I've never felt with anyone.

I wasn't sure if I'd ever have this feeling. The warmth as it blooms, the rumbling excitement in my gut, and the burning intensity between my thighs.

I don't let myself be drawn to people.

I've seen what happens to people with broken hearts,

to those who use women for their bodies, toying with their minds.

I will not be someone to toy with.

This will not happen.

Nope.

Never.

Stop it.

Removing my hand from his, I gulp down the lump in my throat. I hate what he does to me. *Fucking shithead.*

I clear my throat and push my lips together, attempting to look away from him but his hold on me is like an explosion I can't look away from. An array of bright colors bursting and claiming all the darkness in my life.

I've never been in love with anyone before. Never had that urge to jump their bones and see a future with them. But with Scotty, everything is different. He's genuine, caring. Thoughtful. And how he cares for his sister is the sweetest thing. I'm sure if we hadn't hooked up almost a month ago, it wouldn't have mattered. Our conversation that night was eye-opening. Easy. Everything is just easier when he's around.

His tongue slowly darts out of his mouth and licks the corner of his lips. I'm sure he feels it, too. That connection we have is growing. I don't want it to, but it is. Something is starting here and there's no denying it. No matter how hard I push him away, there are some things we can't ignore.

But I swallow hard, watching as a smile spreads to his lips. "Do you have any tattoos?"

I tilt my head to the side, still unable to look away from

him. "You've seen me naked, Scotty. You know for damn sure I don't have any tattoos."

He forks rice into his mouth, smiling like a kid on Christmas morning. "I was very inebriated that night, sweetheart. I remember our time together, but fine details like that didn't stick." He sits back in the chair, licking the cherry sauce from his lips. "Maybe you should remind me? You are only wearing a towel."

I roll my eyes as he leans forward again, elbows on the table. "You can fuck off, shithead."

That laugh. Something so manly and deep shouldn't be allowed to leave someone's lips without a warning that it may cause a rainforest. Because holy fuck, I'm drenched and he hasn't even touched me.

There we go again, staring at each other with an intensity so strong, it's making my cheeks burn up. He feels it, too. I can see the redness crawling up his neck and settling on his cheeks.

That's what's so different about him. He oozes confidence, but deep down, there's this shyness to him that I enjoy unwrapping every time we speak.

It's intriguing.

And it's scaring the shit out of me.

He reaches a hand out to me, his fingertip grazing the side of my forearm that shoots an anvil through my stomach, then up into my throat. He knows what he's doing to me.

Taking in a shaky breath, my tongue drags across the seam of my lips before he does the same. That's when that magnetic pull between us takes hold. The same pull that locked our lips the first night we met.

I lunge forward, grabbing the back of his neck and kissing him.

Stupid fucking hormones.

He kisses back, smiling against my lips as he does. The kiss is soft and sensual, until a moan seeps from me and he pulls me out of the chair. I shouldn't do this. *We* shouldn't do this. Doing this again would only cause feelings to brew. And if feelings brew, then we're both fucked.

Royally and completely fucked.

He spins me, lifting the towel and undoing his pants. It's a fast thought, a movement that we know if we don't complete, then I'll start overthinking and stop it.

Maybe I should stop this. I don't want feelings. Feelings cause pain.

I have to focus on the task at hand and that's getting my medical degree. Not a relationship. They don't last. They end, only causing heartache.

But holy shit, my mind is not thinking of anything but the feeling of Scotty's mouth on mine again.

His lips caress my shoulder, biting down as he lowers his pants. "Ready for me, baby?"

I reach back and run my fingers through the hair on the back of his head, tugging softly to bring his mouth closer to mine. Our tongues slide against each other as his hands explore my body, yanking the towel off me.

He pulls away, fishing for his wallet, and drops nearly all his cards trying to find a condom. Those would've come in handy our first night together.

As soon as it's on, he pushes me forward, and there he is, easing inside me slowly. He's a lot bigger than I remember, a lot bigger than I've had in a long time. Yet, something about this moment is exactly what our life is supposed to be like.

Why does this feel so right?

A guttural groan leaves him when he finally gets all the way in, and thumps roughly, taking me from behind. I'm gripping the edges of the dining table, letting my moans slip free.

It's different.

This feels like it's a want filled with desire. Not just the high from a one-night stand.

This is new.

He pulls out of me and yanks his t-shirt over his head, causing me to turn back and look at him. "Come here," he says, sitting down and lifting me on top of him. "I'm not finished with you yet."

His voice when we're in the throes of pleasure sends me over the edge, weeping for him. I've never been this excited to fuck someone…ever.

He positions himself back into me and I ride him fast, hard. Knowing this would be our last encounter if I had it my way. Who are we kidding, though? This is another of many.

He leans forward, licking the space between my breasts, and grunts. "You're so fucking beautiful, Alora."

Tugging his head back by the hair, I kiss him, shutting him up. My heart can't handle the best lay I've ever had and the most caring person I ever met. "Shut up, shithead."

Moaning, his hands grip my ass, kneading, and

massaging. We're a mess of heavy panting and moans, my tits bouncing against him. "I need in here, baby. I fucking *need* it."

Biting down on his neck, he cries out, thrusting upward and sending me into oblivion. "Scotty!" I scream, riding him harder, faster.

He suckles my breast, then reaches down, struggling with something.

I glance beside me, slowing my movements. "What're you doing?"

"Getting outta my jeans," he says, standing up with me and kicking them off.

His lips find mine as he travels to my bedroom like he knows my damn place.

No one familiarizes themselves here.

Not even Annie.

This is *my* space—albeit, my father pays for it, but still. It's my safe haven where everything is mine and I control it all.

Yet with Scotty, he's taking over everything. Even my refuge.

Scotty lays us on the bed and adjusts himself inside me again, pounding deeply as our moans fill the room. He twists his hips, angling them upward so mine move with him, and grunts, letting us enjoy the intensity of this moment.

But that's all this is, a moment. A lapse of judgment on my part.

I couldn't take the intensity in the room. The thirst that needed to be quenched.

Sliding my legs to his shoulders, I gasp as he thrusts so

deeply, his dick attacks my cervix. Our eyes meet and he smiles again, licking the side of my ankle in a moan. The shithead thinks he won, I'd put money on it.

A throaty groan leaves him and he thumps twice before stilling, holding my gaze as he does. "Fuck," he draws out. "You're killing me, Alora." He opens my legs and lowers on top of me. "Fucking killing me."

"This never happened," I say, sucking in heavy pulls of air.

He chuckles, leaving a kiss on my lips before rolling off me. "It did, four times now." He slides the condom off and cleans himself with a shirt on my bed. Normal. We are acting like a normal couple.

Nope, don't like this.

Covering my face, I groan. It's intense. Everything is so intense my head spins and a wave of nausea rolls in. Definitely don't like this feeling. "What are you doing to me, you crazy man?"

He laughs, leaning on his elbow beside me. "Changing your mind, sweetheart."

I scoff, sitting up. "Don't call me sweetheart."

He takes my wrist, sitting up with me. "Oh, c'mon. Don't be like that."

But I am like that. Because now, I'm regretting everything we just did, all because my heart is tripping over itself for him.

Fuck this man.

Argh!

"I don't do relationships, Scotty. This was…this was a

mistake. Another stupid mistake," I say and rise, taking a t-shirt dress from the laundry basket to throw on.

He sits there, frowning at me, obviously upset that I led him on. But I can't help myself sometimes. He came here with food for me because he knew my week had been hectic. He helped me clean my apartment when he didn't need to. He gave me his sister's painting, dropping it off in the middle of the night because he knew I'd wake up and smile when I saw it.

He knows how to treat me well and yet I just want to get away from him. Push him away from all the chaos that is my life.

I don't need this.

I don't need him.

Love is a construct that we create.

It's not real.

It's not fucking real.

"I think you should leave," I say quietly, uncomfortably staring at him as if being around him is tainting my thoughts and ways. "Please."

He scoffs, rising from the bed in his birthday suit, and stands in front of me. Tempting me with all that is this godlike man. "We could've been good, Alora. You and me. But I don't understand why you won't give me a chance. We're good, can't you see that? So damn good." He shakes his head and reaches up to touch my face yet stops himself. "But if this is what you want, then fine. I'll leave you alone."

With that, he walks out of my room and quickly gets dressed in my kitchen, looking back as I remain standing at the threshold.

The weirdest feeling blooms inside me.

Regret.

And not the kind I get after sleeping with someone. No, regret that I'm not running after him and wrapping my arms around his neck in an apology.

He clears his throat after he stands tall, completely dressed. "I'll, uh, let you know when my sister's in town so you guys can have dinner. Anyone who's a fan of her art is a friend in her book." He meets my gaze. "Don't worry, I won't be there."

He gives me one last once-over, then leaves. Letting the cloud of hurt suffocate me.

How did I end up here, catching feelings for someone our friends said wasn't allowed to happen?

How did I find myself needing to run after him?

Fucking shit, why do I let myself run after him?

I throw open the front door and find him already at his Range Rover, sitting in the front seat, and staring at his phone.

For some reason, the need to go after him halts when I see the saddened look on his face. I hurt him. I did that because of my beliefs. My refusal to have a loving relationship.

Gripping the doorknob, I ready myself to close the door when he looks up at me at the same time my phone chimes.

A lopsided grin spreads to his face and he nods at me, holding my gaze for a moment before reversing out of the spot and speeding down the road.

He came here tonight—sat in traffic, too—to feed me my favorite after a long week.

And I kicked him out.

Closing the door, I growl behind it. "This is why I don't fucking do this shit!"

I don't fall for guys, period.

Cracking the bones in my neck, I snatch my phone from the dining table, heading to the washroom for that much needed bath I planned on having.

But when I glance at my phone, a text from Scotty lights up the screen. Of course, he texts me, probably asking me to hold on a little longer. And I find myself agreeing to do it. Why am I agreeing to hold on if relationships mean diddly-squat to me?

SCOTTY: *Sorry to have bothered you tonight. I just wanted to tell you that it was a treat to meet you, and sorry we couldn't figure this out. Have a good one and I hope life brings you joy.*

SCOTTY: *Good luck with your new job.*

If I didn't feel like crap before, I sure do now.

And look at me, tears are welling in my eyes. I never once cried over a man. And now, I'm crying because I don't know how to change without anyone getting hurt. And I hurt him. Someone who was nothing but kind to me. I pushed him away because that's what I do.

I open my legs and ruin things.

Just like my father.

CHAPTER TEN – SCOTT WESLEY

The national anthem is sung by everyone in the stands—men, women, and a few patriotic kids are belting out, too.

Us guys on the ice, we're too antsy to hum the melody. Adrenaline is high. We want to go. We want to play and win this game. A game that will bring us one step closer to the finals.

I crack my neck, roll my shoulders back, and look over at Kelvin blowing a kiss to Annie. Something I wish I had. A woman in the stands just for me. It never bothered me before. Sometimes my sister would be there, but she stopped coming a while ago. My dad only comes when we play a game in LA.

And yet, now that I glance at Kelvin smiling, I want that, too. I thought I could start something with Alora, but she's so dead set on staying away from the potential us, I wonder if I should even bother trying anymore. I haven't seen or heard from her in over two weeks, and I hate the thought of never seeing her again. But she made her decision, right?

Then my heart thumps double-time when I glance at the family section in the stands and see those luscious green eyes smiling at Sophia. She's not here for me, I know that. She never comes to the games. She never does anything having to do with hockey. But she's here now.

She's fucking here and I can't stop thinking she's trying. She'll give us a chance.

I have to look at the ice in front of me to hide how wide my smile is. I just…can't.

As if on cue, the end of the song rings out and I look up, meeting Alora's gaze. I think she's as shocked as I am that she's here. But my entire being is soaring. Vibrating with glee that she might actually be here for me.

Slowly, I lick my lips and let my smile shine through. I think she likes it when I smile. There's always a touch of pink on her cheeks when I smile and my dimple pops out.

She winks, bringing a beer to her lips, and holds my gaze a fraction longer before Annie steals her attention for a selfie.

Give us a chance, Alora. I'll make you so damn happy.

The guys shove into me, breaking my trance on that goddess. It's go time!

Being on the ice is a rush. Bodies crashing into the boards. Sticks slapping. Chasing after a puck that shoots like a bullet from one end of the rink to the other.

It's thrilling.

Hockey is my life.

But lately, I've been aching to come home to someone. Something that isn't hockey.

Someone like that green-eyed bombshell sitting in the family section.

I'll give her my jersey so people know she's—no, she's not mine. She made that perfectly clear the last time we saw each other. But she'll still wear my jersey. Wear it while cheering me on. Giving me false hope that something will happen.

The whistle blows and we're off, doing play after play and skating up and down the ice. There's such a high, my heart is beating in my ears. I'm playing my ass off, showing her how skilled I can be until I'm checked into the boards; my helmet flies off and as I'm falling to the ice, my cheekbone gets nicked.

Fucker.

I skate after him and shove his head, ready to get into a full-out brawl when Kelvin nudges me, handing me my helmet and skating us to the bench. "Not worth it, Scotty. Let this one go, man," he says, out of breath.

Glaring at the fuckhead who jabbed me into the boards, I growl because the fucker is smiling. "This fucking—"

"Wesley," the medic on hand says, taking my chin. "You're bleeding."

Removing my head from his grasp, I sit on the bench. "I'll live." I squirt water in my mouth, spitting some out at my feet.

I've been pushing myself tonight because Alora is here, but she didn't need to see that and worry. The last thing I want is for her to see how ruthless hockey can be and not want to come back. I want her at all of my games.

Need her at all of them.

Glancing over my shoulder, Alora stands, staring right at me, and she looks concerned. I won't lie and say my heart isn't dancing wildly. But holy crap, it's getting hard to breathe.

You okay? she mouths.

Fuck, it's going to be hard to stay away from this girl.

I'm good, I mouth back and smile.

She looks so radiant tonight. Loose leather jacket with a tight black sweetheart neckline dress underneath. What I wouldn't give to watch that dress fall to her feet.

Run my tongue over her silky skin.

Hear her moans ringing in my ears.

Fuck.

Gregory nudges me, hocking a loogie. "Got you good, huh?"

I spit as well, wiping sweat from my forehead with a towel as I bite on my mouthguard. "Yeah, wait. We have ten minutes left in this game and I'll be on the ice for half that. He'll get what's coming to him."

Gregory chuckles looking back at the family section before leaning into me. "You notice how well everyone's playing because Alora's here? Bitch never comes to any of these games, and yet she's here. My guess is she's fucking one of the guys but no one's saying shit."

Squirting more water in my mouth, I spit some out, and nod at him. "She does seem like that—"

Coach nudges the back of my head. "Wesley, you're on."

Gregory cocks an eyebrow, glancing back as Alora and Annie cheer when Kelvin skates onto the ice. My heart races, seeing her smile and clap, biting her lower lip as her focus is on the game.

She's utter perfection.

As soon as my skates glide on the ice, I catch Alora's eye and grin. I'm winning this game for her. Maybe then, she'll give me another chance.

I pump my legs, coming to a stop and spraying the side with shaved ice, tapping my stick down. "I'm open!"

Kelvin's blocked, unable to get the puck to me. It's my job to make sure he gets his opening. And the guy blocking him is the fucker who gave me the cut on my cheekbone.

Corey and I share a glance and he nods, trading places with me as we switch up the plays. Kelvin slaps the puck to Corey, skating for the net like he's got the cops hot on his tail while my eyes are set on the asshole in front of Kelvin.

When Kelvin sees me sprinting, he darts for Corey, giving me the opening I need.

I check the fucker into the boards, smiling as I do it, and then skate to the net like I'm on fire. I'm making this winning goal for her.

Corey sees me and slaps the puck to the boards, bouncing it behind the net. It lands right at my stick. With a windup, I hit the puck and it slides right between the goalie's legs, sending the crowd into a whirlwind of clapping and cheering.

We won the fucking game!

The guys and I cheer, slamming into each other and hugging. We're undefeated in the goddamn playoffs.

"Fucking A!" Corey yells, banging our helmets together.

"We're heading west, baby!" Marshall cackles, arms

around two of the guys.

I'm laughing, giving props to Kelvin, and glance up at the family stands. There she is, smiling and hugging Annie, then Sophia, but her eyes are on me. Why is she constantly staring at me tonight? I'm not complaining, but my overthinking is making me believe there's more to her gaze than she's letting on.

She winks and flashes me a thumbs-up as Annie tugs her toward the locker rooms. Oh, fuck, yes, she's coming to the locker rooms. Maybe I'll get a celebratory hug after all.

I skate to the bench, following my teammates off the ice as the crowd is still going wild. Alora looks even better up close. The way the dress cuts off at her thighs shows how long her legs are. I'm smitten and she doesn't even want me.

A few of the guys give props to fans leaning over the railing, waving at us, and holding markers out to sign jerseys. I smile at one of the kids, holding my hand out to him. "Hand me your marker."

He's smiling so largely as he stares at his father, jumping in place. I sign my name on my stick and hold it out to him. "Maybe one day we'll see you on the rink."

"Oh, thank you, thank you, thank you," he says, holding the stick to his chest.

I know Alora's staring at me, eating up how kind I am. Not all of the guys are like me. They won't give back and take a few seconds of their time to sign some jerseys. I always do. It's the smiles and admiration on the faces of our fans that make me appreciate my job.

No, it reminds me of the first time I realized I wanted

to play hockey. My favorite player took his jersey off, signed it, then tossed it at me and told me to work hard, so I'd skate my ass off on the ice like him. And I did. I skated as hard as my legs would allow, working my way to the big leagues by the time I was eighteen. I was fucking good, I still am. And if I can give that inspiration to some kid, giving them a dream to work at, then I will. I'll sign a million things just to see that pride in their gaze.

My mom was the one who pushed me to play hockey after that encounter. Her father was a hockey player but broke his back and couldn't make the pros. My entire childhood was skating with my grandfather, playing hockey until the sun went down and the street lights came on, and then watching hockey games on TV until I fell asleep on his lap.

I live and breathe hockey, but now that I'm in the big leagues, something's missing. Something I never wanted until a set of green eyes smiled at me.

Handing the kid the marker back, I remove my helmet when I glance at Alora, keeping my head down even though a smile spreads across my lips. That look on her face. That beauty. She sees the kindness in me. Maybe she'll see it enough to kiss me goodbye tonight.

Corey whistles, taking Alora by the hand and spinning her. "Damn, girl, where're you going dressed like that?"

She chuckles, arching a brow. "I haven't been out in weeks because of finals. Annie dragged me here for girl's night."

"Well, welcome to your first game," Corey says, heading to the locker room.

They have this brother-sister relationship, filled with harmless teasing. But I can't stand how he stares at her or talks about her like she's a piece of meat. He says he's kidding every time he takes it too far, but he better stop soon before I beat the apologies out of him.

My gaze falls on Alora, eating up her glowing skin. She truly looks radiant tonight. Fresh, alive. Maybe the stress of finals has lifted off of her shoulders and she can finally breathe.

Kelvin is kissing Annie and Alora shoves his head away. "Go shower, you stink."

He laughs, looking back at me. "Yo, you wanna come to dinner with us? Alora will be a third wheel if you don't."

I smirk, running a hand through my sweaty hair. "Yeah, I have no plans. It'd be an honor to be the fourth wheel."

Alora slowly licks her lips like she knows I'm watching her. Fuck, it's driving me insane. "Hurry up, then, boys. I'm hungry."

Kelvin leaves Annie with a quick kiss and heads for the locker room. I hesitate a moment, eyeing Alora's legs before I head that way, too. I'm already over a foot taller than her, and now in my skates, she's a tiny little moon beside me.

Soon to be under me again.

Plopping on a bench, I toss my gloves and helmet into my locker and use a towel to wipe the sweat from my face.

"What a fucking game," Gregory says, sitting beside me and leaning forward to untie his skates.

Corey snickers, shoving my head slightly. "Think we

got ourselves out good luck charm. Miss Alora Ashton and her sexy self."

The rumble inside me to grab his face and yank it to me, telling him to watch his fucking mouth nearly takes hold. But I distract myself by leaning forward and getting out of my skates, too. The faster I shower and change, the faster I'll be able to get out there and see her.

"She looks fucking fine tonight," he goes on, making my face heat up.

She does and parts of me want to believe she dressed up for me. "Y'know she's more than her looks or reputation, right? She's a freaking med student," I say, pulling my jersey off.

Corey nods, taking my towel and wiping his face. "I'm just kidding, we're all fun and games her and I. I swear, we get along better than I do with my older sister."

I have a soft spot for that type of relationship because of Frannie. I will always look up to her and I believe Corey looks up to Alora in a similar way. That sibling bond he doesn't have.

Kelvin chuckles, taking out his phone. "Speaking of floozies, check out these chicks sliding into my DMs. I swear, if I wasn't married to a smoke show, I'd be hitting up Brooklyn and Queens tonight."

Sticking his tongue out, he starts handing his phone around, showing off half-naked women. I don't look. Why should I? I have a beauty waiting for me right outside. A beauty who will soon open her eyes and welcome me into her life.

As soon as I'm undressed, I head right to the showers and quickly wash the sweat from my skin. Veins protrude in my forearms, trailing to my chest and decorating the lines to my dick. Something I noticed she likes a lot. She may deny her feelings, but I see her looking at me like a starved lion. And one thing's for sure, she loves staring at the muscles that line my hips.

My slides squeak on the tiles floor as I step out of the showers and wrap a towel around me. A few of the guys are singing our winning anthem, hooting, and howling in celebration of our victory.

Kelvin follows me, towel loosely draped on his hips, and he takes me by the elbow, looking around quickly. "Need I remind you to stay away from Alora; I see how you've been eyeballing her tonight. For the sake of my sanity, please do what my wife asks and stay away from her."

Scoffing, I shrug out of his grasp and shake my head. "For the sake of your wife, you shouldn't warn people who they can and cannot be friends with, Kelvin."

"That look in your eyes tells me you want more than a friendship." He crosses his arms accentuating his dark chest. "And she's not someone to introduce to family."

Rolling my eyes, I step away attempting to be the bigger man, but I stop, looking back at him. "For someone who used to be a player, you're sure easy to judge someone you clearly don't even know."

"And you do?"

Yes, yes, I fucking do.

"Not the point, jackass." Shaking my head, I pull

myself away from an argument I know I'd win over a woman who has stolen my heart and refuses to accept it.

Drying off the best I can, I quickly change, grinding my teeth as I do. Sure, Alora and I aren't a thing. Sure, she's been a pain in my ass and pushes me away every time we get close. She's made it known how much she doesn't want a relationship and yet I keep trying. I have no right to defend her like she's mine to claim, but no person deserves to be talked down upon.

Corey nudges my shoulder, sitting beside me with his back to my locker. "You wanna tell me what that smirk is about?"

Frowning, my smile grows. "What smirk?"

"You've had a smirk on your face since the anthem. My guess is it's because of that green-eyed beauty waiting for you outside the locker rooms."

My heartbeat speeds up, a mix of *did we get caught* and *finally someone noticed how much I like her*. But Kelvin's voice eats away at me, the asshole he is making me wonder why. Why the warnings? Why the constant "don't do this"? Alora is nothing but nice to everyone she meets. A hilarious personality, so smart it's actually terrifying, but an idiot when it comes to relationships.

"Nothing's going on. Her best friend is Kelvin's wife. I'm just being nice." The lie tastes sour on my tongue, but I can't very well tell him the truth. Frannie is the only person I've opened up to. And that's how it will stay until Alora lets me in.

Corey chuckles, arching an eyebrow. "I call bullshit,

but whatever floats your boat, big man," he says quietly. "Plus, think of our double dates. Steph and Alora get along. You and I are practically brothers." He laughs, making me chuckle, too. "She could use a little love in her life. All the razing aside, she's a good person."

Tapping my shoulder, he gets up and heads to his locker, leaving me with that incessant need to hold Alora. The same urge I've had since I met her. The need to kiss her and tell her how I feel. The want to have those succulent lips wrapped around my cock as I praise her and shout her name for all eternity.

Soon, someday, eventually, it'll happen.

I'll make damn sure of it.

CHAPTER ELEVEN –
ALORA ASHTON

Watching Scotty walk away, all dressed up in his hockey gear, makes my decision not to be in a relationship kind of a stupid idea. He's sex on a stick. Especially with those skates on. They'd be a hazard in the bedroom, but holy fuck. The second I saw him skate onto the ice, I clenched my thighs together. And when he spotted me—that instant shock yet happiness that bloomed over him made me hate myself so much more for leading him on.

And now, as the locker room door closes behind him, I realize this dinner that has turned into a double date is going to be torture.

"Y'know, maybe I should just head home and let you and Kelvin have a date night. Lord knows you guys aren't going to get them once the baby comes." I fold my arms, leaning against the wall as I stare at the locker room door, expecting Scotty to walk out and sweep me off my feet.

Stop.

Annie pouts and whines. "No, then Scotty will be a third wheel. Just come and jet after we eat."

I lean my head back as the cheers of the men blast through the door. Another evening around him is going to eat at my psyche. I've been denying myself the feelings that are growing and ignoring the way he makes my heart beat faster. But what would come of us, anyway?

I'm in medical school and doing my residency, which means I'll be working crazy hours and never get to see him. He's a freaking pro hockey player who has practice and games in and out of town. We'd never have time together. And the time we do have, we'd be too exhausted to even bother with each other.

There is no way we'd work, even if we tried. Relationships are bound to fail if effort isn't put in. We'd fail not even two weeks out of the gate.

It's better to leave stones unturned and shove these feelings down until they break me. And when they do, he'll be nine inches deep in someone new.

Annie takes her phone out, skimming through missed messages from someone with a warning emoji as their contact name. Annie has never been secretive, but her shoulders tense when she reads the messages, and she shifts her weight from one foot to the other.

"Who's blasting your phone like that?" I ask, my curiosity at its peak. She used to run her texts by me whenever she wanted to send something raunchy to her boyfriends. Even her arguments with Kelvin, she sends me screenshots. And I won't lie, I love the tea.

The fact that she locks her phone and tucks it away with this guilty look washing over her face, I know something's off. "It's nothing important," she says, forcing a grin. "Just work stuff."

I scoff, pushing off the wall. "Work stuff on a

Saturday? Lemme see. I'll tell those fuckers where to shove it for bothering a pregnant woman on the weekend."

She shakes her head and tucks her purse under her arm. "No, it's fine, Alora. I'll just ignore it and deal with it on Monday."

She's refusing to look at me, shifting her attention from the wall, to the floor, as the sound of the roaring fans slowly trickling out of the arena surrounds us.

Something's up, something she doesn't want her best freaking friend to know about.

"Annie, you okay?"

She flashes me a tight smile and nods, her grin growing when the locker room door opens and Kelvin walks out in a pale blue striped dress shirt and dark gray pants. His smile hasn't left his face from the moment they met, and I don't think it ever will.

As if the gods know I won't be able to look away, Scotty comes out behind him, running his hands through his messy wet hair. He's in a gray t-shirt and dark wash jeans with a dark blue blazer to liven up his casual look.

Holy shit balls, the way the jeans hug his muscular thighs, the t-shirt has wet spots from the shower and in its usual fashion, tight as shit.

He's killing me.

Fuck, why did I agree to go out tonight? I just know one of us will make a move and the next thing I know, I'll be naked and on top of him, and then I'll regret it in the morning.

Who are we kidding? No, I won't.

"Hey, babe," Kelvin says, pulling Annie into a kiss.

I roll my eyes and shove his head away from hers. "You guys are so cute it's gross. But if I stare at you two sucking face any longer, I might lose my appetite, so let's go."

Scotty smirks, keeping his head down as we follow Kelvin deeper into the arena, and down a long corridor that leads to the back entrance. I wonder if he played one helluva game for me, showing off what an athlete he can be. And how he generously gave the boy his stick and signed jerseys for fans. God, he's the entire package, and yet, my mind won't agree with my heart. They're battling it out and it's making me nauseous.

Scotty even smells delicious; that sandalwood scent will always remind me of him.

"Did you drive here?" he asks, and I know it's directed at me but he's keeping his gaze ahead. The two people walking with us warned Scotty and me not to get into a relationship. We're going to have to keep our secret for as long as necessary.

"Alora and I took an Uber." Annie threads her fingers with Kelvin's, swinging their arms slightly. "I didn't have to order one now, did I?"

Kelvin shakes his head. "Scotty's got his car."

Even more incentive not to go tonight. He'll drive me home, walk me to my door, and end up soaking my pillows and bedsheets with his body spray.

Think of an excuse to leave.

Think of an excuse to leave.

Think of an excuse to—

"What do you feel like eating?" Annie breaks into my

thoughts, locking our arms together. "I'm feeling a nice juicy burger, mmm. Yeah, I want meat."

Laughing, we step into the evening and head for Scotty's car parked across the street. "Your cravings are getting worse. Pre-pregnant Annie hated burgers."

"I fucking love it," Kelvin growls, groping Annie. "I want her big and plump."

She wiggles her finger at him. "Nope, I'm going back to the gym as soon as this baby is out of me."

Scrunching my nose, I have never thought of or wanted anything to do with children. They can either make or break a relationship, and I'm perfectly fine with the way things are in my life. I adore being Auntie Alora who spoils the kids with things Mom or Dad said no to. Like swearing and candy. "Gross."

"You say that now, but one day when you meet the right guy, you'll want kids." Annie folds her arms, arching an eyebrow at me. "So, for now, you will smile and make it seem like babies are the best."

My nose is still scrunched as Kelvin gets into the front seat and Annie opens the back door. "But it'll tear apart your vagina."

Annie sighs, getting into the backseat. "Oh, my God."

I'm chuckling as I make my way to the other side and stop. Scotty is standing there with the back door open for me, a sultry grin spread on his lips.

I don't bother acknowledging the sweetness of the act, I just get into the backseat and huff quietly.

How the hell am I supposed to deal with this tonight?

He's far different from any man I've ever been with or any man I've ever thought of dating.

He's kind to me and not just because he wants in my pants. This freaking guy wants to date me and see where our relationship goes.

Is he for fucking real?

No, relationships die.

People die.

Hearts break and sometimes never heal.

I won't be wounded.

I won't feel loss.

It'll be me and me alone until the day I die.

He'll find someone new.

He'll find someone who opens his mind and can have great conversations.

He won't need me.

He won't want me.

As far as we know, this is nothing but infatuation. Soon, the temptation will dwindle and we'll both be moaning someone else's name.

Soon. Very, very soon.

CHAPTER TWELVE – SCOTT WESLEY

Every time I glance in the rearview mirror, I catch Alora looking away. Devilishly green eyes making me squirm in my seat.

Fuck, I hate the warnings.

I hate the pep talk, like I'm some horndog who will eat her up and spit her out. But no, I actually want to make an honest woman out of her.

Need I remind you to stay away from Alora; I see how you've been eyeballing her tonight. For the sake of my sanity, please do what my wife asks and stay away from her.

Kelvin made my insides burst into flames. I don't know why I needed the reminder or the warning. She wants nothing to do with me. Made that very clear numerous times.

But here she is, sitting right behind me in my car and smelling as yummy as ever.

Pulling into the parking lot of a sports-themed restaurant, I get out and open Alora's door before she has the chance. I think she likes it, too. She's huffed twice now, and I'm certain it's because she hates how much she likes my gesture.

I'd give her every romantic gesture I could think of if it meant being hers for all eternity.

Kelvin slides his arm around Annie's shoulders as they lead us inside, giving me the itch to do the same to Alora. But I wouldn't put it past her to slap my hand away. Sadly, I'd do it again to get a rise out of her. Seeing how she hates to love me has become my new favorite thing.

Sports memorabilia hangs on the walls, highlights from tonight's game play on the TVs, and loads of people are sitting around the bar wearing our jerseys. My heart races, knowing that people will come up to Kelvin and me, asking for pictures and autographs. As much as I enjoy it, I want peace tonight—

Then I realize I have Alora standing beside me and people will think we're together. Maybe taking pictures with her won't be so bad.

Kelvin smiles at the waitress, letting her know we'd like a booth somewhere private. But the crowd is huge tonight, so no matter where we sit, we'll be bothered.

He leads us toward the booth by the terrace, holding onto Annie's hand as we roam through the crowd with our heads down. Alora reaches back, gripping my wrist as we walk, but I slither my hand to fit into hers. Her palms are slightly sweaty, and for some reason, tingles swarm my insides and make my entire body ripple with excitement.

She's coming home with me tonight, I'll make damn sure of it.

She slides into one side of the booth and Annie pulls

Kelvin into the other side. Smiling when I sit beside Alora, she rolls her eyes and opens the drinks menu. She can roll her eyes all she wants, it doesn't change the way her cheeks darken around me or how the sounds of her moans still ring in my ears.

She scans the menu twice and nibbles her bottom lip. Christ, this girl has me whipped. "Am I drinking alone tonight or are you big goofs going to join me?"

"I'll have a beer," I say, sliding my arms out of the blazer and naturally fanning an arm on the booth behind her. "But I'm driving, so I can't go crazy."

Kelvin whistles, leaning forward. "Like that fucking game, bro. Holy shit, my heart's still pumping."

"It was a helluva game," Annie says, opening her menu. "Alora finally got to see you play."

Alora tilts her head and side-glances at me quickly before folding her arms. "It's just a bunch of sweaty men skating back and forth. I wasn't missing much."

Kelvin grins, tapping the table. "But you made half the guys on our team play their asses off just by being there. You've officially become our good luck charm and have to come to every game."

"Oh, really? If I'm such good luck, then how'd this guy get checked into the boards?" She nudges my side, smirking. "They didn't do your patchwork very well, though."

I remove my arm from the back of the booth and touch my cheek. "I told them I just wanted a Band-Aid."

She hums, rummaging through her purse and pushing me to get out of the booth. "We'll be right back. Order me something fruity to drink and if they come for food, get me a Cobb salad, no avocados."

Stammering as she takes my hand, she pulls me to the restrooms. "Bacon burger with fries and any beer on tap," I call out to Kelvin.

There it is again, our fingers braiding together as she leads me through the crowd. I keep my head down, just until I have her alone. I don't feel like stopping for autographs or pictures until she fixes my cut to her standards.

She pulls me into the family stall, locking the door behind us, and points at the vanity. "Who hires your medical team? Jeez, Annie can do a better job than this and the woman can't draw a straight line."

I chuckle, leaning on the vanity with my legs open so she can stand between them. Being this close to her is sending my heart rate into overdrive, stealing my breath with it.

We lock eyes for a second, making her cheeks blush slightly before she removes the bandages and sputters. "You need freaking—" she grumbles, shaking her head. "You're lucky I have these, shithead." She takes out butterfly closures and cleans my cheekbone with the alcohol wipes in a little pink pouch that looks like a makeup bag.

"Do you always carry this stuff around with you?" I blink quickly when she leans closer, fighting the urge to place my hands on her hips.

"My dad gave it to me the day I told him I got into med school. Said if I'm choosing to take this path, then I have to always be prepared in case I'm ever needed." She blows softly at my wound and it sends goosebumps all over me.

This woman will be my ending if I don't have her again.

She meets my gaze for a fraction of a second, a ghost of a smile spreading to her lips, but it immediately disappears, frown lines replacing it. I hate how much she holds back. How much she keeps guarded, like she's scared to open her heart.

I would never dream of hurting her. Her smile makes life worth it, a fucking joy to witness. But she's cursed. That's all I can pin it to. Cursed with the thought that love breaks us.

It can, but not for us. Never for us.

"There. Good as new." She grins, tapping my chest. "Don't get it wet."

I can't take it anymore. I grab her face and capture her lips in a sinful kiss. She doesn't even hesitate, her tongue parts the seam of my lips as I attack her mouth with mine. She tastes good, fucking sweet. And this thing she does with her tongue, makes my hips thrust forward restlessly.

Fuck.

"No." She pulls away, putting a hand on her mouth. "No, we shouldn't…um, they're probably waiting for us."

I stand taller, looking down at her swallowing hard and fighting the urge to stare at my lips. She's failing miserably. "Why won't you let this happen?" I slide my hand to the back of her neck, letting my fingers get lost in her long hair. "We're perfect together, baby, admit it."

She lets out this breath that knocks me back a step, desperately aching for her lips on mine. "No, Scotty. This—I can't. Please, just remember that."

I can fight her on this and I know I'd win.

I can fight her on this and have her bent over this vanity, moaning my name.

Or I can give in because of the distraught look on her face that tells me she doesn't want me pushing buttons tonight.

So, I won't.

"Okay," I say softly, removing my hands from her. "Just know that I'm not going anywhere."

She winces slightly, taking her bag and walking out the door. I don't follow after her. I give her the space she needs, despite the ache that's eating away at me. The goddamn knife in my chest.

Cleaning up the mess on the counter, I look at her handiwork. A lot cleaner than the medical team that's paid more than she is, I'm sure. If she's even paid at all yet.

Maybe when she's done with school she can work for us, be my personal doctor.

I'll pay whatever she wants. Sky's the limit when it comes to her.

With one last glance at myself in the mirror, I run my fingers through my hair and ready myself to step back into the crowd of rowdy fans. I'm sure they've already asked Kelvin for pictures and autographs.

The second the door opens, Alora is standing there, nibbling her lower lip as three men stop her from leaving the corridor. They have jerseys on and keep pointing at the restroom I'm walking out of.

Nope, don't like the urge that washes over me to pummel these fucks to the ground and make them apologize to her on their knees.

"Hey," I say, stepping closer to her. "You okay?"

Relief blooms on her face and she comes closer, her back flush against my front. "They wouldn't let me leave without getting a picture with you."

My entire body tenses, sliding a protective arm around her and squeezing her closer to my chest. I keep my gaze on them, the three men gulping and flickering their attention between her and me. My jaw clenches at the thought of them touching her or hurting her in some way. "What did they say?"

"They wouldn't let me pass without getting autographs and pictures from you." She lifts her head, exhaling sharply. "Even when I asked to move, they wouldn't listen."

The one with a backward-facing cap puts his hands up. "We don't want any trouble, we're just huge fans and wanted a photo. We figured your girlfriend would get you to agree—"

"You could've just asked me instead of making her feel uncomfortable." I urge her forward, pushing past the guys. "And because of how you made her feel, you're not getting a photo. Next time, I won't be so nice."

The men scoff, muttering profanities at me. I don't care if it gives me a bad reputation, no girl should ever feel threatened or uncomfortable in a situation like that. My sister said it best, *do good in the world, and good will be granted to you. Be an asshole, and you'll be treated like a dirty asshole.* Those men are dirty assholes.

"You okay?" I ask Alora again, keeping a protective hand on her lower back.

She nods, glancing over her shoulder. "They're following us." I stop, nostrils flaring, but she grips my arm to keep me from turning around. "It's not worth it, they didn't do anything. Let it go, please?"

She tugs me to the booth and Kelvin looks back as our food is already severed, and he's frowning. "What took you so long?"

She pulls me into the booth, swallowing thickly. But I can't get my eyes off these guys coming over. My blood's boiling, making me want to fucking scream. "Three guys cornered her, trying to get my picture, and they're right fucking—"

"Hi, I just wanted to apologize for what happened—"

I slide out of the booth and rise, Kelvin following suit. "Didn't I say that next time I wouldn't be so nice?"

"I-I know." The shorter one has his hands up as Kelvin puffs out his chest. "We just—"

"You were just leaving, no?" Kelvin interrupts him.

The silent one of the bunch nods, urging his guys away from us, but that doesn't stop the fucker with the backward cap from snapping a few pictures.

I growl, stepping forward, but Kelvin puts his hand against my chest. "Do you really wanna start something now? We're in the middle of playoffs. This shit can wait. Let it *fucking* go."

Exactly what my sister said when something like this happened to her. People can be so cruel, so ruthless. She's one of the nicest and wisest people I know, and yet, people still point and laugh because she's different. But that's what I love most about my sister. She knows she's different, but it doesn't stop her. And that makes her strong. So fucking strong.

I huff and plop back down in the booth, looking over at Alora, who's chugging her drink. "You okay?"

I can't stop asking her. I want her to feel safe with me. To know I can protect her from any walks of life. That includes dumbass fans.

"Drink, you'll relax a little," she says as Annie looks up at Kelvin.

Kelvin sucks his teeth, watching as the guys head back to the bar. He sinks into the booth, shaking his head. "Reminds me of what happened to your sister."

Alora glances at me as I chug a half-pint of beer, licking the foam from my upper lip. "What happened to your sister?"

"Bunch of trolls took pictures of her at one of the games and posted them online, saying such fucked-up and cruel things." Shaking my head, I finish off the beer and belch quietly behind my hand. "One of the only reasons she doesn't come to my games anymore."

Worry lines appear on Alora's forehead and she nibbles her lip the way she does when she's anxious. She doesn't like this as much as me. I miss having my sister at the games. I used to always salute her after every goal I made.

Now, I have no one to look at in the stands.

"People are fucking assholes," Alora finally says, draining the rest of her drink, too.

"Hear, hear." Kelvin brings his soda to his lips. "Let's

just forget those fucks and go back to celebrating another big win."

I smirk, taking a breath in an attempt to stop this incessant urge to charge at the fucks that keep glancing over here.

But I won't.

For her, I'll sit here and eat a meal I don't think I can stomach anymore.

For her, I'll swallow my pride and let it fucking go.

CHAPTER THIRTEEN – ALORA ASHTON

Scotty drops off Annie and Kelvin first, I have a feeling he planned it that way since my apartment is much closer to the restaurant than their house is. But I'd be lying if I said I didn't have fun tonight. Being around him took this weight off my shoulders and calmed the chaos in my head. I hate how much I like it.

Jumping out of the backseat, I wrap my arms around Annie's neck in a sweet embrace before I hop into the front seat. "Call me tomorrow, yeah?"

She smiles, waving at us. "Love you."

I stick my tongue out and close the door, glancing at Scotty smiling beside me. He has no idea how turned on he made me by protecting me from those guys. Yes, I'm an independent woman who truly didn't need him to step in. I could've owned those men with the snap of my finger.

But Scotty's demeanor changed when he saw me, the scene unfolding in his head like I was in trouble. No one's ever cared for me like that. Protected me like that.

The feeling of his arms on me, knowing I was safe in their embrace. Shit, I should've shoved him back into the restroom and finished what we started in there before I walked out.

But I didn't.

And I won't tonight. I made myself clear from the get-go that Scotty and I won't happen. He wants more, but I can't give him more than what I've already given him.

Nothing more.

God, I'm a fucking broken record on repeat.

"Thank you for dinner, you didn't have to pay for my meal."

He smirks, adjusting the beaded bracelet on his wrist. "It's my pleasure, Alora."

"Mmm, I needed that, though. A night out of drinking without a book in front of me, or notes I have to study, or my residency weighing on me—" I pause, frowning as I realize I'm opening up. Why is it always so easy to talk to him?

"I told you, sweetheart, I'm always here if you need someone to vent to. Just give me a call and I'll listen to all your worries." He smiles, tapping my leg and leaving his hand there. "And if you need to blow off some steam, I'm always available for that, y'know."

Swatting his hand off my leg, I suck my teeth and fold my arms. "Shut up."

He adjusts his hand on the steering wheel, lowering the volume on the radio. "You didn't correct them."

I inhale slowly, looking out the window. "Hmm?"

"Those fuckheads called you my girlfriend, and you didn't correct them." He leans his arm on the center console, hand hanging off it loosely. Was he holding onto that thought this whole time? "You could've told them to fuck right off, but you didn't."

I smirk, rolling my head to look at him. "No, I didn't, because they cornered me for you. Not my fight, shithead."

"Yet, you didn't correct them," he repeats, waggling his eyebrows.

Flicking his hand, I fold my arms across my chest. "No, I didn't. But I'm not your girlfriend."

"Keep denying us, sweetheart. One day you'll give me the time of day." he says, raising the volume on the radio. "You'll own that title, I guarantee it."

It's past midnight, and frankly, I'm way too tired to put up a fight. This feels like a tomorrow problem. Or a never problem. Love is not for me. It hurts. It kills. It'll make my life a living hell.

Sinking into the seat, I close my eyes and listen to the soft folk music playing through his speakers. Yet as soon as I close my eyes, I see the love I've witnessed before. The love of my grandparents. The love my friends found. The love that blooms in the halls at school and on the streets in the city. It's real for them. They found their person, their better half.

But I won't. I saw what love did to my mother. It broke her, tore her apart. She wasn't the same happy-go-lucky woman I knew growing up. Some mornings she barely got out of bed. Some mornings, I'd find her sleeping in her puke as a bottle of vodka and sleeping pills were left open on her nightstand. When I'd come home from school, supper wouldn't be ready because she'd been "too sad" to do anything. On my weekends with my father, I'd see how happy he was. How much he loved life with the numerous women he'd bring home. He didn't have a care in the world; as long as I was happy, he was happy. He didn't need to love someone other than his daughter. Then, when I'd come home, I'd see what love did to my mother. It destroyed her. She may have passed away from a brain aneurysm, but she died long before that of a broken heart.

Truth bomb, I've never had the title of girlfriend before. Belonging to someone who vows to make you smile, make you feel loved. And I don't want it because love isn't real, is it? It's just a made-up concept so companies can make millions on Valentine's Day.

I inhale slowly, open my eyes, and glance over at Scotty as his hand finds my thigh. I can't help but wonder what it would be like to go home with him after a game. The two of us lying in bed, talking or not, but just lying there in a completely comfortable way that only we understand. In a way that would make me nuzzle up to him and fall asleep, knowing I'm protected by someone who can give me the world.

No.

What I need is to focus on school. That's my job right now.

After about twenty minutes of silence, he pulls up to my apartment and parks, letting the engine idle before killing it completely and removing his hand from my leg. "Thank you for coming to the game."

Unclipping my belt, I arch an eyebrow. "No need to thank me, it was Annie's idea."

He takes my wrist, stopping me from opening the

door. "You're always welcome. Every single game there will be a seat just for you."

"Why?"

He unclips his belt and smirks, brushing hair off my shoulder. "Because you are my good luck charm, sweetheart."

"I don't want to be."

My body responds on its own, leaning closer to him. I give him an inch, and he takes a mile, lifting me onto his lap. My breath hitches, making my entire body heat up. He knows what he's doing. Even after I was harsh with him, even after he knew I didn't want this and he said he'd leave me alone, he's still trying.

I straddle him, placing my hands on his chest, and feeling the rapid beating of his heart.

"If you don't want to be my good luck charm, then why are you sitting on me?" He stares at my chest, moving more of my hair behind me. "You're breathing so quickly."

I slam my lips onto his, taking all the shit I keep telling him and myself, and toss it out the window. I need him right now.

Struggling with taking off my jacket, he lowers the zipper on his fly, and that monstrosity in his boxers springs to life. "Condom—I don't have one."

He kisses me again, fumbling in his jeans for his wallet. "I restocked after the last time."

I snatch it from him and tear it open with my teeth. He growls softly, taking himself out and sliding the condom on before I'm even out of this freaking jacket.

With a gasp, he yanks my underwear to the side and slides inside me. This isn't the first time I've had sex in a car, don't think it will be my last, yet there's something about the way he's staring at me, the way he's moaning with me and grabbing my ass.

Sex with Scotty always felt…different.

New.

Like this was more than just a one-night stand.

Like this thing we have is never-ending.

But things end. They always end.

He thrusts upward, groaning softly as a throaty grunt escapes his lips. "Fuck, Alora. You feel so fucking good. So tight, just for me, isn't it? Just for me, baby."

I don't want to hear it.

I don't want him to try and make me swoon, not when he's nine inches deep.

I want nothing but that rush of adrenaline I get with sex. That euphoric high. But let's be honest, I've never had a high like I do when I'm with him.

Every time he thrusts upward, stars cloud my vision. He knows every part of me, every spot to hit that will guide me closer to my orgasm. And when he licks his thumb, rubbing my clit, I can't contain myself any longer. My moans grow, increasing my movements. I don't know who will come first, him or I.

He exhales sharply, legs twitching under me. "I'll wait for you, baby. *Fuck*, come with me."

We tumble over the edge, the car bouncing around as I throw my head back and moan, his mouth biting down on my breast.

God, why does he make my head spin?

We're a mix of deep breaths, dry lips, and intense gazes when he grins. There it goes again, that look he continues to give me because I let down my walls. I have to stop doing that and stop letting him in. I won't end up like my mother. I won't fall in love, only to be hurt, my heart ripped apart.

He's a hockey player, traveling often and meeting numerous fans. Who's to say he won't find someone prettier, more accepting. Someone who'll win him over while I'm back at home with my heart on my sleeve, letting him destroy me.

I don't want to be destroyed.

It's like an affirmation in my head, a motto I repeat to myself.

My eyebrows pinch together, making me whimper softly. His expression doesn't change; I think he believes I'm reacting this way over his smile.

I'm not. No matter how perfect it is. My sanity matters more.

"Always a pleasure." I get off him and fix my thong, tousling my hair. "Well, g'night."

He frowns, tucking himself away. "Wait, what?"

Shooting out of the car with my things, I head to my apartment, squeezing my eyes shut because of the guilt riding through me. I'm never fucking guilty when it comes to sex. Yet, as I make my way to my front door, the pit of my stomach is in knots. I don't want to treat him like everyone else, but it's all I know.

"Alora? What was that?" He runs up behind me, out of

breath. "You have sex with me and just leave, like this doesn't mean anything to you?"

I scoff, wiping a hand down my face. "How many times do I have to say it, Scotty?"

"You're just going to stand there and tell me you don't feel anything for me? Not a single thing?" His chest is heaving, jaw tight.

Tears well in my eyes, but I blink them away. *Never show them you're weak.* My father's voice moves through my thoughts.

I was never one to easily communicate my feelings or emotions. Much like my father. I bury everything as deep as it'll go, forcing myself to forget my problems and hope they evaporate.

But as Scotty steps closer to me, pinning me against the door of my apartment with his lips capturing mine, I know I'll never be able to give him the happiness he deserves.

"I'm sorry," I whisper, pushing against his chest. "I have study group in the morning."

He scoffs, stepping away from me, and shakes his head. "Whatever, Alora. I'll…yeah, goodnight."

He walks off, leaving me standing there with my heart beating like it's at a rave concert. All the while, my brain is denying me that ounce of happiness I might be able to have. It's denying me the natural things that people do.

They find each other.

They love.

They live.

I keep telling myself I won't find that happy ending.

Not while the man who's going to break me is pulling out of a parking spot with a bewildered look on his face like I destroyed him.

But no. He's destroying me by removing the negativity I have against the word love.

How can I feel something for someone when I don't even know what the hell to feel in the first place?

CHAPTER FOURTEEN – SCOTT WESLEY

Parking in the usual spot outside her apartment, I sigh. It's been almost a week since I last saw her. Since we fucked in my car and she just walked away like it meant nothing when her face said so much more than her words.

So here I am, making another attempt at winning her heart, thinking maybe, just maybe, she'll have dinner with me.

Am I an idiot? Most probably.

Desperate? No…yes, also most probably.

Do I care for Alora and that's why I keep trying? A great deal.

My stubborn mind will not take no for an answer when it comes to her. If we tried and it didn't work, then at least we tried. But we would make it work. Of course, it would be a huge change to mesh our lives together; with her schooling and residency, my hockey and practices…yet I know we would make it work. We always would.

Frannie is the only person I open up to about my love life. She's the one I go to with all my problems. And when I told her about Alora and how she's pushing me away, the first thing Frannie asked was if she was worth it. *Yes. Alora is worth every argument and every nerve-wracking gut punch she gives me.* Frannie chuckled over the phone and told me to prove to her with one more try that I'm everything she's never had, starting with the basics.

I open the chat thread with my sister, staring at the last thing she sent me.

FRANNIE: *Make her your spaghetti bolognese. It'll make her smile.*

FRANNIE: *And don't forget to bring her flowers. Sunflowers, of course.*

I breathe out through my lips, looking in the back seat at the bag of ingredients I just picked up. Alora's told me time and time again she doesn't want a relationship, but we originally agreed on being friends. So, we'll be friends. And friends support friends when they're stressed and have probably been eating nothing but ramen noodles while studying and working.

That's exactly what I saw when I helped her clean the apartment. Empty packages of ramen and takeout scattered all over her counters. And coffee, so much coffee.

Sunflowers and red roses sit on the passenger seat and I have two coffees in the cupholders. Hopefully, she appreciates this. Hopefully, she won't slam the door in my face. Hopefully, it'll make her smile. Friends, we will settle on friends.

I hang the bag off my arm, tucking the flowers in it, and hold a coffee in each hand. "Don't bring up relationships," I whisper to myself as I climb the steps and walk to her door. "Don't look at her too long and make her nervous." I expel a breath, repeating this mantra. "Don't bring up relationships. Don't look at her too long and make her nervous." I groan, balancing the coffees stacked one on the other, and knock at her door. "And don't fucking kiss her."

Music is thumping on the other side of the door, which makes me smile. It's the song I had playing in the car the other night when I brought her home. It's things like this that show me she cares. Those walls she has built up around her have something to do with why she's against relationships. And the stubborn fucking asshole inside of me has to figure out what it is.

The door opens to reveal her shocked face, bright green eyes wide and mouth slightly agape. And holy fuck, as if testing my resolve to not do all the things I said I wouldn't do, she opens the door in a black bra and matching thong. This woman is killing me. "Scotty? What—what're you doing here?"

Oh, shit. She's going on a date. Fucking fuck. *No.* No, I won't have that.

"I just wanted to make you dinner." I hold out a coffee, forcing a smile to hide the stone in my throat. I can't lose her before I ever truly had her.

"Oh."

I raise my eyebrows as she stares at the coffee I'm holding out to her. "Oh?"

She shakes her head like she's shaking away a thought. "That's—no one's ever made me dinner before."

"You've had some pretty shitty boyfriends, Alora." I smirk, putting one coffee on top of the other again to hand her the flowers. "And don't think anything of it, they're just flowers to brighten up your kitchen."

She releases a slow breath, still staring at the coffee. "Scotty, I don't know what to say."

Yep, she has a guy over.

"Why?"

Her glassy eyes meet mine, her chest rising and falling quickly. "No one's ever bought me flowers before."

Putting everything at my feet, I take her by the shoulders. She looks petrified, like I just told her I was moving away and she'd never seen me again. "Alora, don't see this as anything other than what I'm offering. Dinner with a friend. We can even cook it together."

Her watery eyes are bouncing all over my face. Flickering between my eyes and my mouth. "Scotty, I—"

I growl, releasing her shoulders, and dropping my head back. "You have someone over, don't you?" Pinching my eyes shut, I shake my head. "No, you're allowed to do whatever you want. I shouldn't be upset or jealous—okay, here. Take the food, I'll text you the recipe—"

"I don't have anyone here," she interrupts me.

I'm so relieved, I might actually kiss her.

"Then what's the problem?" I ask, slightly out of breath.

"You're doing everything no one has ever done for me and it's scaring the fucking shit out of me because I can't give you more." She wipes an escaping tear from her cheek. No, I didn't want her to cry. That wasn't my intention. I wanted to make her smile. Flowers always make the women in my life smile. "Scotty, please tell me you're not here for that."

Tilting her chin up, I brush my thumb on her bottom lip. "I'm here to make you dinner. You're been stressed, and the thought of you being stressed bothers me. I don't want you to worry about anything anymore. Not even us." I smile, planting a soft kiss on her cheek. "We're friends, remember?"

She sniffs, stuffing her feelings deep and letting out a soft chuckle. "You're lucky I'm hungry, shithead."

She picks up the coffee and goes back into her apartment, flashing me her tight ass in that thong. Where is she going? Her makeup is done, hair falls in subtle waves. There aren't any cleaning products around, so she's not cleaning while looking like this. Question is, why is it bothering me?

"You, uh, you're sure you're not expecting anyone?" That jealous side of me shines through as I place the bag on the counter and hold the flowers out to her. "I'm not making any promises that I won't shove my tongue down your throat once they get here."

She laughs, taking a vase from under the sink and filling it halfway with water. "Do you remember my friend from the night we met? We're supposed to have drinks later on."

Arching a brow, I lean my hands on the counter on either side of her. "Where? Here?"

She rolls her eyes and pushes me away from her, grabbing an oversized flannel shirt from the back of a dining chair. "The reason I'm drinking at three in the afternoon is I wanted a night away from life for a moment."

I don't like the worry on her face. "Everything okay?"

She nods, fixing the flowers. "My dad's just—it's fine."

I shouldn't push out of her the reason for her worry. Pushing will lead to her putting more walls up. So, I nod, too, and start taking ingredients out of the bag. "I hope you like spaghetti with meat sauce. This was my mother's favorite and the only thing she taught me how to cook. My sister says if I ever want to win a woman over, I should make her this and she'll fall in love with me like in one of her fairytales."

Alora laughs, taking pots and pans out. Even her laugh is different. It's…sad. "And how many women have you made this for, huh?"

"None."

She pauses as she fills the pot with water and looks up at me. Her pupils are dilated and her chest is heaving. "Scotty—"

"Friends."

She pinches the bridge of her nose as a slew of texts blasts her phone. Luckily, the thing is sitting in front of me and I glance down, seeing a girl's name on the screen. At least Alora wasn't lying about tonight. Not that I didn't believe her, but the dark side of me believes the fuckheads in the locker room that talk about her promiscuous side when I've seen her more than they have. She doesn't have that lifestyle, far from it.

She snatches her phone and reads through the texts, sucking her teeth and groaning softly. "Great. First my dad and now this."

My heart trips when I see the disappointment on her face. I'm sure the reason why she doesn't believe in relationships is probably because she can't depend on anyone. Everyone she's ever cared for has let her down in a way.

I reach out and take the phone from her, scanning through the messages from the bitch who bailed on their plans tonight.

LEILA: *So…don't hate me, but can we do this another night? I'm ovulating!!!!!*
LEILA: *I know you've had a shitty week and the whole thing with your dad. You can drink for two now!!!*
LEILA: *Don't be mad, please!*

I lock her phone and place it face down, looking up at her as she stares at it. Drink for two alone? What kind of friend bails on someone who's having a shitty week? Not a true friend, that's who.

My instinct is to go up to her, wrap my arms around that delicate body, and tell her I'll always be here, no matter what life brings. But I don't think she wants that from me right now.

She sniffs, her fingers grazing her phone, and sighs heavily. "I've been in school to become a doctor for almost six years. The plan was to take over my father's practice when he retires." A tear slips free and she wipes it away quickly, thinking I wouldn't notice. I do and the urge to hold her is prominent, but not until she finishes. "He dropped a bomb on me that he's moving out west and closing his office. All his patients have to find a new doctor and all the nurses are out of a job. I begged him to wait, but he said he's tired of giving me handouts. Tired of paying for my schooling, my car, my apartment, when I'm old enough to afford this shit on my own."

She releases a slow breath, letting more tears slide down her cheeks. "Which, let's face it, I am, but I can't afford any of those things without getting a job. And if I get a job, I'd have to work full-time to afford the life I'm living. I won't be able to finish school, either, because I'd be exhausted and overworked. I feel like I wasted all this fucking time and—argh, I'm shit out of luck and my life is fucked now, all because of his stupid new girlfriend who's my fucking age. But it's fine. It's fine. It's totally…fine. So, yeah—" She glances up at me, eyebrows furrowed. "Um, sorry."

Sorry?

She's apologizing for unloading all this shit swimming around in her head? Jeez, her father is one gigantic asshole for giving up on his daughter like this.

Putting my hand on hers, I squeeze with a reassuring grin. "If you need anything, just ask."

She chuckles weakly, moving her hand away. "No, shithead. It's fine. I'm sure I'll think of something." She sniffs again, wiping her nose on her sleeve. "I'll think of something."

What can I do to change this? What can I do to make her smile again? I like it best when she smiles. Or when she's giving me shit. It's the cutest. That's the Alora I'm falling for.

She takes the bottle of rum from the counter and fills the shot glass again, throwing it back. "He did the same thing to my mom when he left her. She quit school when they got married because he said he'd support her. Which he did—until he didn't. He left her with nothing but the clothes on her back, and growing up with a mom who was depressed all the time because of a man who promised her the world does things to a kid." She meets my gaze, another tear slipping free. "False hope from someone you love only leaves you heartbroken."

She's scared to love because of this man.

Scared to open up because of him, too.

She's never had her heart broken before because she's never let herself love. Never experienced the joy of coming home to someone after a long day or calling someone when something exciting happens—or when something drags you down and you need to hear their voice. I can be that voice.

I'll be the only voice she needs.

I pour her another shot, sliding the glass closer to her, and take the other shot glass for me. Without hesitating, we shoot the rum back and exhale sharply at the same time. "I'm not going anywhere tonight, Alora. You and I are getting drunk and forgetting life for a bit."

She chuckles in this saddened, forced way. "And then we'd end up in bed together. I'm not okay with that."

I swat a hand in the air and start prepping dinner. "I'll crash on the couch, promise."

Her tongue glides along the seam of her lips as she

contemplates my offer. But it's not an offer. She needs a friend right now. Someone to be on her side, holding her hand, and listening to her troubles. And she fucking found him. "Mmm, fine. I'm already tipsy, shithead. Catch up."

I grin as she makes us another drink. Tonight I'll open my heart to her. I'll show her what it can be like to be a couple. I'll show her that not all men are assholes. Not all men only want one thing. I'll show her that men like me want happiness, and I'm eager to prove it to her. This shithead will keep a smile on that beautiful face.

Clapping my hands, I nod and start taking things out of the bag. "You can help me or you can stand there and keep looking pretty. Dealer's choice."

She arches an eyebrow, pouring another shot for us. "I'm a mean cook so this will be a treat to watch."

"I'll teach you the steps. My mother was the best cook I know," I start, taking the shot Alora holds out to me. "Big shoes to fill, sweetheart."

She throws back the shot, narrowing her eyes at me. "Don't call me sweetheart. And stop expecting…things."

Like the coy little ass that I can be, I put my hands up and back up toward her stove. "Just making conversation."

Rolling those beautiful green eyes, she looks into the bag and begins removing a few things. Red wine, Parmesan cheese, puréed tomato jars, herbs, and a pack of minced meat. "You seriously never made this for anyone before? No exes or friends?"

Heat crawls up my neck, settling in my face. I avoid looking at her as I open the jars of puréed tomatoes. No one was worth it enough. No one deserved to be treated to something I created. Sure, my exes have had this before when my mom made it. But never by me. "I haven't been in a relationship in over two years. And before that, when my mom was alive, the exes I had were so picky with their diet. None of them were worth it."

Brushing the hair out of her face, she frowns, staring at the olive oil and garlic I'm tossing in the pan before adding the puréed tomatoes. "What makes me so special? Like I keep saying, this better not be a tactic to win over my heart."

We stare at each other as soon as the word heart leaves her lips, our chests rising and falling. Who are we kidding, our hearts are so far intertwined at this point our souls are holding hands, waiting for us to catch up.

Taking a large spoon from the vase on the counter, I stir the sauce and smile. She knows as well as I do, we're both fucked. "And why would I do that when I know if you wanted me, I'd be in your arms right now." Inhaling a shaky breath, my smile falters because of her stubborn voice. "But you don't do relationships, so I'm settling on being your friend."

Even those words make me sick to my stomach. But it's what I'll agree upon until she wakes up.

Taking another pot from under the sink, I arch an eyebrow at the pink metal and chuckle. "I thought your favorite color was gray?"

Laughing, she stirs the sauce and tastes it, adding a pinch of salt. "Yes. And pink."

Bumping my hip into hers, I smirk at the way we're

standing at the stove like a couple. Just the two of us making a meal together we'll share over a glass of wine and end in a kiss goodnight.

She scratches the back of her neck and sighs, folding her arms. "Sorry about the other night...I shouldn't...we're friends and I shouldn't have jumped out of your car like that after we just—"

"It's fine, Alora," I interrupt her, moving hair off her shoulder to reveal that beautiful neck. "I get scared, too, when my heart beats like crazy around you."

The breath she expels sends a chill through me. It's a breath of fear and acceptance of something we can't control.

Slowly, her eyes find mine, and redness blooms on her cheeks. "You promised you wouldn't do this."

"Do what?" My fingers trace the veins on her neck, stopping at her collarbone and collapsing my hand there. "Your heart is going crazy."

"Scotty," she whispers.

But I can't take it, tilting her chin I press my mouth on hers in a delicate kiss that won't lead to anything more than this. Her eyes are glazed, lips parted, and that fucking tongue drags along the seam of her lips.

But I won't push. When she's ready, she'll come to me.

"You should stir the sauce," I say, my voice cracking. I feel it, too. The magnetic pull brings us together, binding us with this chemistry that's out of this world.

She blinks, and just like that, she breaks away and stirs the sauce. Her manicured hands grip the handle until her knuckles turn white. The sick bastard that I am imagines those hands wrapped around my cock, pumping until it sprays all over her tits. Her perfect fucking tits.

Swallowing thickly, I step around her and grab her ass, chuckling as I do it.

"Hey!" She scowls. "First a kiss now an ass grab. Friends don't do stuff like this, shithead."

Laughter booms out of me, shaking my head. "The guys and I slap each other's asses all the time on the ice. Corey's the only one who went as far as slapping my ass in the shower. What makes this so different?"

Arching an eyebrow, she takes the rum and pours a shot. "Difference is, Corey was doing it because he's a little shit, and you're doing it because you want in there."

Tilting my head from side to side, I take the shot from her. "You're not wrong. It would be a pleasure to slide inside that tight ass of yours, baby."

Rolling her eyes, she shoves my chest playfully. "For your information, no one has ever been in there. Not a single one."

The thought of being the first sends a growl through me, caging her in as I grip the edge of the counter around her. "And yet, you let me slide a finger in there our first night together."

Placing her hands on my chest, she rises, lips feathering mine. She knows what's she doing, I swear she can feel the way my heart is hammering and how sweat beads from at the base of my spine. *Fuck.* "And yet you let me do the same on our first night, shithead."

Closing the distance between us, I press a kiss on those

pillowy lips and step back. "Touché."

Shoving me back a step, she smirks. "Get back to cooking, shithead."

God, this woman is everything I never had. I wish my mother was alive to meet her. SHe'd be in such awe at how Alora holds a conversation. How she describes things and has such a unique outlook on life. It's what drew me to her in the first place, her entire uniqueness.

Stabbing the meat, I look over to catch her checking me out. Her gaze roams up and down my body, pausing on my arms before those cat-like eyes travel to my face.

"Hope you're hungry, sweetheart."

Throwing the shot back, she wipes her mouth with the back of her hand. "Don't call me sweetheart, shithead."

I don't know how much time has passed, but it's enough for the water in the pot to boil and for my hold on her to falter. The intensity of that stare backs me up a step, leaving me delusional about her essence. This woman will be mine. Broken, but she's my broken beauty. Someone I'll fix, someone I'll help heal and keep smiling.

Someone who will call me on her bad days. Flourish with me on her good days. And scream my name on her best days. I know, from this moment on, the woman of my dreams is just out of reach.

CHAPTER FIFTEEN –
ALORA ASHTON

Scotty and I are laughing, tears streaming down our cheeks. He has a heart of gold, he's kind as shit, and thoughtful. He didn't have to spend the evening drinking with me. But he did. Leila was the one who planned this night, and yet, where the hell is she? She's been flaking on a lot lately. Annie's still upset Leila didn't show up to the gender reveal because she was also ovulating.

I didn't mean to open up to Scotty, either, but everything piled on top of each other and kind of erupted out of my mouth. Yet he didn't judge me. He cooked us a meal and shared a few laughs with me. Anything to keep my mind distracted. He's all right, I'll give him that.

It's nearly nine o'clock when I glance at the time on the stove and whistle. "Holy crap, six hours went by in a flash."

He sinks back on the couch, dangling his ankle off his knee. "Now imagine what it would be like to date me."

I roll my eyes and shove his face away. "I don't do relationships, shithead. I told you this."

No matter how fast my heart beats when he's near, or that fluttering sensation in my belly. I don't need added pain and disappointment in my life. I'm happy with how things are. And yet, when we lock eyes, there's that sensation again.

Allowing the alcohol to take hold before my brain can stop it, I straddle him, holding his head in my hands. His breathing shudders, hands gripping my hips, and he wets his lips, tilting his head back. "Can you do this without strings? Without wanting more?"

His lips feather over mine, nipping at the bottom one. "I like you a lot, Alora. Way too much to be one of your booty calls."

"Don't paint this image of me like everyone else does," I say softly, my vulnerability shining through.

"I would never." He holds the side of my face, fingers getting lost in my hair. "From the start, Alora, I saw you. Not the person these people think they see. I saw *you*. Smart, beautiful, and so fucking funny." His thumb brushes my cheek. "You, baby. Just you."

That was the first thing he told me. How he sees me for me and not my reputation. The thought of being seen causes me to act on instinct, taking over my common sense. I kiss him, letting our tongues slide against each other. He tugs me closer, grinding his dick against me. Sober me wouldn't allow this. Sober me would tell him I'm not the type of girl he'd want to take home to his family. I'm broken, lost.

I'm the type of girl you pick up in a bar and never call again. But this isn't true anymore. I'm not that girl. I never was. To him, I'm me. I'm finally me.

With this realization hanging over me, something just snaps.

I pull away from his lips with a whimper. "I-I can't, Scotty."

"I won't abandon you like your father, Alora. I'll be here." He takes my hand and pushes our palms together. "Right fucking here, baby."

My father didn't abandon me. He abandoned my mother. Abandoned our family life for that of a player. He forgot about her and left her for dead…and now, I guess Scotty's right, my father's abandoning me for that skinny bitch in LA.

Scotty wants to be there for me. Care for me. A fucking man wants me and all I want to ask is *why*. Then, flashes of my mother strike me, seeing her crying, sleeping face-first in her vomit, and cursing the day she met my father. No, I won't end up like her. A ruined mess until her life ceased.

Tears well in my eyes and I get off Scotty's lap, shaking my head. "You should go. I—goodnight, Scotty."

He sees the tears as I head for my room, not fast enough to catch me before I slam the door and lock it. "Alora, what happened?" He knocks, jiggling the knob. "Hey, talk to me. What's going through that head of yours?"

"Nothing, Scotty." I cover my mouth as I sob. "It's nothing."

"Open the door, please." There's a panic in his voice. Something that's making me weep even more when he jiggles the knob. "Alora, talk to me. Tell me why you're crying. What did I do?"

"That's just it, isn't it? You did everything right. Everything someone else deserves. But that someone isn't me, Scotty. I don't need this. I don't need you. My life is fucked as it is without a relationship. I have no idea how to add that to the mix. Please." I cover my mouth again, trying to keep calm. "Please, go home. Just go home."

He tries the knob again and growls. "Alora, open the door."

I slide down until my ass hits the floor and hug my knees. I don't want him here. I want him gone. I want to be alone. I want nothing more than to get smashed and forget all this happened in the morning. My head is throbbing, my heart is racing, and all the walls are closing in. I haven't had a panic attack since my mother died. And while I try to calm my breathing, it only causes me to gasp for breaths.

The knob jiggles again and his heavy sigh expels on the other side of the door. "Just breathe, Alora. I'm right here."

Clenching my shaking hands into fists, I close my eyes and his smile comes to life. His face lights up the darkness, easing my nerves and bringing my breathing back to steady breaths.

And when I hear Scotty slide down the door and sit on the other side of it, I know I'm in for a long damn night.

***

I fell asleep in a ball on the floor and jolt into wakefulness when I hear an alarm go off. Scotty groans on the other side of the door, cursing under his breath. He slides up the door and tries the knob once more before his footfalls move through my apartment. An incoming text makes my phone chime before he huffs and curses again, leaving through the front door. Must be a practice, they do have playoff games and they're jetting off to Vancouver soon.

Sucking my teeth, I hold onto my neck as a blinding

pain shoots through it. Not the brightest idea, but in the state I was in last night, I wanted to remain close to Scotty without him holding me. Stupid, right? If I just opened the door, he would have held me and eased my nerves.

Hesitantly, I open the door and head straight for the front window, seeing his Range Rover back out of the spot and shoot like a bullet from the parking lot. I don't feel any better this morning than I did last night, maybe a little hungover. I'm glad I didn't have to face him. I need space. Loads of fucking room to breathe and figure out what the fuck I want to do.

My phone goes off again and I rub the sleep from my eyes as I head for it.

SCOTTY: *Hey, I don't want to leave, but I gotta. I have a training I can't miss. But please call me when you wake up. I need to hear your voice and know you're okay. It's me, Alora. You can talk to me. Please, baby, don't shut me out.* ♥

And that's exactly what I'm going to do. I'm going to keep on doing what I'm doing and hopefully convince my father to give me a shot. I am his daughter, after all. That trumps skinny bitches from LA.

Yet, as I look down at my phone and read the text from Scotty, my heart hammers like a jackrabbit. My head continues to tell me that I'll end up alone like my mother. But my heart tells me to take a leap of faith.

Life was so much easier when I didn't have a heart that continues to betray me.

CHAPTER SIXTEEN –
SCOTT WESLEY

It's been weeks since Alora and I last spoke. I don't know what I expected of that night. A relationship, maybe? I thought I'd be able to change her views on the matter with how I make her feel because I know I make her feel *something*. But I don't think there's a way to change very much about her. She's set in her ways.

I tried not to ask about her whenever I hung out with Kelvin and Annie. I kept things casual and asked about her schooling and if her exams were done. They didn't seem suspicious of my prying, but fuck, did I ever want to just call her up and ask her myself.

She's been quiet on her social media, quiet among her friends, too.

She's frazzled when she's in her head. Calm and collected when she breaks her walls down. It astounds and intrigues me how this woman is able to keep it together so well. But even the toughest people break down every once in a while, and I witnessed her most recent one. I fell asleep on the floor outside her door and had a kink in my shoulder for six days because of it. But I'd do it again in a heartbeat. Anything to be near her and prove that we will work. That's it's me, it's *us*.

I've tried to text her twice, but I never brought myself to hit send.

I know nothing will come of this and I'm already in over my head, but this connection we have when we're together is electrifying. I know she feels it, too. No matter how much she denies it. We're perfect when we're together.

The team is leaving today on a private jet to Vancouver. I hate flying, hate it more when I'm sober. But Coach won't let us take anything before the game tomorrow night. Not even a relaxant.

I wonder if Alora will come today.

We've been waiting for Annie and Sophia to arrive. They were stuck in traffic on their way here. The team had an early morning meeting to go over plays, and the girls were to meet us later. Just not an hour later.

Kelvin nudges me as I scroll through my Instagram account, unfollowing random chicks I used to fool around with. They're not like Alora; no one is as appealing as she is. Woman has me swooning but wants nothing to do with me. Am I coming off as too desperate? Am I making a fool of myself trying to force this? Maybe, but how can I deny the connection we have? Something neither of us has had with anyone else.

"Hey, you good?" Kelvin asks, taking me away from my scattered thoughts.

I lock my phone and frown, sliding it into my pocket. "Yeah? Why wouldn't I be?"

"You've seemed distracted the last few weeks. Even at

practice. You never let Marshall get by, and he did. Twice." Kelvin grabs my shoulder and brings me closer. "Is it because it's almost your mom's birthday?"

I can't very well tell him it's about Alora, he'd have my head on a platter. So, I shrug, swallowing hard. "Yeah, kinda."

"We're all here for you, man, you know that," he says, opening his mouth to speak but stops as soon as Annie, Sophia, *and* Alora come strutting down the runway.

It's impossible to hide my smile, and Alora notices, flashing me a smile, too. I guess things are good with us. Maybe we're okay and we can be friends again. Please, let us be friends again.

"Alora?" Gregory laughs. "The fuck you doing here? Couldn't resist being our good luck charm?"

She shoves her carry-on at his chest. "Who says I'm coming to the game? I've been promised a spa day, I won't say no to that."

Corey snickers with a wink. "Maybe a visit to a massage parlor, too?"

She cackles, following Annie and Sophia up the stairs to the door of the plane. "I brought my vibrator for that, thank you very much."

Woman is killing me in that pastel green dress with dainty little flowers that's short enough to show me she's wearing those hot pink panties.

I let out a rush of air and follow behind, looking back at the guys. Are they staring up her dress? No fucking decency. I make sure to walk closely behind to cover her ass a little and continue to remind myself that she's not mine. But Christ, if they weren't like my brothers, I'd beat them until they apologized.

She claims the aisle seat in the middle of the plane with Annie beside her. They're giggling and taking selfies. It's cute how much she cares for Annie. Protects her in a weird sisterly way. She never told me if she has any siblings, my guess is she doesn't. Kelvin told me that she and Annie have known each other since grade school. It's evident by the way they laugh and poke fun at each other. It's not the same friendship she has with Sophia, not by a long shot.

Like some sick lost puppy dog looking for his mate, I googled the meaning of Alora; it means *my beautiful dream*. This woman is all that and then some. She's my dream, a dream I didn't know was missing until I spotted her sitting at a bar.

The guys are sitting sporadically on the plane, talking among themselves, some listening to music, and others taking selfies to post for their fans. Kelvin sits in front of Annie, and it allows me to sit in front of Alora. The woman smells like citrus, and I can't stop inhaling.

Coach stands up and claps his hands once we're settled in and quiet down. He's one of the top coaches in the league. I was lucky as sin to get on his team. Even luckier when he told me he had his eye on me for years.

"All right, fellas," Coach says, standing in the aisle of the plane. "No drinking, no drugs, and no extracurriculars." He shoves Brett's head. He's the only one of us that snorts cocaine. He's one helluva hockey player, but he'll ruin his career if he continues with that shit. "We have a five-hour flight ahead of us. So, get some rest, yeah? We'll be on the ice tonight, practicing the newest plays we went over today. I want it locked down in time for tomorrow's game, got it?"

"Yes, Coach," every single one of us says at the same time, making Alora chuckle.

"All right." He claps again. "Buckle up, fellas...and ladies."

A lot of the guys, including Kelvin, start fist-pumping and barking like dogs. They bang their hands against the chairs and overhead compartments. I laugh softly, watching these men act like fools. But we're a team, and on the ice, we're a unit. Their spirit for the game is just as high as mine. So, I let out a howl, slapping hands with Kelvin.

Undefeated and going strong. Winning the championship is ours this year, I can feel it.

Coach puts his hands up, a cheeky smile on his face. "Settle down, settle down."

Alora and Annie are laughing, getting comfortable in their seats as Annie fake gags. "The testosterone in this plane is making me nauseous."

Alora clicks her tongue. "You mean the egos. Fifty bucks says someone has their shirt off as soon as the captain removes the seatbelt sign."

"You just can't handle this, sweetness," Mitch says, leaning over with a wink.

Alora grimaces. "In your dreams, pal."

I smile, looking down at my phone that I'm turning off. I like her, there's no denying that. I probably would have liked her, too, if I just met her at one of Annie and Kelvin's get-togethers.

She's smart, which leads to great conversations.

She's gorgeous, and that definitely inflates my ego to have her in my arms.

We click, but she's got a head of stone.

The plane starts moving, readying for takeoff. I take a few deep breaths as we speed down the runway. Another deep breath when we're up in the air.

And release it when we reach cruising altitude for the next five hours. Sleep—I'll catch up on that while listening to the ramblings of my dream girl behind me.

listening to the ramblings of my dream girl behind me.

CHAPTER SEVENTEEN –
ALORA ASHTON

I thought it would be awkward to see Scotty again. Aside from his constant staring, it isn't. To top it off, he's sitting in front of me as if he's claiming me like Kelvin is, sitting in front of Annie. I'm not going to lie, Scotty's been all over the place in my head. I can't take it. I've never been this hooked on someone before.

And with the news that will crumble my entire life, he's been on my mind so much more.

Annie nudges me, causing me to inhale and glance at her with a forced grin. "Where's your head at? You look lost."

"Just thinking about school and my dad's practice…" I shrug, licking my lips and looking at her. "Stress is not fun. And I could really use a damn drink."

She chuckles. "Spa day is a must."

I nod, getting comfortable as Scotty leans his seat back a little, the top of his head coming into view. His hair is a mess today and I don't think he did that on purpose like he usually does. But at least he smells like sandalwood. It's the only scent that reminds me of him.

"How're you feeling lately? Baby still giving you nausea?" I ask Annie, trying to veer the topic of conversation away from me.

She's good at prying into my life even when I don't want to tell her anything about it. I used to tell her everything growing up, until she met Kelvin and the judging started. His words and actions rubbed off on her. She never judged me and used to wish she could be as extroverted and wild as I am. Then Kelvin changed her, which I guess is fine. But things between us don't feel the same. So, I keep to myself, trying not to tell her as much as I used to. Especially when it comes to shocking news.

And lately, the biggest secret of them all is Scotty. I tried to erase him from my head, but I couldn't. Fuck, I don't think I'll ever be able to. Then he posted a shirtless picture on his Instagram last week with the caption, *Open your eyes, sweetheart, this one's for you.* I nearly hit my head against the wall. The shithead knew I was watching. He wants this to work, and I don't know how it could.

Annie rubs her stomach, smiling down at it. "I think we have a name picked out."

Humming, I cross one leg over the other at the knee. Something she hasn't been able to do because of the pressure down there. Smiling at the genuine happiness on her face, I raise my eyebrows in anticipation. "Lay it on me."

"Landon Issac."

I puff out my bottom lip and nod. Not the name I would go for, but it's cute, a tribute to her father, as well. "Baby Landon, I like it."

She smiles, leaning her head on my shoulder. "Good, I'm glad. I was worried you'd think it was too…jock-ish."

Letting out a laugh, I take her hand. "You could name

him Thaddeus and I'd still love it."

"Thaddeus the Third, Duke of…New York?" she says, laughing until she snorts.

"Oh, God, I remember Thaddeus from middle school, the nerdy kid with the lisp who always announced himself when he entered a room." I scrunch my nose and shake my head. "Didn't you go to second base with him?"

She palms her face, shaking her head. "Don't remind me."

Kelvin rises from his seat, looking back at us. "You thirsty? Hungry?"

She shakes her head and lifts her reusable water bottle. "It's orange juice, so I'm good until lunch."

He jerks his head to the side. "Can you pass me the headphones? Scotty's passed out and he's a loud snorer."

He snores, huh?

Why do my insides love that about him? Like it's some flaw—shit, stop it, heart. You're not allowed to like him. Not with this burden of his.

Annie hands Kelvin the headphones and leans her head on my shoulder again as she takes out a book. She's obsessed with romance novels. The smuttier, the better. And *I'm* the creep for actually doing all the kinky shit in these books she fantasizes about?

I get comfortable beside her, letting my eyelids droop, too. Might as well catch up on some sleep with the nonstop weekend I have ahead of me.

CHAPTER EIGHTEEN –
SCOTT WESLEY

Screams wake me.

The shaking plane is beeping and vibrating.

Oxygen masks fall out and Kelvin shoves me, waking me up fully. "Put it on! Put it the fuck on!"

Half dazed, I do as he says and I strap the mask on, looking around at all the panicked faces. What the fuck is going on? Are we crashing? Is it turbulence? Shrieks drown out the orders the captain is yelling over the intercom. People are crying, squeezing each other's hands.

The person I'm most worried about is behind me.

Annie's wails pierce my eardrums, her panicked voice taking over the rattling plane and everyone else's screams. "My oxygen mask didn't come out! It didn't come out!"

She's hyperventilating, and Kelvin goes to unclip his belt, but I stop him, squeezing his forearm.

"Take mine," Alora says. I look back and see her placing it on Annie's face. Tears are staining her cheeks. "Just breathe, okay? Like me." Alora's voice shakes, but she steadies it. Steadies it for her best friend and breathes slowly, in and out, with a forced smile on her face. "Just breathe."

Everyone is in a panicked frenzy. The plane is going

down. We're going to die.

We're all going to die!

I glance back again and Alora has her eyes closed, head leaning back, her breaths coming quickly. The selfless act she did for her friend is astounding. Not one of the fucks around me would even think to do something like that.

Taking my oxygen mask off, I jolt as if the plane hit a speed bump, and hold it out to her. "Alora! Put it on."

She opens her eyes and shakes her head, wetness clouding her vision. "It's okay."

"Alora, please," I whisper as she closes her eyes again. I want to hold her, crash with her in my arms. Instead, we're gripping the handles of our seats and breathing quickly.

I look out the window and the top of the trees are coming into view, the bottom of the plane scraping them. It'll be over soon and I didn't even get to kiss her goodbye.

We're bouncing and twisting, slamming into different branches and trunks.

Screams get louder, praying gets quieter, and the thought of surviving is diminishing.

The plane hits a tree, sending our carry-ons tumbling down, knocking into us.

The screams.

So many screams.

When the plane takes a nosedive and hits the final tree, I jolt forward, hitting my head on the plastic part of the seat in front of me. Warmth blooms on my head, and everything else blurs, fading to black.

CHAPTER NINETEEN – ALORA ASHTON

The screams have settled, turning to moans and groans once the plane has touched down.

I'm shaking so much, I'm shivering.

I've flown planes a handful of times, enough to know shit like this isn't supposed to happen.

It's not supposed to crash.

It's not supposed to catch fire.

It's just not.

My dad always said *you're more likely to die in a car than on a plane.*

Well, Dad, you're fucking wrong here. We almost died. Fuck, some of us probably did.

I'm trying to catch my breath, looking around at everyone checking themselves for damage.

This is what I do, I'm almost a doctor. This is my time to shine.

But I can't move.

I can't fucking move.

"Alora?" Annie's weak voice jolts me from my fear. "Kelvin?"

I moan, looking down at my leg. It's bleeding and throbbing. Bags were falling and things were flying.

Something must've nicked me. But it's okay. It's just a scratch. Even though it fucking hurts and is bleeding, I'll be okay.

"Annie." My voice is strained. I clear it and unbuckle my belt. "Hey, look at me."

Annie's hands are shaking when she removes the mask and places a hand on her stomach. "The baby," she whispers.

"It's going to be okay," I say, trying to reassure her. But I have no fucking clue if any of us will be okay.

She starts crying, hugging herself. I'm frantic, unable to fathom any clear thought other than the fact that we landed, and we're okay. But she needs me, needs something.

Taking her hand, I squeeze, forcing a lopsided grin. "It'll be okay, Annie. We'll get outta here."

She nods, knowing I'm always the strong one of the two of us. Just like when we were kids. Always getting us out of the trouble I got us into.

I get up and look around; the back of the plane is completely crushed, and the front of the plane is nonexistent, having separated during the crash.

How in the hell did this happen?

Kelvin turns in his seat to look at Annie. "Hey, babe, hey."

She's crying softly, holding on to her stomach for dear life. She's pregnant, and under this much stress, there's no telling what could happen to the baby. "What happened? This doesn't make sense. We should've been—"

He reaches over and takes her hand, his dark skin against hers is so different yet the same as goosebumps rise on their skin. "I'm right here."

"I love you," she says, her voice wavering.

"Me too, babe." Kelvin's eyebrows pinch together, and he looks at Scotty with pure horror. "Scotty? Hey, man." His panicked voice takes over everyone else's panic. "Scotty? Scott!"

Snatching my cardigan from my purse, I tie it around my leg, yanking it tightly before I move to Scotty. He's bent over, limbs limp. Fear licks up my spine when I see blood. This isn't like me to care about someone more than myself. But fear licks up my spine as I touch his face, then check his pulse. He's alive. Tendrils of relief spread through me like wildfire, my heart still beating like a drum.

Kelvin helps me push him up, gently resting his head back against the chair. Scotty's beautiful face has a cut above his eyebrow, blood leaking down into his eye. A harassing anxiety strikes me at the thought of losing him. I thought I could do this without him, but I can't. *I can't.*

Panic blooms in my chest when the screams of others hit my eardrums. Am I able to help these people? The ones who judge me? The ones who think I'm nothing but a whore? Will anyone trust me?

Will Scotty forgive me?

It's your time to shine, Alora.

"Scotty?" I tap his face lightly, then tap a little harder when he doesn't answer. "Scotty, I need you to open your eyes for me, okay?" Turning his face to mine, I look at the cut. It's fairly deep. I might have to stitch it up if we don't get out of here.

Kelvin shakes his shoulder. "Scotty?"

A groan leaves Scotty, sending my heart into a tailspin as he turns his head to the side. "Hey, Scotty. I need you to open your eyes. Can you do that for me?" My hand is still cupped to the side of his face, my thumb brushing along his cheek. "Scotty?"

His eyes flicker open and he looks at me, furrowing his brows. "What—" He winces and lifts a hand to his head. "Fuck."

"Don't touch it," I say, pulling his hand away. "I'll take a better look at it once we get off the plane."

He groans again, coughing and shifting in his seat. "The plane." He gasps, taking my hand from his face. "Are you okay?"

I nod and look at Kelvin. "If you can find my bag, I have my medical kit in there. I'll be able to close that cut."

Scotty takes my leg, studying the blood soaking into my cardigan. "You're hurt—"

Touching his face again, I flash the most reassuring grin I can muster. "I'll be fine."

Annie leans over, holding out her silk scarf. "Put this on your head."

Taking it from her, I wrap it around his head, tying a knot to keep it in place. "Don't get up too fast, okay?"

Kelvin gets on his knees on the chair and leans over it to grab Annie's hand but gets immediately distracted when he looks at the seat diagonal to mine. Corey's whimpering, looking beside him as his teammate has a piece of metal lodged into his neck, blood squirting everywhere.

Gasping, I take a step back and stare at the metal shard

penetrating Corey's thigh. He's wincing and whimpering as he holds onto his legs. I'm in too much shock to move. I know these people will depend on me for help. I'm doing my residency, I'm almost a doctor. This is what I signed up for. I help people, that's my only job.

How can I do this? Am I up for the task? I have no idea if I can stomach this much blood and death and—

"Alora, please. I can't die here," Corey cries. "I can't fucking die here."

It's my time to shine. I can do this. I can fucking do this.

My dad's always been someone I look up to. My mother was my guiding light for many years, but she let my father run her life. For years I viewed her as weak. She was never weak, she was brainwashed. So deeply in love that she forgot who she was. I looked to my dad for advice. And for many summers, I helped out at his practice. I've seen blood and I've sewn up wounds.

This is something I know how to do and no one will judge me for it.

My breathing quickens, staring at the blood soaking into Corey's jeans. Working at my father's practice, I've been around injuries, but never anything this chaotic. Never to the point of seeing someone's insides, or brains splattered on the seat in front of them.

Never like this.

Twisting my hair into a high ponytail, I ignore both the dread crawling around inside me as well as the pain in my leg. It's a similar pain to the time I tried to jump a fence and missed. A feat that earned me a cut on my inner thigh, requiring seventeen stitches, and it took months to heal.

The coach stands, staggering as he holds onto his side. "Hey, hey!" he yells. "Everyone all ri—" That's when he sees the dead guy bleeding out beside Corey. "Jesus Christ."

I limp toward Corey, eyeing the smoke at the back of the plane. Two guys are sitting in front of him, taking quick heavy breaths to calm themselves. But it's not the time to relax, it's time to act fast and get out of here.

"Hey." I snap my fingers at them. "Help me get him outside."

Without hesitation, they climb out of their seats, widening their eyes when they see Corey's leg. One lifts him by the arms, and the other carefully takes his legs.

Corey winces and whines, looking at me with teary eyes. "Alora, please."

"It'll be okay, Corey." I try to keep a straight face when all I want to do is scream and cry with him. "We need to get you off the plane."

Slowly, all of us file out, Kelvin holding onto Annie, Gregory holding onto Sophia, and Scotty right behind me. I reach back and he immediately grabs my hand, squeezing it tightly. I know I shouldn't give in to these feelings, but if not now, then when? Even if just for a moment to ease my nerves.

As we make our way to the exit, I count three more dead guys. One of them has a broken neck from the food cart crashing down the aisle, the other has a piece of metal poking out his chest, and the third is face-first on the floor, blood pooling around him.

Four of these men are gone. They have families, kids,

and wives back home. Gone, all for a fucking hockey game that will guarantee them winning the championship.

Not. Fucking. Worth it.

We get outside and take in more of the damage. The back of the plane is smoking, the wing beside us is missing an engine, the tail is crushed, and the front is gone. Could it be engine failure that caused this? Mechanical issues?

Negligence of the missing pilots?

Planes don't crash like this. They just don't!

I limp to Annie and Kelvin, ignoring the cries and pleading for help from the others. My best friend is my priority right now. "Hey." I take Annie's hand. "Lemme check you out, okay?"

Kelvin slides my purse over but I don't need anything in there. Just her wrist.

Looking at my watch, I find her pulse and count the beats. Her blood pressure is high, but it's understandable. I close my eyes, listening to my own heartbeat as it pounds in my ears.

"And the baby?" she asks, a hand pressed onto her stomach.

With a breath, I open my eyes and stare at her stomach, there's no fucking way I'll be able to tell if the baby is okay. I didn't think to bring my stethoscope with me to try and listen to his heartbeat. Why would I bring it?

But I have to keep her calm. The less stressed out she is, the better it'll be for baby Landon.

I take my watch off and give it to her. "I want you to monitor him until I come back. Two-minute intervals—I want to know how many movements you're feeling, okay? Count his kicks."

She nods, sniffling, and takes the watch with her shaking hand. "Count the kicks."

"Alora?" Corey groans, holding his leg. "Alora, please!"

Looking at Scotty, he's leaning on a boulder, out of breath when we lock eyes. My ears are ringing. Everything is vibrating. I don't know what to do. They're calling my name. They're crying. They need medical assistance.

We crash-landed and by some miracle, we're alive.

We're alive and in the middle of nowhere. How the hell are we supposed to get out of here?

How the hell am I supposed to help these people?

How the fuck can I keep it together when all I want to do is scream, too?

I start breathing quickly, hyperventilating and unable to control the oxygen coming in. Kelvin takes my hand, speaking to me but his words are masked by my gasps. Annie's doing the same, tears streaming down her cheeks like mine.

I can't fucking do this!

I don't even notice it until Scotty is on his knees beside me, taking my head in his hands.

Nothing's registering.

All I hear is my thundering heart and the ringing in my goddamn ears.

But he steadies me as his thumbs brush the tears away, pulling me out of my shocked state. "You got this, okay? You can do this, Alora. Everyone needs you. Okay? We *need* you." He releases my face and takes my hands. "Breathe with me."

Pushing my quivering lips together, I release a shuddering breath. "This is too much."

"We're right here, Alora," Annie says. "We're here to help, okay?"

I sniff, glancing around. The guys have scattered throughout the area, groans and crying filling in the silence. Pushing this panic aside, I shake my head and exhale. "Just count the kicks, yeah?"

Scotty glances around, too. "Tell me what you need me to do."

I slowly rise to my feet as my chest tightens and know I have to head over to Corey. "M-my medical kit."

Scotty takes it from my purse and squeezes my shoulder. "Just breathe, okay?"

Sniffing, I limp my way to Corey. He tries sitting up when he sees me, his face sweaty and pale. The blood soaking into his jeans causes a worry that gnaws at my churning stomach. Fuck, what if it hit an artery? I'm not prepared for that.

Carefully, I get onto my knees with a wince between his legs and clear my throat. "Lemme see."

One of the guys who helped get him out of the plane looks at me, annoyance spreads to his face. "What the fuck are you going to do? He has a piece of metal in his leg."

"She's a medical student, jackass," Scotty says, getting on his knees on the other side of Corey's leg.

"Oh, s-sorry," the guy says, gulping loudly.

Now's not the time for my snarky remarks. Survival mode. Safety. And a way to help these people is what matters. "What's your name?" I ask the unhelpful jackass as my shaking hands are pushing around the puncture on Corey's leg. His shrieking is not making it easy for me.

"Donovan."

I point at the plane. "I need you to find me a knife to cut his pants. Scissors, anything."

He gets up quickly and jogs into the plane. Gregory comes up to me next, holding his shoulder. "I think it's dislocated." He winces, trying to move it.

"Okay, let me deal with this and I'll pop it back in." I've snapped thirteen shoulders back in place since I started med school. This is a piece of cake.

Corey's leg, on the other hand, is making my usual steady hands shake, as if I'm standing outside naked in the middle of winter.

I open my kit with an exhale. "Anyone have vodka?"

"Now's not the time to party, Alora," Kelvin calls out. I ignore him as a tall man with cornrows searches through his bag and pulls out a large bottle of tequila.

"Will this work?" he asks, tapping his chest. "Brett."

"Thanks, Brett," I say right as Donovan comes back with a pair of cuticle scissors. "This is all I could find."

"It's better than nothing." Handing the bottle of tequila to Scotty, I look at Corey as his deep brown eyes bore into mine. "It'll be okay." I force a grin. "I have to cut off your jeans."

He nods, sniffling and glancing at Scotty. "If anything

happens to me—"

"Nothing will happen to you," Scotty interrupts him. "You're going home to your girl and your son."

My eyes well with tears at that thought, knowing Corey has a seven-month-old baby at home, and a wife with postpartum depression.

I have to make sure he gets home to them.

Corey whimpers, looking at me as I cut his pants from the ankle up to his groin so I can see the wound. It's gushing blood, painting my hands in seconds. If this hit an artery, there isn't anything I can do. But I have to try.

I have to fucking try.

Opening the tequila, I take a swig, shaking my head before I pour some of it on the wound to help disinfect it. Corey yells and tries to stop me, but Brett, Donovan, and Scotty hold him in place.

Blood is seeping out the sides, painting his leg crimson. The metal shard couldn't have gone that deep. Maybe an inch or two. It's not out the other side, which is a good sign.

It is a good sign, right?

The way the blood is pouring out, I can't help but think he'll never see his son grow up, and that's a fucked-up thought on my part. But I don't know how to stop this bleeding.

"Fuck," I say under my breath.

Corey whimpers. "What?"

Furrowing my brows, I look up at him. My voice wavers when I try to speak. But I can't. All I can think about is that baby growing up without a father.

Scotty puts a hand on my shoulder, causing me to look away from the blood and to those eyes that look more hazel than green today. "You got this, Alora, okay?"

Do I, though?

Clearing my throat, I wipe a falling tear. "O-one of two things can happen. Uh, i-if it hit an artery, you're as good as dead." Corey groans, and I shake my head and look down again.

A dull ache pounds in my chest as I release a breath. "If I leave it in and you get an infection, we might have to chop your leg off," I say, tears sliding down my cheeks. Corey sobs, pushing himself up off the ground, but Brett slides an arm around his shoulders, steadying him.

A dizzying sense of anxiety washes over me when I look at Scotty for that ounce of support I need from him. "Um, i-if I pull it out and…and I—" I look down at his leg again. "I just…I don't know what to do," I whisper.

Corey's eyes darken with worry, and he grits his teeth. "Just take it out." He chokes on a sob. "Just fucking take it out."

Scotty squeezes my hand, Corey's blood spreading onto him. "Just tell us what to do, Alora. We're right here to help, okay?"

The thought of having the death of someone on my hands is like a million needles jabbing my skin. What the fuck do I do?

Closing my eyes, I tilt my head heavenward, taking a few deep breaths. This trip was not intended. I never planned on coming, but then I *had* to.

Now look at me. What if we're stuck here? What if no one finds us?

I sniffle, wiping my tears on my forearms. "Okay. Shit, okay."

Grabbing the tequila bottle, I pour it on my hands to sanitize them, staring at the metal poking through his skin. How am I going to do this? How am I going to make sure he survives?

This is a lot of pressure for someone who's never done something this drastic. How does my dad do this, being under the strain of having someone else's life in his hands?

I try to close my eyes and remember what I can from class and from my dad. All I can see is blood. So much damn blood. "I, uh, I'll have to cauterize the wound as soon as the metal is out. I need a spoon and a lighter. And towels—or shirts."

Scotty presses his lips onto my shoulder, his breath fanning my skin. The last time I saw him, I hurt him badly. Told him I wasn't good for him. I'm a mess. I don't do relationships.

All this time, he's the only thing that's been on my mind, keeping me steady. And having him right here beside me is easing my nerves, allowing me to do this.

I can do this.

I look around and see the coach holding onto his side and watching me in action. "Hey, Coach, I need your belt."

He nods, wincing as he removes his belt with Donovan's help. It's a leather belt; it'll hold tight around Corey's thigh.

Scotty takes the belt from Donovan, getting ready to wrap it around Corey's leg. "Where?" he asks, looking at me.

Fixing the belt on his upper thigh, Scotty ties it as tight as possible. Corey yelps, a loud and gut-wrenching cry. But we have to do this.

A fist of panic twists inside me at his sobs. "I-it's just to help limit the bleeding," I explain, nodding quickly.

Corey sucks his teeth, tears streaming down his cheeks. "Hurts like a son of a bitch."

A spoon is held out in front of me; it's now or never. I've never cauterized a wound before but I've seen it done on survival shows. My mom was obsessed with those. We'd watch them religiously. Sometimes I'll still indulge in a binge-watch of a few episodes, but it doesn't feel the same without her.

"Okay, I need people to hold him down. Scotty, when I pull it out, you're going to push the heated spoon on the wound, got it?"

He nods, coming closer to Corey.

I begin heating the spoon, but Scotty takes it from me, heating it himself so I can do my job and try to save this man's life. Cracking the bones in my neck, I suck in a few rushes of air, relying on everything I've read in my textbooks about punctures to arteries. It can decrease blood flow to the heart, and cause excessive blood loss, which can cause him to bleed out quickly. I'd have to insert a stent to fix the issue, but I have no idea how to do that and I'm not equipped to do anything so drastic in a fucking forest.

I'm praying it isn't bad. *Please, don't be bad.*

Corey catches my eyes, his are red and wet with tears. "Alora?" he whispers.

Closing my eyes, I groan, dropping my head back. More breaths, deep and shaky. *You can do this.*

"Fuck." I put my hand on my stomach and breathe again. It's as though not enough oxygen is filling my lungs. I'm drowning, my lungs burning, desperate for air. "Okay, hold him as steady as you can, please."

Swatting my shaking hands in the air before gripping the metal shard, I look up at Corey. All the times he made fun of me and treated me with disrespect have completely gone out the window. He sees me now, the real me. Not the trollop that sleeps with men. He sees what I'm capable of. For fucking once, I feel wanted.

"Fucking shit, Alora. *Fuck!*" He grinds his teeth, staring down at my hands. "Please, please."

I don't even countdown, I just pull the metal out as steady as I can, tossing it aside. Scotty immediately puts the spoon down, helping to stop the bleeding. At least, I'm hoping it'll do that. Grabbing the shirts that Brett placed on the ground beside me, I apply pressure as I breathe through my anxiety. He'll be okay. He *has* to be okay.

Corey leans back into Brett, his face pale and moist. "Fuck…fuck…I think I'm gonna pass out."

"Just breathe," I tell Corey without looking up at him. My focus is on his leg.

The bleeding has stopped slightly; and the metal rod didn't go in as deep as I thought, which is a good sign.

I sigh, wiping my forehead with my forearm.

"Okay…okay, this is promising." I look up at Corey and smile, reassuring him. "But this next part will hurt like a motherfucker, so brace yourself."

Corey stammers, looking down at his leg. "What do you have to do?"

"You need stitches, but before I do that, I have to clean it well to avoid infection," I say, wiping my hands on the shirt I used to clean his leg. "It's, uh…going to be okay."

Scotty squeezes my shoulder again, causing a grin to tug at the corner of my mouth. Why do his reassuring squeezes make this situation a little bit better?

I release another breath and grab my medical kit, glancing back at everyone else around me. So many injured players and only one measly medical kit. We'll have to use it sparingly; only for the most desperate cases. Cuts and bruises will heal, but wounds requiring stitches are a priority.

With a gulp, I turn back to Corey who's breathing slowly with Brett's arm still around his shoulders. "Can someone search the plane for a first aid kit? I might need more supplies." Two men run off, going into the plane as Scotty gives my shoulder another squeeze.

"You did good, sweetheart."

I know what I have to do, and that's to be a leader for these people. Help them and heal them; it's up to me to make sure we go home in one piece.

CHAPTER TWENTY –
SCOTT WESLEY

Seeing her work her magic is breathtaking, astounding. I'm so proud of her.

She speaks to them soothingly, reassures them that everything will be fine. She panics, but she breathes through it, looking at me for her calm. *I'm her calm.*

We have no idea if we'll be fine or not. But she finds a way to soothe everyone.

It's inspiring.

She patched up Corey, popped Gregory's shoulder back in, cleaned scratches, and made sure everyone was okay. She checks on Annie often, feeling her pulse, asking about the baby.

But no one checks to see if Alora is okay.

She's sitting on a rock away from everyone, her hands stained with blood from multiple people. They're shaking, but she clenches them into fists and releases them in an attempt to stop it.

She's been going nonstop the past couple of hours, fighting through her panic with me right beside her. She has no one to turn to, worried about everyone's well-being but her own. So, I stayed by her side. *I'm her calm.*

A few deep breaths leave her before I make my way over. The cut on my head hasn't been tended to, but I don't expect her to do it now.

I tossed the scarf from my head after we dealt with Corey. The bleeding has stopped, but it still stings and I wince every time I squint from the bright sunlight.

"Hey, Alora? You okay?" I ask, sitting beside her.

She lifts her head and glances at me quickly before looking back down. Those green eyes are glassy; she's been crying. Hiding her pain and worry after getting her shit together with Corey. I don't like seeing her tears. "I'm fine."

Hesitating, I put my arm around her, inhaling a breath. "You're doing great, you know that? We're lucky to have you here."

She lowers her head and starts sobbing—quiet sobs that shake her body. I press my lips onto her temple until she calms down. I don't care who sees this, I don't care about the warnings or the backlash. She needs someone right now.

I will be that someone.

Shushing her quietly, I rub her arm as her crying slowly subsides. She needed that, fuck, we all do. We crashed in the middle of nowhere and we have no experience being in the wilderness.

We're lucky to be alive at all. Even luckier to have Alora here. Medical student or not, she was a trouper today and a lot of us should be thankful for that.

She shakes me off, tensing as if she let her guard down for a moment. "You don't have to do that." She sniffs, getting to her feet. "I'm fine."

She's pushing me away.

She's building her walls.

She's blocking me from being there for her again.

I just want her to open her damn eyes and see we're meant to be.

"Hey!" Marshall calls out. "Hey, guys, I found water. It's a lake or something."

Alora walks to Annie with me hot on her tail. "Annie, let's go. You have to cool off."

"I don't want to go in the lake, I'm fine sitting here," Annie retorts, rubbing her stomach.

Alora winces when she leans down in front of Annie, putting the back of her hand on Annie's forehead. Alora's leg is still wrapped with a sweater. She hasn't even tended to her own wound, she's so focused on everyone else.

She stands taller, hands in fists on her hips. "Look, you can fight me on this all you want, but you know I'll win. So, let's skip over the *I don't wanna, but you gotta* bullshit, and just come with me."

Kelvin kisses Annie's head, rubbing up and down her arm. "You should cool off a little. It's hot outside."

She sniffs and puts her hand out to Alora, getting to her feet, and following the group who survived the crash to the water. Four died; four men I used to know are gone. How the hell are we supposed to tell their families?

Fuck, it could have been any of us. I could have lost her. She could have lost me.

How the fuck are we surviving this nightmare?

Marshall moves branches out of the way, revealing a

beautiful, glistening lake. The water is so smooth, it's reminiscent of glass. Until the wind blows, disturbing the peace. But that just makes the scorching sun dancing on the surface of the water look like sparkling stars.

As beautiful as this place is, it'll all slowly become a nightmare if we don't get out of here.

"Put your feet in the water, it'll cool you off quickly," Alora says to Annie.

With a gulp, Alora steps out of her wedge sandals and takes a step into the water. Aside from Corey, she's the only one who's covered in blood. I wouldn't blame her if she dove in head first to clean off. Instead, she leans down to rinse her hands.

They're still shaking.

If she'd let me in, I'd help her. I'd calm down that scattered and panicked mind of hers.

But she won't. Even after everything we went through today, she's not letting me in.

Forcing myself to look away from her, but I'm not fast enough before Kelvin notices. He scoffs, shaking his head. Again, even after all of this, the fucker can't even let me stare at the most beautiful and selfless woman without giving me a warning.

I don't care anymore. I don't care who it hurts. This woman will see how perfect we are together.

"Any luck calling for help?" I ask Marshall as he steps into the water, helping Annie take a few steps over the rocks.

Marshall shakes his head. "My phone is shot."

"Mine, too," Donovan says.

"Same," Kelvin adds.

Alora winces, taking the cardigan off her leg to clean the blood. "I haven't checked mine yet."

Brett pulls his shirt off to rinse Corey's blood from his arms. "No service, unfortunately."

"No one has a satellite phone? Aren't the new iPhones equipped with that?" Alora swats her wet hands in the air and stands upright.

Brett shrugs, looking at me. I've heard about the new iPhones receiving satellite signals, but I doubt any of us had our phones on during the crash. Half of them are damaged, and the ones that aren't can't catch service. Just our luck, isn't it?

I dunk my hands in the water, washing off the dried blood. I don't even know who it belongs to. Could be Corey's, could be Marshall's. I'm pretty sure some of it is mine. This is maddening. I don't know how she does it. How she keeps her cool. It's exhausting and frightening.

She stands near me, sniffling as she looks off at the horizon. Something like this shouldn't have happened. The rarity and magnitude of it leaves me in disbelief.

We're all in shock, wondering if anyone is going to find us.

Save us.

Wondering where we are and how long we'll be out here.

How long will we survive?

Long enough to turn savage and forget what's it like to be human?

Long enough for us to turn on each other? Everyone fends for themselves.

No, I won't let it get that far. I'll stand by her side and keep this group afloat.

We're survivors.

We're a team.

We can do this.

Kelvin clears his throat as Mitch and Coach make their way to us. "I think we should salvage what we have. Be prepared to stay the night and find our bearings in the morning."

I nod, stepping closer to Alora as our hands touch at our sides. We don't hold each other, not yet. "Find us some food and blankets."

Coach holds onto his side while looking off at the horizon as well. "All right, I want you uninjured fucks scoping out the plane. Take out the luggage and rummage through that, too. For the injured ones, we have to figure out how to start a fire. There are probably wolves and bears in these woods. We don't need anyone else getting hurt."

Alora shifts on her feet, her pinky grazing mine. I hook it with hers, a grin tugging at my lips. "I should have another lighter in my luggage," she offers.

Brett puts his shirt back on and nods. "Marshall and I can collect firewood."

"I'll get the luggage off the plane," I say as Alora squeezes my pinky.

Kelvin glances at me and Alora but can't see our hands. I'm standing too close to her for that. "I'll help them."

"What do you want me to do?" Annie asks, wiggling her toes in the water.

Alora releases me, stepping over to her. "Just relax. Stay here and don't walk unless you have to." A smile touches Alora's face. "Keep counting the kicks."

Her eyes meet mine as she limps out of the water and picks her shoes up off the ground.

"Are you sure you're up for it? You should rest up, too," Coach says, looking at the red and swollen cut on her leg.

She stands upright, fixing her dress. "I'm sure."

Kelvin and I follow Alora to the plane, and Mitch comes to help, too. I don't know what we're supposed to find in our luggage, but I highly doubt it'll be anything useful to surviving out here. At least not enough for us to last more than a day or two.

Kelvin and Mitch step up to the plane first, Kelvin putting his hand out to Alora. She winces when she steps up, allowing me to help her by lifting her with me. "You sure you're up for this?" Kelvin asks. "You did a lot today, you should rest."

"I'm fine." She groans at the two dead guys in front of us. "Let's just get this over with."

She limps toward the back of the plane and opens one of the carry-ons from the floor that must've fallen out when we were going down, rummaging through it.

I stay close to her, but also give her some space. Her shoulders relax when she looks over at me. And I can't help but smile at that gesture. *I'm her calm.*

Mitch opens a clear garbage bag and starts filling it with snacks and whatever food he can find from the cart. He takes another bag and fills it with water bottles, juices, and sodas. We should have enough for a drink each, a snack or two per person. But not enough to last us days. We have a pregnant woman on our hands. Someone who needs it more than any of the rest of us. And knowing Alora, she'd give her portions to Annie because of the baby.

Glancing around, I wonder where the flight crew is. Were they sucked out of the plane when it started falling apart? There were two pilots and a flight attendant, where are they? I release a slow breath, placing a hand on my stomach at the lives we lost. Life can be so fucking cruel.

"We've got enough blankets and pillows for all of us. Not as many neck pillows, though," Kelvin says, piling the blankets on a chair.

"Get sweaters for everyone, too. It gets cold out here at night," Mitch says, eyeing Alora's legs. "Maybe some pants, too."

Stepping into his line of view, I'm disturbed by how disgusting some of the guys can be. I'm sure he meant nothing by it, either, but hearing their locker room talk about how they've degraded women is appalling. I feel bad for their significant others, and the women they have one-night stands with.

I never understood why Kelvin spoke so negatively about Alora. He had never mentioned her name before the gender reveal, only referred to her as "Annie's slutty friend," as if she's not a human being. So, what if she likes to screw around. Before meeting Annie, that's what he used to do. Maybe it has something to do with the fear that Annie will go back to her ways of acting like Alora instead of being faithful to her husband.

"You should take a soda or juice to Annie, she could use the sugar," Alora says, finding a bag filled with jerseys and sweaters.

Kelvin takes orange juice and a cookie from the bags. "I'll bring it to her."

Mitch nods, lifting the bags. "Should I stash these in the upper compartments?"

Kelvin shrugs, looking at us. "Coach said there could be bears or wolves. Think they'd sniff this food out?"

"Can't be too careful." I eye the bag of drinks. I'm so thirsty but we should ration what we have.

Mitch lifts the bags into the front overhead compartment and shuts the door. "All right, we have blankets, pillows—"

"And sweaters," Alora interrupts him, pushing the heavy bag in front of her before I lift it and toss it closer to Mitch.

"Okay, I think we'll be able to last the night and do a search for the front of the plane in the morning," Mitch says, eyeing Alora again with a lick of his lips. "Thank you, Alora."

Kelvin nods at me and steps off the plane. Mitch awkwardly follows, fixing his jeans, and leaving Alora and me alone. It's the first time we've been together since the night she broke down.

A night I just want to forget. I was helpless, but

afterward, I understood her so much better. I saw her reason to hate love, and I also saw the fight in her eyes that stops her heart from beating for me.

Clearing my throat, I reach for her hand again. She lets me, but only for a moment. As soon as she looks at our hands, she retracts hers. "How're you doing?"

She shrugs, sniffling as tears shimmer in her eyes. "I wasn't supposed to come on this trip." Her tears slip free, and all I want to do is hold her. I doubt she'll let me. "But something—I had to come in the end and look at this shit. How are we supposed to get out of this?"

Fuck it. I pull her to my chest and kiss the side of her head. "We'll get out of here, okay? I promise you, sweetheart, we'll be home soon."

She rests her head on my chest, but her arms don't wrap around me. She's leaning into me, breathing slowly, then groans. "Don't call me sweetheart."

"Too bad," I whisper, kissing the top of her head again as her arms finally slither around my waist.

I smooth out her hair, moving the ponytail off her shoulder, and nuzzling my cheek on her head. "Anything you need, I'm here."

She nods and squeezes me closer, letting more walls down. But she's still tense in my embrace. I can blame it on the crash. Though, I know it's because of the unspoken words she's too afraid to tell me.

Leaving another kiss on her head before she releases me, I tilt her chin up. Her eyes are a deeper green today, pupils dilated. There's no shame when I stare at her lips as they slowly part, and her tongue drags across her bottom lip.

Fuck.

As fucked-up and dangerous as our situation is, my dick rises, confined in my jeans. *Time and place, Scotty.*
But if I know how she thinks, I know she's thinking of ways in which she can back away from this moment. Leave us before we're even one.

I plant a soft kiss on her lips, faintly tasting the tequila on her tongue from earlier. She immediately pulls away, touching her lips softly. "I can't, Scotty—"

"I know."

Her breathing shakes when she looks around the plane again; her nerves are probably shot. So many of us are depending on her in this madness. "No, you don't know. Things are different now and they're so fucking complicated—"

I let out a wry chuckle. "Nothing has to be complicated, y'know. I get it. You don't want to be in a relationship with me. It's fine. You said your piece already. But that doesn't mean I don't care about you."

"You shouldn't."

"I know."

Her eyebrows pinch together, studying me for a brief second before she exhales a breath. I wish I knew what was going on in that head of hers. Stubborn little moon, I'll give her that.

Reaching around my neck, I undo the clasp of the white gold necklace with the moon, holding it out in front of me. She's staring at it, always so fascinated with this piece of jewelry from the moment she gave it back to me.

"Turn around," I tell her, smirking.

"Why?"

Lifting the necklace, I hold it against her chest and fasten the clasp behind her neck. She's pressed up against me, a tear sliding down her cheek. "Scotty, I can't accept this. It was your mother's."

I fix her ponytail again and trace her jawline. "I want you to wear it until we get out of here, okay? Don't think anything of it. Not...not now, anyway."

"This is—"

"Don't overthink it," I interrupt her, tilting her chin up and planting a soft one on her.

She groans quietly, touching the necklace and pushing past me. I don't think she likes the fact that she's warming up to the idea of us. As soon as her walls come down, she'll want this, too.

"Scotty?" she says softly at the top of the stairs.

The corner of my mouth quirks up when I turn to look at her, seeing the thankful look on her face. "Yeah, sweetheart?"

She takes a breath, licking her lips. "Thank you, shithead."

You're welcome, baby.

As soon as she's down the steps, I take a breath and release it on a sigh. I've never been without that necklace since my mother passed. But Alora deserves it. She needs that reassurance more than I do. Soon, I'll be more than her calm. I'll be her world. Her everything.

CHAPTER TWENTY-ONE – ALORA ASHTON

Coach and Brett are attempting to start a fire. It's much cooler than it was when we crashed. The sun is disappearing behind the trees, a golden hue poking out around the branches.

I'm sitting under a tree as I was before, trying to compose myself after patching everyone up. I don't know how I did it, but I managed with Scotty at my side.

I don't want to admit it, but Scotty's kept me grounded. He's helped me through the process of trying to figure out if what I'm doing is right. If the healing I'm attempting is how it's supposed to be done. I've stitched people up before. Hundreds of them. But for some reason, this matters most. People could get infections out here. I'm not equipped for that.

My first patient ever was a little boy who split his chin open. He was a tough little guy, he didn't cry one bit. Only a couple of tears in his eyes and he held onto his mother's hand until she asked him to let go because she couldn't feel her fingers. As I glued his cut closed, he looked at me and smiled, asking if I liked Spider-Man. I hated telling him I didn't like superheroes, so I told him that Spidey was my favorite. I now have a first-edition Spider-Man comic hanging in my guest room. Although, as nervous as I was that day to actually work on a person, I don't think I was as anxious as I've been all day today.

Most of the evening, we've been scavenging for materials, clothes, food, water, and weapons in case we need them—it's just their hockey sticks, but it's better than nothing.

Sadly, not a single one of us has cell service out here, and the fuckers with the newest iPhones, didn't protect their phones, so they're cracked beyond repair.

Scotty's staring at me as he sits by Corey, talking to him but giving me some of his attention.

He can give it to me all he wants, but he doesn't understand the burden he's given me. I've let him in today, yes. I was worried when he wasn't waking up, linked my pinky with his, and let him hold me on the plane when we were supposed to be finding supplies. I've been weak enough around him. I can't let my heart win anymore.

I have a rule, something my father taught me. *After sleeping with someone more than three times, they start to feel things. That's when you back out.*

It's odd to think I've allowed myself to believe that. To live by that rule. Yet I did.

But with Scotty, after our first night together, I planned to never see him again. He'd be another notch in my bedpost. Yet, he's snaked his way into my life, allowing me to fall in love with the thought of a relationship. Allowing me to break my rule of three. I tried to stay away from him. Shit, I tried so hard to get away. But I couldn't, not with this racing heart that's so attracted to him, it's sickening.

I want him in so many new ways. Ways I've never

wanted anyone. And not just because of sex, but because of how he makes me feel. The way he looks at me ignites this inspiration to be better. I'm a wilting rose coming back to life and blooming again.

And here we are, survivors of this flight. Stuck in a forest with nowhere to go. I might even let my guard down for a moment and speak with him.

I don't know if I'll be able to fully commit. I don't do relationships. I never have. This is no different.

I don't think Scotty's like me—a whore people labeled because it's what they believe defines me. Not my medical schooling. So, I embraced that persona from a young age. Letting the first boy who told me he likes me to have sex with me. It was an awkward experience, and when I told Dad about it, that's when he gave me the talk.

Three times, he said. *After that, they'll develop feelings. You don't want to end up like your mother. Three times, Alora. Remember that.*

I did.

I still do.

Except with Scotty.

With a groan, I get to my feet and start to make my rounds, doing what a doctor does and checking in on her patients.

I smile at Gregory and Sophia, crouching in front of them dispite the soreness in my thigh. "How's the shoulder?"

"Hurts like a son of a bitch," he says, trying to move it.

"We'll try doing some exercises tomorrow to make sure it's not locked in place," I say, standing tall. "Get yourself something to eat, okay?"

Sophia nods, glancing at Gregory. "Thank you, Alora."

"No sweat." I chuckle wryly and continue.

I check in on Coach, whose ribs are cracked. There isn't much I can do other than tell him to take it easy. I check in on a couple of the others who hit their heads. I'm sure one has a minor concussion, the other seems fine. He isn't sensitive to light or slurring. He's alert, which gives me some sense of ease.

I check in on Kelvin and Annie, then Corey last. Kelvin's doing fine, he has a sore arm from knocking it into the side of the plane when we crash-landed, but nothing major.

I'm more worried about Annie. She's tired, weak, but the baby is kicking up a storm, which is a good sign. That's all that matters, really. But I still worry that severe damage could have been done during the crash, and from the stress. If we don't get out of here soon, starvation is a possibility.

"Only get up when you have to," I say to Annie, checking her pulse again. "Sleep if you're tired, and the next time you get up to pee, I want you to cool off with your feet in the water."

"Thank you, Alora," Annie says, yawning.

"If you're feeling weak or dizzy, let me know. Your blood sugar could be dropping," I add, getting to my feet.

Kelvin frowns, holding my watch out to me. "Isn't that Scotty's necklace?"

Lifting a shoulder, I swallow the saliva building in my mouth. "He said I earned it for everything I did today. And it's pretty, so I wasn't going to say no."

Strapping my watch back in place, I glance at Corey over my shoulder. He doesn't look as pale anymore, but that doesn't mean there isn't a possibility of infection setting in.

Kelvin doesn't seem to believe a word I say, but I don't really care. The less he knows about my life, the better. And he already knows everything because of Annie. If only her lips were as closed as her legs have become. Every time Kelvin says something about my loose ways, he forgets that his wife used to be my right hand. She's kissed more guys than I have, but I get the backlash because she's married.

Stupidity.

I head to Corey, getting on my knees in front of him with a sigh. Here we go, my last patient. "Hey," he says, wincing as he tries to reposition.

I grin and remove the bandages to inspect the stitching I did. Not bad, if I do say so myself. There are no signs of infection, though it is red and a little swollen. There's no telling what will happen if he doesn't get to a hospital. "How's it feeling?"

He chuckles weakly. "Like I got stabbed in the leg."

I lean in closer, poking around the area. "Doesn't look like infection is setting in, which is a good sign."

Scotty clears his throat, nudging his head toward the plane. "The captain was talking about a toothache. Think maybe he has meds in his luggage?"

Corey scoffs, narrowing his eyes at the plane. "Front half of the goddamn plane is missing."

"Doesn't mean his shit isn't mixed in with ours," Scotty

shoots back.

Securing the bandage in place, I lean back on my heels even though my leg is throbbing. "Once morning hits, we'll go rummaging through the luggage and see if we can find anything. If not, take some Tylenol to ease the pain a little."

Corey groans, adjusting himself again. "What's the worst case, Alora?"

Licking my lips, I gaze at the fire crackling behind me. Worst case? We have to cut off his leg, I guess. Or if an infection begins, it could get into his bloodstream and…well…he'll die.

Worst case?

I face him again and the corner of my mouth twitches. "Why don't we take it day by day, yeah? See where that gets us."

Corey coughs, nodding slightly. "Yeah, okay. Thanks."

Standing up with a groan, my leg becoming more of an irritant than anything, I brush off my knees. "No problem."

Scotty gets up with me, opening his mouth to speak but stops when I walk away. I don't want this to start again. Starting something only leads to ending something. I won't go through the pain Mom went through, that heartache she lived with for years.

It won't happen.

I won't let it.

But if I don't get this shit taken care of, it just might.

"Alora?" Scotty says, his fingers curling around my elbow. "Can I ask you something?"

I sigh heavily and turn around. "What, Scotty?"

He points at his head, ignoring my harsh, snarky tone. "Can you take a look at me?"

After all the chaos that happened today, I completely disregarded his injury. Trying to push him away led me to be neglectful where it matters most.

"Oh, my God." I put a hand on my mouth. "I didn't mean to forget you. There's just been so many—"

He chuckles, putting his hand on my shoulder. "It's okay. Patch me up now while we still have some daylight and we'll call it even."

Finding my medical kit on a boulder by the fire, I force him to lean on it so I can see what the problem is. There's a gash above his eyebrow, an inch or two in length. Taking his chin, I turn his head from side to side. I notice the way his short beard covers his jawline, climbs down his neck, and decorates above his upper lip. He's gorgeous, labeled as a typical pretty boy. But he has different layers to him, our time speaking together proved that.

But I'm not here to learn more about those layers.

I'm not here to understand or comfort him.

I'm here to help these people.

No more, no less.

Flashing a light in his eyes to check for a concussion, I sigh when nothing of the sort registers. I'd stay up all night with him if necessary.

Then, I tear open a packet of rubbing alcohol and clean his wound. He winces once but keeps his eyes on me. Watching as I inspect, clean, and think about what to do.

His stare makes me nervous, and I hate being nervous.

Men don't make me nervous. They're used by me for a good time. For a release.

I don't swallow hard or feel my pulse increase when a smirk touches their lips.

This is not me.

I don't act like this. I don't fall for men who smile at me. I don't fall for men, period.

But goddammit, with this news burning a hole in my chest, my feelings for Scotty have increased tenfold. How did I let this happen?

I catch his eye. "I can glue it. You won't need stitches."

I'm standing close to him, and my crotch pushes into him as I hold the cut together and apply glue. I can feel him twitching a little. Enough to show me he likes this.

Why does he have to like me?

His hands somehow slide to my hips as I'm blowing softly at the glue I just applied. I'm having a hard time keeping it together. And even though we're stuck in this forest, it feels like the world is dead around us. It's only Scotty and me on this boulder. There aren't other people here. There isn't a crackling fire.

No, it's just him and me as I blow softly on the cut above his eyebrow.

But those feelings rush away when his thumbs move back and forth on my hips.

The world comes back into focus and my walls build back up.

This is not happening.

Stepping back, I clear my throat, my cheeks flaming.

"Done." I meet his eyes quickly, then look back at the cut. "Don't get it wet for at least two days, shithead."

His hands fall from my hips and he smirks. "I won't."

I swallow hard, stepping away and glancing at Annie as she rises to her feet. "Excuse me."

He takes me by the elbow, that gaze of his piercing a hole in the side of my face. "Stop avoiding me."

I remove my arm from his grasp. "Stop expecting more from me."

That smirk spreads to a smile like he knows something I don't.

I know guys like him. They want you because the sex is good, but when push comes to shove, there's nothing he wouldn't do to avoid being that perfect boyfriend. Hockey comes first; his sister, too. I would just be a thought in his mind when he wants to blow a load.

No, guys like him don't want a lifetime, they want a *for now*.

So, I won't give in. I don't do relationships. Never have. Never will.

My heart will stay intact, thank you very much.

My mantra on fucking repeat.

I make my way to Annie, glancing over my shoulder at Scotty when I feel his eyes on me. Why does he have to be nice *and* handsome? It's just not fair, and it makes my head hurt. I'm so freaking confused. Shit, looking back at him, maybe I don't know guys like him at all. Maybe he's that diamond in the rough.

"Kelvin and Marshall went to get the blankets from the

plane before nightfall," she says, smoothing a hand over her stomach. "I think we all need some shut-eye."

"That's a good idea." I sniff, wiping my nose on the back of my hand. "I'm gonna sleep next to Corey, keep an eye on him tonight."

"You were amazing today, Alora. I don't think any of us would have been able to hold it together without you." She takes my hand and holds it. "I love you, y'know."

I chuckle, squeezing her back. "Love you, too."

She swallows, looking around to see if anyone is within earshot, and tugs me closer. "What're you going to do? You finally going to accept this—"

"No," I interrupt her. "As soon as we get out of here, the plan is the same."

"Are you sure about this?" she asks, as if she can change my mind.

"Yes."

She sighs, releasing my hand and looking behind me. "You and Scotty seem to be getting along."

I shrug, hating the fact that she knows nothing about our time together. Nothing about the fact that my heart beats for the first time because of him. "He's Kelvin's friend. I have to be nice if I'm going to see him at all your get-togethers."

"Don't be stupid, please," she says, stabbing me right in the gut with her words. "I know he gave you a necklace because you earned it, but that was his mother's, and she died on my wedding day. That's pretty recent to give something like that away without expecting something in return."

Shaking my head, I glance at Scotty talking with Brett.

She doesn't know half of why Scotty gave me this necklace. Frankly, I don't even think I know why he gave it to me. He cares for me, more than I realize.

He's sweet to me.

He's loving.

Funny.

Easy to talk with and be around.

But I can't tell her that. Even with this madness around us, she's still warning me to keep my legs closed. Something I should've already done and I wouldn't be in this mess of feelings.

"I...I didn't know that," I lie and reach back to remove the necklace, tucking it into the pocket of my dress. "I thought it was a nice gesture for everything that happened—I'll give it back to him, I promise."

It feels like I just slapped him in the face in front of everyone, but I can't tell Annie what I've done.

I can't tell her the truth.

I can't tell him the truth.

Wake up, Alora. Just wake the fuck up!

She nods, smiling at someone behind me. "Hey, babe."

Kelvin hands her a pillow and blanket; one for me, too. "It'll get cold tonight."

"Thanks," I say, smiling.

Annie punches his thigh and he groans, looking down at her, then at me with this look of annoyance and regret. "You...um...thank you, Alora. You're a huge asset and...yeah, just sorry."

Is he apologizing for always treating me like crap

because of my sex life right now?

I chuckle dryly. "Sorry for what?"

Yep, I need to hear him say it.

Over a year of hearing his fucked-up ways of referring to me. All the times he put me down for no reason. I need to hear him apologize for being the biggest asshole anyone has ever met.

He side-eyes Annie and sputters. "I-I've been a dick to you—a lot. And…I don't know what we'd do without you."

I smirk, tucking the pillow under my arm. "Nice to know you see me as an actual person and not a whore."

"Alora!" she barks quietly.

I widen my eyes and chuckle. "What?"

"I deserved that. Shit, I probably deserve more. I've been a dick to you for no reason, and…a lot of us would be in way worse condition if it weren't for you. So, yeah, thanks," he adds, nudging my shoulder.

Smiling, I look down at Annie as she prides herself on how her husband just apologized to me as if it was some big win on his part. It wasn't. He's still a dick, but he's her dick, so I guess all is forgiven. "Anyway, get some sleep, guys. We'll figure a way out of this in the morning."

I squeeze Annie's arm and make my way to Corey. Scotty is still sitting on the boulder, talking to Brett. I don't think Brett recognizes me from the night Scotty and I met. It was dark in the bar, and over two months ago. I prefer it that way, too. The fewer ties, the better, right?

Smiling when I approach Corey, I sit on the ground beside him. "Hope you don't mind if I crash here tonight. I wanna keep an eye on you."

He chuckles, tapping my arm. "Of course not. You're the reason I'm hopefully going home to my girl and kid."

I swat my hand in the air. "I'm far from qualified enough to save lives…but thanks."

Kelvin and Donovan are handing blankets out, and sweaters, too. Scotty takes three sweaters, two pillows, and two blankets, making his way to Corey and me. He eyes the two of us with this intense gaze as if he's jealous.

Fifty bucks says he asks to sleep beside me tonight.

"Hey." He nods his head at Corey, dropping a pillow and blanket beside him. "Here, put this on." He hands him a sweater. "Gonna get cold tonight." He dangles one in front of me. "You should, too."

Taking the sweater, I pull it over my head. "Yeah, thanks."

"Bunking with us, too?" Corey grunts, pulling the sweater on. "Doc is keeping an eye on me."

Scotty smirks, dropping his pillow and blanket on my lap, and getting to his knees. "Why not?"

Clearing my throat, I study the wound on his head. "Any headaches?"

He shakes his head, grinning. "I'm okay, sweetheart."

"Don't call me sweetheart." Lifting the hoodie over my head, I fix the pillow on the ground, helping Corey lay the blanket on his legs. "Can you wiggle your toes?" I ask, about to fix the blanket over his foot.

He wiggles them and chuckles. "I wanna see if I can try walking tomorrow, doc."

I nod, smirking at the sound of him calling me *doc*. It's cute and it's something I'll have to get used to. "One step at a time."

Corey snickers. "Ha, ha."

Scotty props his knees up and wraps his arms around them, holding onto his wrist as he scans the area. Everyone is settling down, finding a spot close to the fire. We're nowhere near it, so I know it'll get cold tonight, but I don't want to move Corey right now. Not until absolutely necessary. And if his wound still looks the same in the morning, we'll attempt to walk and get him to the water to wash off some of the blood on his thigh.

Scotty bumps into me, lowering his voice. "Where's the necklace?"

How did he notice that?

Jerking my head at Annie, I fish it from my pocket. "She warned me to stay away from you. Said you're only giving this to me for a chance to get me into bed." I dangle the chain out to him. "Maybe she's right, maybe you're only giving this to me as a way to *open my eyes*." I quote the photo caption he posted on his Instagram for me.

He shakes his head, taking the necklace and putting it back on me. "I wanted you to have it until we get out of here. It brings me peace, maybe it will do the same for you."

I chuckle nasally, licking my lips. "Who says I need peace?"

His eyes trail to my lips, staying there for several seconds before his gaze meets my eyes again. "Me."

Scoffing, I stare at the fire. He doesn't know me well

enough to know I need peace. What I need is a release, space, and a breath of air. I love my life but I feel trapped in it. Like the label slapped on me is who I'm supposed to be, not this doctor I'm striving to become.

I've grown tired of the endless nights of taking home strangers or sleeping with my regulars. When I took Scotty home, our connection was different. It felt unique. *We* felt unique.

Then *this* happened, and now I'm feeling that our uniqueness was supposed to bind us in a way I never knew I wanted.

But in all the ways I can't have.

"Just think about it," he whispers.

I inhale sharply and look at him. "Think about what?"

He smiles, winking, and pulling the sweater over his head.

Us.

He meant to think about us.

I close my eyes for a moment and think about nothing at all. A clear mind is what I need for a good night's sleep.

Pulling the blanket over me, I turn away from Scotty. "Get some rest, Corey. You'll need it."

He chuckles. "Thanks, doc."

Scotty grunts, lying beside me with enough distance between us that no one will ask questions. But simply knowing he's right there makes me want to snuggle up to him. My heart is running a race my mind can't catch up with.

Shit.

It's going to be one long night.

CHAPTER TWENTY-TWO – SCOTT WESLEY

Alora fell asleep after everyone else, tossing and turning to try and find a comfortable spot on the hard ground. She wanted to keep an eye on Corey to make sure he was okay and didn't need anything during the night.

Selfless and perfect.

She's shivering, though.

Teeth chattering.

Curled in a ball beside me.

I don't hesitate; I scoot closer to her and wrap my arm around her, tucking her close to me. She tenses but gives in, letting me hold her and warm her up as her ass pushes into my crotch. She's killing me and doesn't even know it.

"I got you," I whisper so quietly, it's practically inaudible.

She takes my hand and twines our fingers together, curling our hands under her chin and it sends my heart into overdrive. What I wouldn't do to kiss her right now —she can push me away all she wants, but her heart is beating just as fast as mine.

I won't push my luck, though. Instead, I leave a kiss on the back of her head, knowing I'm that much closer to calling her mine.

Just as her shivers start to die down, a growl sounds nearby, causing her to flinch and me to squeeze her closer. I'm going to protect her whether she wants me to or not.

Another growl echoes, making Corey wince as he sits up and looks beyond, into the dark forest. "Scotty? Hey, Scotty? Wake—"

The growls grow closer and I shoot up, keeping her close to me as I try to see in the darkness. She groans, sitting up with me, then jolts when the growl creeps closer to us.

"Hey!" I yell, urging everyone to wake up as glowing eyes glimmer in the darkness. Are those wolves? *Jesus, fuck!*

"What the fuck?" Coach shouts. "What's your problem?"

Corey winces and grunts, trying to get away without moving his leg. "There's fucking wolves, man. Wolves!"

Brett runs over, hockey stick in hand, trying to see where the wolves are. Donovan gets up, too, and Kelvin as well, all snatching hockey sticks off the ground.

I help Alora to her feet, pushing her behind me. "Go by the fire."

"Move Corey," she says, the natural nurturer and caretaker in her taking precedence over her survival.

Coach turns on a flashlight, casting shadows of our bodies on the ground as we hover around him. There's nothing in the darkness, at least nothing we can see. Marshall and Mitch run with Corey to the fire, where Sophia, Annie, and Alora stand. She has a worried look on her face.

I'll protect you, baby. This I swear.

Growls sound again, farther away this time. A second set of growls sounds, also moving farther away. Four of us stand guard, staring off into the shadows as Coach moves the beam of light around the area.

Then, my worst nightmare happens. Annie and Sophia scream, growls, and thrashes sound next. A wolf has Alora by the forearm, her shrieks consume me. Blood drains from my face, and my entire body is numb with fear. All I see is red.

I don't even think. I just act.

I charge for them, shoving Sophia out of the way. Gregory and I kick the wolf until it lets go of Alora's arm. My heart is lodged in my throat as I watch the fucker release her.

Marshall attacks it until it scurries away. "Fucking cocksucker!"

"Oh, my God!" Annie cries, slapping a hand on her mouth.

Alora scoots away from Marshall, holding her arm to her chest. "I'm okay, I'm okay."

She doesn't look okay. Tears are falling down her cheeks, and her face is pale by the glow of the dying fire. Worry squeezes the air from my lungs as I go to her, picking her up and sitting by the fire with her on my lap. "Lemme see it." My voice is hoarse and shaky.

She moves her shaking arm away from her chest and I tear open the sleeve, revealing the bleeding bite marks that wrap around her forearm. "Fucking shit."

Annie sniffs, coming over to us, but Kelvin stops her and holds her head in his hands. "Are you okay?" he asks.

"Don't worry about me," she says, searching for the

medical kit that got knocked over in the ruckus.

A few of the guys still stand guard with the hockey sticks in hand, glancing back at the woman who helped us yesterday.

A fucking godsend if you ask me.

Annie locates the medical kit and holds it out to me. It's nearly empty of its contents; we won't last another day if someone else gets hurt.

Annie's breathing trembles as she looks down at Alora. "She saved me from the wolf."

Everyone stares at Alora on my lap. She's a savior, so much more than how everyone speaks about her.

A soft chuckle leaves Alora, followed by a sniff. "Remember that time you kicked the neighbor's dog so he wouldn't attack me? Guess this makes us even, huh?"

Annie chuckles, choking on a sob. "Guess it does."

She glances up at Annie with a forced grin, tears still rolling down her cheeks. I hold onto Alora, trying to figure out what I can do to help her. How the hell can I help this woman who's done nothing but take care of all of us?

Marshall crouches down beside us, looking at her arm. "What do you need from us?"

Alora turns her arm from side to side, inspecting the bite mark again. "Get the tequila to disinfect this." She groans. "And a t-shirt or something to wrap around it."

"Isn't there gauze?" I ask, keeping her pressed to my chest. "The stuff you used to patch Corey up."

She nods. "There isn't much left. I'd rather save it for him."

Even though my fear comes tumbling back with a vengeance at what could've happened to her, I sigh, tearing the sleeve of the hoodie off her shoulder. "You need it, too, Alora."

Those wet eyes glisten in the glow of the flames. "I'll be fine."

Seems to be her motto. Like she's holding in all her feelings, unable to let them out. She's not used to being vulnerable in front of these people; they put her down and label her some floozy. She's so much more than that.

I don't think she's ever been vulnerable in front of anyone but Annie.

And me.

"Add more logs to the fire," Coach says, holding his side as he looks back at where we were sleeping.

We have to figure a way out of here, and fast. Any longer, we'll be dropping like flies.

One by one.

Until the wilderness consumes all of us.

CHAPTER TWENTY-THREE –
ALORA ASHTON

So much for sleep. Scotty helped me wrap my arm in a t-shirt and helped me out of the hoodie and into another one. One that says WESLEY on the back of it. It's one of his sweaters and a little part of me blooms at the thought of being his. I didn't even bat an eye when he held me, even after my arm was wrapped, I remained on his lap by the flames.

Now that everyone is asleep, I'm wide awake.

This could have been a lot worse than it was. The wolf could have attacked my throat, could have dragged me off into the darkness with his pack.

Annie was in trouble, vulnerable because of the baby; it's like the wolf smelled that on her. I saw him creeping, an ugly snarl on his face, ready to attack. I let it assault me instead.

Maybe these people will look at me differently.

Maybe they won't.

But as long as my best friend is okay, that's all that matters to me.

When the sun begins to crest the tops of the trees, I take this as my opportunity to change out of this bloody dress.

Tiptoeing around the sleeping bodies, I climb up the steps into the plane to retrieve my luggage. I'm immediately hit with the stench of rot. The bodies are decomposing, probably why the wolves were here last night.

Groaning, I place two fingers under my nose as I find something to wear. Tears well in my eyes, not because of the smell, but because of the reality we're stuck in.

Our plane crashed in the middle of nowhere.

Four people died. Shit, maybe more with the pilots and flight crew.

There are multiple wounded men.

My best friend is pregnant out here.

We got attacked by wolves.

And now, we have to figure out how the hell we're supposed to survive this nightmare.

I take what I need and get off the plane again, inhaling a sharp breath of fresh air. Everyone is still asleep; snores and heavy breathing are moving throughout the quiet. It is peaceful here despite it all. Calming, too.

It's crazy how much something this serene is needed when you live in the hustle and bustle of city living and school life. I never take steps back and breathe, and just live in the moment. I guess that would be my biggest takeaway from this. To live and forget all the bullshit. Just live.

Maybe Scotty's right, maybe I do need peace. Something to rid the negativity I surround myself with when it comes to relationships. *Just think about it.*

I think I just might.

Taking my chances despite my fears, I step into the forest, looking around every corner for safety. But I don't think the wolves will return as the sun rises. There's more of a chance we'd spot them in the daylight than in the dark.

I find an area far enough away with a knocked-over tree trunk and place my clothes there. I wince when I pull the sweater off; my forearm has been throbbing all night. Part of the reason why I couldn't sleep. But I'll pull through like I always do. I have people depending on me. There will come a time to break down. This is not that time.

As soon as I have the bloodied dress over my head, twigs snap behind me and I gasp, whipping my head around, only to see Scotty coming toward me and rubbing his eyes. "Jesus, Scotty. You nearly gave me a heart attack."

He smirks sleepily, giving me a once-over. "I saw you walk out here alone. Don't think that was too smart on your part," he says quietly.

Tossing the dirty dress aside, I look at the fresh one. "I needed out of these clothes."

He steps toward me, determination in his gaze. "Let me help."

Tilting my head to the side, I arch an eyebrow. "I think you're better at removing my clothes than putting them on, shithead."

He chuckles softly. "I'm only here to help, Alora. Honest." His finger traces down my neck, stopping in the middle of my chest, where I'm sure he can feel the pounding of my traitorous heart. "You already told me multiple times to back down. If you're not interested, you're not interested."

I swallow hard when he removes his finger as if he pulled me by a string before severing the tie. "What happened to *just think about it?*"

He shrugs, taking my fresh underwear and getting on his knees. He helps me out of my thong, kissing my hip bone before pulling up the fresh pair. "You're as stubborn as a rusted bolt. I can try and try, but will it even be worth it?"

That hits me harder than it should have. Especially now. Tears unwillingly slide down my cheeks, causing me to whimper and look away from him. I know how I am. I know how my mind works, but for someone to lay it out, it's like he's giving up.

Maybe he should.

Maybe giving up on me will prove I have a lot of work to do on myself.

My views on relationships are backward because of my parents. Yes, they weren't the best example, and yes, maybe I should have learned from that. But I didn't. I gave into the knowledge of being a player from my father thinking that's how life is supposed to be.

A series of fucks until you die, he said.

I don't want Scotty to just be a fuck.

I don't think I ever did.

But I push him away because I don't know any better. My life is a series of men revolving through my bed like I run a whorehouse and I'm the main attraction.

I only know how to be a sleaze; I don't know how to be a girlfriend who loves and adores. I only know one thing. My rule of three.

Taking my clean pale blue dress, I slide it over my head as quickly as I can just to get away from him. I don't even know how to get away from someone I'm trapped in the wilderness with. But I manage to take one step before he has me by the elbow, holding me in place.

"Talk to me," he whispers.

A heavy breath leaves me, riddled with regret as the words leave my mouth before I can stop them. "Why? It's not like this would last, right? You'd get tired of me or I'd get bored with you, and you'd be off with the next pretty thing to throw themselves at you. Be realistic, shithead. You and I would never work."

He laughs, and that makes me angrier than I've ever been. Like my words don't fucking matter. "You really think that?"

I yank my arm out of his grip and scoff. "Be realistic, Scotty."

"I'm trying, but you keep pushing me away, baby."

There it is. The cork lodged in my throat.

The air is sucked out of me and leaves me like a dried-up raisin.

Men only call me *baby* for one thing and one thing only. Sex. But hearing it from Scotty's lips again is so much more…permanent. Normal. He's said it before and it always felt right.

He moves his finger down my nose, tracing my lips and his fingers slowly move down my neck. "I don't care how many men you slept with. Ten. Fifty. Hundreds. We were idiots to think this wasn't going to be more than a one-night stand…I want to be the only man you wake up beside. The only man who you call yours. The only man to make this heart beat as fast as it's beating now." He stares at my chest and presses his hand there, lowering his voice. "Just me."

Love isn't real.

That's what I've been taught all my life.

I should never settle down because it just leads to heartbreak. But maybe I was wrong.

Dad was wrong.

Mom was wrong.

Maybe love is real and not some construct developed by Hallmark.

Maybe it's real and it's standing right in front of me.

I place my hand on his. He's staring at my lips, a subtle smirk spreading to his. A good morning kiss might mend these wounds my heart created. I'm giving him false hope, but I'm also trying. I can try, can't I?

As I part my lips and tilt my head up, twigs snap behind us, causing my body to naturally step away.

"Scotty? Alora?" Kelvin's voice startles me. "What's going on here?"

Scotty grins, tapping my shoulder. "You okay?"

I open my mouth but no words come out. I stare at Scotty, tears clouding my vision.

"I heard her crying. Figured she could use a hug after everything she's done for us and with what happened last night," Scotty says, nodding at me and stepping away.

"Oh," Kelvin says, staring at me as I take my dirty clothes from the tree trunk and wipe my cheeks. "It looked like—"

"I'm not some whore who sleeps with anything that moves, Kelvin. Sorry to disappoint," I scoff and brush past him, shaking my head in sheer awe and disturbance at Kelvin's stupidity. More so at Scotty for opening up like that. How does he always know the right things to say?

Fuck, how can I even begin to breathe with him stealing the air from me?

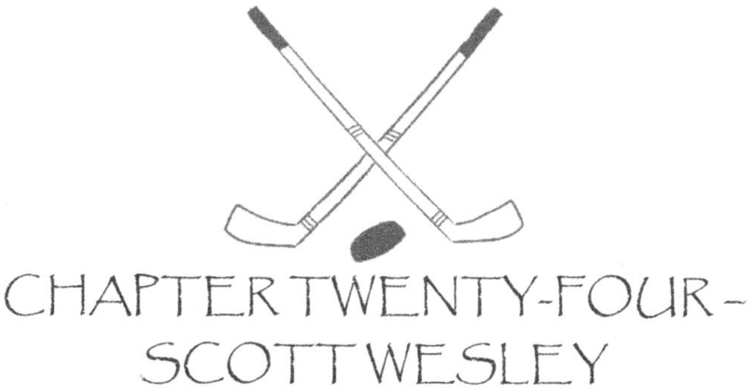

CHAPTER TWENTY-FOUR – SCOTT WESLEY

I unzip my fly and relieve myself as Kelvin stands nearby, arms crossed and looking behind him as Alora walks away. I was seconds from wrecking her with my mouth, taking her against this tree trunk, and showing her how great we could be.

She'll realize soon enough that she can't hold in those feelings much longer; I see them written all over her face. We're that one in a million. I'll prove it to her. I'll show her that we can love like no other without heartbreaks.

She won't have a life like her mother.

She won't look for joy in being with someone different every night like her father.

She'll find that joy in me. She'll come home to me. Laugh with me. Love with me. Start a great life with me.

And I think she's starting to envision it.

Kelvin clears his throat and spits, letting out a breath. "Look, man, I don't know what you and Alora are doing, but I already asked you not to start anything out of respect for my wife."

I drop my head back and chuckle, shaking my head. "So, when someone who has been a superstar the past twenty-four hours is crying because of this bullshit we're all in, I'm just supposed to ignore it? Just supposed to let her cry and act like everything she's doing is wrong? I'm supposed to ignore the only person that's helping us." I suck my teeth and fix my pants. "Poor girl has been going nonstop since we crashed, helping every single one of us, saving your fucking wife from getting attacked by wolves, but that doesn't matter, does it? I still get warned to leave her the fuck alone as if this is the fucking moment I'd try and fuck some girl when she's seconds from breaking down."

Okay, so maybe I'm trying to get my point across with something I was about to do to her against this tree, but he doesn't need to know that. He needs to understand the warnings are uncalled for.

Kelvin swallows hard, scratching the back of his neck and shifting his stance. *Yeah, fucker, I got you there.*

He pinches his eyes shut, shaking his head. "Yeah, sorry, I didn't think—"

"No, you didn't," I interrupt him. "And if I wanted to sleep with her or start a relationship with her, that's no one's goddamn business. It's between Alora and me." I take a step forward, towering over him by at least four inches. "And if we become friends, then that's also none of your business. You can't tell people who they can and cannot be with, Kelvin. That's fucked-up, even for you. Not to mention how you speak about other girls behind your wife's back; now that's disrespectful."

He nods, looking back to see if Alora is there. She isn't. Which makes me antsy because I want to find her. We weren't done talking. I don't think we ever will be until she's in my arms, calling me hers.

"Sorry," Kelvin finishes and steps around me, unzipping his jeans to relieve himself as I go find Alora.

I said it the first time I heard her name, this girl is a pain in my fucking ass. But I wouldn't have it any other way. So long as she's the only pain.

As soon as I make my way back to the group, she's on her knees beside Corey, inspecting his wound and forcing a smile behind those sad eyes. I did that. I inflicted that sadness on her.

Sadness that's so much deeper than on the surface. Something I have this inkling to fix.

Maybe she'll let me, maybe she won't. But there's a worry inside her; she's broken. And I don't like it.

Marshall comes up to me holding a tiny water bottle that must've been invented for children, not airplanes. The thing is so small, it disappears in my hand. And yet, when I look up at Alora, all I envision is holding a bottle like this with her. Only it's not a water bottle. It's our future.

"Coach started waking us up, saying he wants everyone up and at 'em by the time the sun rises. Think we're going to start hiking outta here," Marshall says in a tired voice as a yawn breaks through at the end.

Glancing at Alora, she's wrinkling her nose at Corey, cleaning his leg and applying ointment, then a fresh bandage. "Think he's up for the hike? He had a shard of metal in his leg yesterday."

Marshall shrugs, giving Alora a once-over as she

stands in a bent-over position with her ass half hanging out. *Goddamn*.

She doesn't mean to do this most of the time but shit like this drives me mental. The number of eyes I'll have to gouge out when she's mine will be many—if she'll ever agree to be mine. I get one step ahead with her, then take twenty back.

"Mmm, now that's a piece of cake I'd lick the frosting off of," Marshall says, biting his lower lip.

It's taking everything in me not to punch him.

"Watch your fucking mouth." I clench my fists at my sides. "If it wasn't for her, half of us would still be fucked."

Marshall cocks an eyebrow, glancing back at Alora. "Someone has a hard-on for her, huh? Did Kelvin warn you, too?"

Wait, he warned Marshall as well? I don't know whether I should feel happy about the fact that I wasn't the only one he warned or pissed that he would think so little of me and put me down to this fucker's level.

I grit my teeth and growl. "Shut up."

Alora crouches down again, the pain in her leg is evident by the look on her face. Yet she does nothing to relieve it. Her patients are her priority. She'll be one helluva doctor one day. But even doctors call in sick.

She's trying to help Corey stand and none of the fuckheads are helping. He slithers his arm around her shoulders as her arms snake around him, too. Nope, don't like that.

Sucking my teeth, I jog over, placing a hand on her

back. "Let me."

"It's okay, just get his other side," she says in a strained breath.

We get Corey standing and he hops on one leg with a wince. "Fucking shit."

She chuckles, still straining. "And you thought walking today would be a good idea."

He laughs. I'm certain he's putting more weight on me than her and he hops again. "Just let me take a piss, wouldja."

I chuckle, helping Corey limp to a tree so he can lean on it. A few of the guys watch us, and Brett stands to offer help—a little too late—but I wave him off. Alora and I got this.

We'll always get this.

Corey pulls his dick out and Alora averts her gaze, looking around at everyone. A few of the guys are moaning and groaning, complaining about sleeping on the hard ground. Some of them are holding their heads. Must be migraines because they're missing their fix. Soon the withdrawals will start and that won't be fun. It's not a lot of the guys, but enough of them snort coke at parties. About three of them are addicted to the shit.

Personally, that's not for me. That crap is something that can get any of them kicked off the damn team—no, kicked out of the league.

I live and breathe hockey, and it's maddening these guys don't have that same mindset.

"You think Coach is for real? Are we gonna try and hike outta here today?" Corey asks, tucking himself away and draping his arm on Alora's shoulders again.

She lifts a shoulder. "Without any sense of which way to go, we'll either be walking in circles or walking deeper into the forest. I don't think it's a good choice without a map and a compass."

"Don't iPhones have compasses built in?" Corey groans as I lift him and help him sit on a stump.

"Yeah, but who knows how accurate it would be," she responds, wiping her brow with the back of her hand. "You all right?"

Corey nods with a grin. "Yeah, thanks, doc."

She eyes me and pushes her lips together, our unfinished business bothering her as much as it is me. I never thought I'd find myself wrapped around someone so tightly that it's lonely without them around. But that's how it is with Alora.

For the past eight and a half weeks, all I've thought about was her. The way we speak to each other is unique. It's different. Forgiving and honest.

Then, she stumped me. Broke me down in ways I never thought words could.

Yet I didn't give up.

I'm carrying hope.

Enough hope to last me a lifetime.

She heads to Annie, putting her hand out to help her up. Alora's beautiful when she worries, even more stunning when she cares. And the way she touches Annie's stomach, there's this glee on her face. Something I never noticed before. There's love for her best friend and that baby, a love she never experienced before.

If she'd let me in, I'd show her that kind of love. A love to last us thousands of years.

Corey nudges me, stopping me from staring at Alora like snapping me out of a trance. "You like her, huh?"

"Hmm?" I shift my gaze to meet his, and a smirk is spread to his face.

"It's all over your face, man." That smirk spreads to a smile as a chuckle leaves him. "You don't think I noticed the change in your whole self at Annie's gender reveal? You spoke about the chick you hooked up with being the best sex of your life, but you never got her number. And then Alora walks into the room and you light up. You've had a spring in your step since then." He jerks his head at her. "She's the girl, isn't she? She's the sweetheart you asked to open her eyes from your Instagram post?"

I sigh, looking at her as she points at the water bottle and Annie nods, presumably telling her pregnant friend to eat. Alora walks off, nodding good morning to some of the guys as she does, and heads for the water. You know damn well I'm going to follow her.

Looking back at Corey, I furrow my brow. "Doesn't really matter, anyway, she wants nothing to do with me and Kelvin keeps warning me to stay away from her."

Corey looks over his shoulder as a bush closes the path Alora steps through and nods, the corner of his mouth quirking up again. "You're not giving up on her, are you? Mr. Scotty Wesley, rocket on the ice, is giving up? Now that doesn't sound like the Scotty I know." He smirks, wincing as he moves his leg into a slightly bent position. "We only live once, and we're fucking lucky as shit to be alive right now." He leans forward and nudges me. "Go get your girl."

I can't help but smile. *My girl*, yeah, I like the sound of that.

"She certainly is something," I say, squeezing his shoulder. "Get us something to eat, I have a feeling I'm going to be carrying your ass a lot today."

He laughs, tapping my hand before I release him and walk off. No one else has followed her to the water, half the guys are still waking up or have fallen back asleep. This is my chance to get my woman. Fucking love the sound of that shit.

I move branches out of the way and push through bushes until I breech the exit, and find her standing at the edge of the water looking off as the sun glistens atop it, hand on her stomach, and taking a few deep breaths. Her hair looks lighter in the dawn, almost a dark caramel instead of milk chocolate.

Breathtaking. This woman is everything I've ever dreamed of. And then some.

I'm making it my goal to have her in my arms when we win the championship. An award-winning kiss on the ice for all the world to see.

"Hey," I say quietly, smiling as I approach her.

She glances at me over her shoulder, her facial expression stoic. The stress she must be under is heightened. These guys all look up to her for help. We're in a panic, too, but Alora's is on a whole other level. And I'm making it worse by poking her heart into accepting our fate. We're simply meant to be.

She turns back to the water and sighs, fiddling with the hem of her dress. "You think we were meant to meet that night? Our lives were already connected and as if by some chance—fate if you will—we met and just…connected on a deeper level."

I come up behind her, fingers delicately brushing her arms. "I do."

"How're we supposed to do this?" she whispers.

My lips graze her shoulder, teeth following suit. "Just like this, baby."

Her breathing shudders, and she wipes her cheeks. "Believe it or not, I've never had a relationship before. So…I don't know how to do this and I don't—"

Shouts travel quickly over the horizon, arguing and yelling jolting our heads in the direction we came from. Over the sounds of the shouting, Kelvin is screaming, and he's usually a gentle giant.

"What the fuck?"

I stare at the trees and bushes, knowing I need to be there to stop whatever is happening. Kelvin doesn't scream. He's not a fighter, not even on the ice. He avoids checking into people. He avoids conflict.

Glancing at Alora, she's choked with horror as I am; what if the wolves came back?

Threading our fingers, I lead us through the forest to where we crashed, the anticipation eating away at me at what could be causing the outburst. A conflict that's rising to full-on fighting as we grow nearer.

Letting go of her hand, I charge for Kelvin and Brett

who are wrestling on the ground. Neither of them are getting a good punch in. I pull Kelvin off him and we stumble backward, but he's out of my grip, fixing his shirt and shoving me away.

"Dude, fucking relax! What the hell is going on?" I raise my voice.

"These two fucks just started arguing when Brett sat with Annie," Corey yells, gritting his teeth as Donovan helps him stand.

Brett laughs, out of breath, and Marshall has a hand on his chest. "Tell them, Kelvin. Tell them why we can't stand each other."

"Fuck you," Kelvin belts out, stepping forward to attack again, but I shove him back and puff out my chest.

"Kelvin, please. Just stop it," Annie begs, tears falling from her eyes.

He turns to look at her, that menacing stare of his making her whimper. "Stop it? *Stop it?!*" He tries to thunder toward her but doesn't move more than an inch because of me. "After what I just found out, you want me to *stop*? Are you fucking psychotic, you whore?"

"Hey," Alora shouts, stepping forward to comfort her best friend. "Watch your damn mouth! She's your pregnant wife—"

Kelvin interrupts her with a manic laugh, one that scares even me. Something went down, and I think it has to do with why Brett and Kelvin hate each other.

Kelvin bares his teeth at his wife. "Why don't you tell your friend why you're as whorish as she is, Annie."

Brett tries to step in as Annie lets out a sob, but Marshall and Gregory hold him back. "You have some fucking nerve calling her that, asshole."

Kelvin turns slightly, fists clenched at his sides. Even on the ice Kelvin never gets this mad. When someone shoves him or checks him into the boards, he lets it go. He's not like us, seeking revenge. We live for that shit. Tossing our gloves on the ice when adrenaline pumps through our veins. Some of the best battles are fought that way. So seeing Kelvin like this, it must be for something huge.

Coach emerges from the bushes, zipping up his fly, and takes in the tension. "The fuck is all the shouting about?"

Kelvin whips his arm from my grip and attempts to go for Brett once more, but Gregory grabs ahold of him. We have to stop this stupidity before they do something they'll regret.

"Fuck you!" Kelvin yells at Brett, spittle forming at the corner of his mouth. "I'm gonna fucking kill you, you fucking cocksucker."

Coach barges in, shoving Gregory and me out of the way. He has Kelvin by the front of his shirt and lifts him with ease, even with his sore ribs. "Knock it the fuck off! We're a team, do you understand me? And teams don't fucking fight when there's a lot on the line. And right now, *all* of our lives are on the damn line."

Kelvin licks his lips, trying to get out of Coach's hold. He's too far gone to be able to see straight, to see anything other than anger, at least. "A team, he says." His eyes darken, brow frowning. "My wife and I were a team at some point, too. Now I don't know if that fucking baby in her belly is even mine. So, tell me, Coach, do you still think teammates are not allowed to argue when something like this gets dropped in their lap? Hmm?"

Everyone looks at Annie, her face red and tears streaming. There's shame painted all over her as she stares between Kelvin and Brett. Of course, Brett would do something like this. He has no sense of honor.

Alora touches Annie's arm. "Annie, is this true?"

She whimpers, looking at Kelvin, then Brett. "It was an accident."

Alora gasps and glances at Kelvin. "What the fuck, Annie?" she says quietly.

Annie scoffs, hands in fists at her sides. "Oh, because you're any better. You open your legs so often, but the second I do, it's frowned upon."

Alora scowls, jerking her head back. "How is this a shot at me all of a sudden? I didn't cheat on my husband."

"You're the one who took me out that night, remember?" Annie shoots back.

Alora stands taller, defending herself. "I put you in an Uber, *remember*?" she jeers, looking at Kelvin with flared nostrils. "I didn't do shit or persuade her into any of this before you come barking at me next like it's my fucking fault."

"No, it's not your fault my wife's a whore," Kelvin says so calmly it sends a shiver through me.

Annie clamps her mouth shut. "I'm not a fucking whore!"

"You're certainly acting like one! You don't even know who the father of that baby in your belly is," Kelvin spits, shoving Coach off him.

Annie thunders forward, pushing Kelvin back a step. "No, being a fucking whore is getting an abortion." She stares at Alora. "That's the reason she's on this trip. To get rid of that thing in *her* belly."

I widen my eyes and shoot my attention at my dream girl. Tears have started to spill over as she takes a step back. My chest starts to constrict, giving my heart a lurch. "You're a fucking bitch," she says, her voice cracking.

"You're pregnant?" I raise my voice, staring at her like this is the first time I've received bad news.

The first time I got bad news was when Frannie called me saying Mom was sick.

Now Alora's pregnant, and all I'm thinking about is who I have to kill if that baby isn't mine.

She whimpers, storming off into the woods as I call after her, but Coach grabs my arm. "This ain't your fight, Scotty," he tells me. But he doesn't know.

None of these assholes know.

"That's my fucking kid!" I shout, shoving him off.

Annie gasps, hand on her mouth. And the last thing I see before running after my dream is Kelvin gritting his teeth at Annie for ruining *his* fucking life.

Oh, how the tables have fucking turned.

CHAPTER TWENTY-FIVE – ALORA ASHTON

Annie came to my apartment early one morning two weeks ago. I scared her into coming over, saying I was having heart palpitations. Frankly, I probably was. Nausea took over my life for a little and I thought it was because of stress.

But then when I finally realized Mother Nature didn't bless me with my period, I put two and two together, peeing on six sticks and screaming into a pillow at how stupid I was.

I stood outside my place, waiting for Annie to pull up and biting my thumbnail until nail polish decorated my lips. I was living a nightmare.

When she pulled up, she carried two coffees and waddled up the stairs to me, frowning as she saw the likes of my worried face.

Bags under my eyes.

Eyes puffy and red.

Dried mascara riddled my cheeks.

I was a mess.

Fuck, I still am.

"Everything okay?" she asked, out of breath, handing me a coffee—probably decaf. "You scared the shit outta me."

I groaned as another sob broke through. "I'm—fuck."

She pulled me into a hug and let me release my tears over my stupidity again. I hadn't cried that much since my mother died. This entire moment ruined any mourning I went through.

Trumped any selfless act I'd done.

That morning I broke and I wasn't sure if she could fix me.

Somehow, we managed to make our way inside and sit on the couch. We drank coffee as I stared at the macaroni and cheese I ate from the pot last night still sitting on the coffee table.

"What happened, Alora?"

I sniffed, looking up at her. "I'm fucking pregnant."

"Oh," she gasped, taking my hand. "Do you know wh-who the father is?"

I nodded quickly, seeing Scotty's face in my head. Those beautiful eyes stared at me as if he'd known me from a past life. That dimple I hate to love. His laugh that made my knees weak. Worst of all, every time I closed my eyes all I saw was the disappointed look on his face when I told him to leave.

It's the same face he'd probably give me if I told him about the baby.

"He's not going to know about this," I finally said, wiping my cheek again.

Annie furrowed her brow. "You're getting rid of it?"

"Well, yeah. I have no real job yet. I'm still in school—and everything with my dad." I scoffed. "Who the fuck am I to raise a kid? I've never had a boyfriend before, let alone a fling that lasted long enough to consider dating. I can't do this. You know I can't."

She was silent for a moment, staring at her Starbucks cup like the answers were going to pop out at her. "Do you have a plan?"

I sniffled, falling back on the couch and looking at the ceiling. "Think I'm going to travel to Vancouver with you and pay my cousin a visit." I turned my head to look at her. "She has that clinic that offers free abortions. I already spoke to her and my appointment is set for the afternoon we land. For the next two days of our trip, I'll have enough time to recoup before we're on the plane home."

Annie smoothed a hand over her stomach. "When did it happen?"

I grumbled out an answer, but she nudged me and I released a shaky breath. "The last time I went out. The night before your gender reveal."

"At Leila's fiancé's bar?" she asked, narrowing her eyes.

Groaning, I moved onto my side and rested my head on her lap. I stared at my phone on the coffee table, contemplating sending Scotty a message. Not to tell him the news, but to hear his voice again.

I missed his voice the most.

"It'll be okay, Alora," she said, smoothing out my hair.

I sniffed, tears forming in my eyes again. "Will it?"

We stayed like that for a little while, basking in my stupidity once and for all. Sooner or later, it was going to come back with a vengeance. I could only be so loose for so long.

Regret fuelled my being until she picked me up a few days later and we were off to the airport for our flight to Vancouver.

I knew seeing Scotty again would be tough, especially with this thing inside me. But I had to stay strong. Who was I if I didn't have my strength?

***

I'm weeping, hand on my mouth to silence my sobs as I make for the forest. I have no idea where I'm going, weaving around the trees. But I need away from them. Away from anyone who knows my secret. I wanted to hide it from Scotty to avoid him trying to convince me to keep it. I want to finish school and get a job before…this.

Do I even want this?

For my entire life having a family or being in love was off the table. Yet, twenty minutes ago, I felt like we were making a breakthrough. Deciding to say fuck it all and be one.

But now? No. Now it can't happen because he's going to try and stop me from killing this thing.

And I don't know how to say no to him.

Christ, I've been so wrapped up with school and exams, I didn't even think to get myself a morning-after pill. People would think I'd protect myself with birth control. But I don't because of the side effects. They're what scares me the most. So, I make my hookups wrap it, and get myself checked regularly.

But this time, I fucked up. Badly.

Fuck you, Annie, for making my problems public because you're a goddamn idiot.

Typical fucking Annie. She's never allowed to be the bad guy, always has to take someone down with her. And I was the easy target because of this *thing*.

And now Scotty and the entire team know not only about the pregnancy but about us, too.

Is there an *us*? We were getting somewhere. I was letting him in. I truly was.

But now, my walls are up and no one will be able to destroy them.

"Alora? Alora! Hey!" Scotty calls out to me, running as fast as he can through the brush.

I keep going; the last thing I need is to see him. To hear the words that'll leave his lips about us and the baby.

No, I need to be alone.

"Alora," he calls once more, footfalls thundering toward me as I step into a small clearing. "Stop a minute, will you?"

Whimpering, I ignore him, and press on. I need to get lost in these woods for a little while. "Leave me alone, Scotty."

He takes my elbow and halts my stomping, looking at me with tears in his eyes. "Is it mine?"

I scoff, looking off at the endless greenery. "Does it matter? I'm getting rid of it anyway."

"Is it mine?" He raises his voice so loudly that I jump, meeting his eyes again.

I wipe under my nose and stare at him. He's angry, not sad or excited. He's fucking mad at me right now like this pregnancy is my fault.

"I'm not that much of a fucking whore that the father of this thing inside me is a mystery," I bark, yanking my elbow from his hand. "Of course, it's yours, Scotty. You're the last person I've been with. And the *only* person I've been with in over eight months."

The tears finally slip free and he wipes a hand down his face. "Were you even going to tell me?"

I cross my arms. "I was getting rid of it, does that answer your question?"

He gives me a once-over, staring at my stomach a second longer than the rest of me. When he meets my eyes, more tears rise in them, making those green eyes an almost emerald color. "We were going to start this relationship with lies? With you killing our kid?"

"We weren't starting anything, Scotty. What we shared were just words."

Words that were left floating on the horizon.

He shakes his head, wiping the tears from his eyes. "I guess I should've just listened and stayed the hell away from you, then."

That stung, and I think he meant it. "Maybe you should've."

He hesitates when he sees more tears leave my eyes but he backtracks and leaves me alone in an alien forest. It's what I wanted, right? To be left alone with my thoughts and this agonizing stone in my throat that hasn't left since I found out about the baby.

As I stand there crying, I find myself looking around in the direction that shithead came from, wondering if he'll ever come back and comfort me.

I know he won't. I ruined this like I ruin everything I touch. It's a wonder anyone stays friends with me for very long.

With one more glance back, I continue into the forest, wondering why my life chose to turn out this way when everything was fine.

Wasn't everything fine?

When did it all go to shit?

CHAPTER TWENTY-SIX –
SCOTT WESLEY

I don't make it more than ten feet before I stop and turn back to see her again.

I never wanted to stay away from her. All I wanted was her. Told her that numerous times.

Now that a baby is involved, I don't know how to react without making her feel bad for not telling me.

She must've been scared when she found out. We're not a couple, and in her mind, she'd have to do this alone.

But she wouldn't. I'd be there for every important milestone. For the baby's and for her, too. Her graduation, her first Mother's Day, all her birthdays, Christmas…everything.

It's too late, though.

She made up her mind and the longer we're out here, the easier it'll be for her to get lost in that thick skull of hers. There's only so many times I can repeat myself and try to prove I'm the right guy for her. But if she doesn't see it now, will she ever?

I follow her as she continues deeper into the forest, crying softly as she does.

She's so damn perfect. I'm such an idiot for reacting the way I did. I couldn't help it. She makes me so angry that she won't open her eyes and see how great we are together.

Stubborn pain in my ass.

She stops dead in her tracks, gasping, then darts into the clearing. "Hey! Hey, are you all right?"

I charge after her, branches whipping me in the chest and face. She's on her knees beside someone who's sitting against a boulder, blood decorating their face. It's the freaking pilot.

"Hey, sir, can you look at me?" she says, checking his pulse. "My name's Alora." She takes his hand, looking over her shoulder as I approach her. "I-I need you to, um…" she stammers, returning her attention to the pilot. "Can you squeeze my hand? I need to know if you can hear me, sir. Squeeze my hand."

A beat passes and I'm caught staring at the rapid rise and fall of her chest, and how she keeps her fingers on his wrist as she checks her watch.

I get down on my knees beside her, putting a gentle hand on her lower back. "What do you need from me?"

"Check the area and see if the front of the plane is close by," she says, smiling at the pilot. "All right, there you go. Can you squeeze again?" She nods, glancing at me. "Isn't there something in the plane that'll help us get out of here?"

I nod slowly, keeping my eyes locked with hers. "And when we get out of here, Alora, we're sitting down and having a long talk."

"Now's not the time, shithead," she snaps, nostrils flaring.

Getting to my feet, I leave a kiss on the top of her head

before I follow the debris on the ground.

I glance back at her as she counts, staring at her watch as she does it.

We're doing this, aren't we? Yeah, we're fucking doing this if it's the last honest thing I do with my life. I may live and breathe hockey, but that changed the moment this plane crashed. I live and breathe Alora now. Nothing but Alora.

I barely make it fifty feet from her and see the nose of the plane is lodged between two trees, metal warped and bent, scorch marks staining the sides from a possible fire.

How the fuck did this happen?

"Hello? Anyone here?" I call, walking around the plane. "Hello?"

That's when I see the other pilot lying face-first on the ground. His back is rising and falling. I dart back to Alora, legs pumping as I move through the forest at record speed. She's standing now, looking around as if to try and calculate where the plane might be based on how this pilot got there.

"Alora, I found the plane," I tell her and grab her hand. "I found the other pilot, too."

She lets me hold her hand as we power through the forest to the man lying on the ground. She approaches him first, dropping to her knees. "Hey, sir, can you hear me?"

The pilot groans, opening his eyes and blinking rapidly. "O-oh, God. Help! Th-the p-plane went d-down, I don't know what happened. M-malfunctions—"

"It's okay." I get down beside her, hand on her shoulder. "We're passengers from the flight."

He chuckles softly, tears following suit. Relief sweeps

over him as he looks at Alora. "I, uh." He sniffs. "I can't move my legs." He props himself onto his elbows and glances at his legs. "I can't feel a damn fucking thing," he sobs, looking between Alora and me.

She moves closer on her knees and stares at his back; blood and shards of metal are sticking out of it. His white dress shirt is stained crimson and covered in dirt.

"Can you lie back on your stomach?" she says softly. Her voice is soothing and nurturing. "I'm not a doctor yet, but I'm a medical student. If you'll allow me to take a look?"

He nods, wincing as he lowers himself down and turns his head to the side to look at her. "I broke my back, didn't I?"

"Well, the fact that you're moving is a good sign. But the fact that you can't feel your legs is not." She lifts his shirt, taking a look at his black and blue back.

Her eyes widen, gulping slowly, and lowers his shirt again. "Okay, well…shit." She stares at me with watery eyes.

The man panics, looking at her. "What?"

I tilt her head to face me; those eyes are so green they match the leaves shining in the sunlight. "Just breathe, okay? You got this, baby."

"We have to get him out of here," she whispers, tears streaming down her cheeks.

"The tail end of the plane has the GPS trackers," the pilot says. "We sent out a Mayday as we were crashing."

Turning to her, I witness the problem-solving taking place again. She's trying to figure out what to do and how to do it. "We'll get everyone to come here so he's not left alone, okay?" I suggest.

She nods, sniffles, and leans back on her heels. "We can't move him, so that works."

I look down at him and force a grin. "What's your name?"

"Nathan," he says, pointing a finger behind him. "Other guy is Mikey."

I smile, getting to my feet. "I'm Scotty, this is my — Alora. We're going to get everyone who survived and bring them here. Get some water and food in you, too."

Nathan smiles back, nodding as Alora takes my hand and rises to her feet as well.

"Stay with him," she says, moving a strand of hair from her mouth. "I'll go get everyone."

I take her arm. "No, let me go."

"I'll be fine, Scotty."

With that, she marches off, leaving me with my heart on my sleeve wondering if I'll ever be able to fix this madness between us.

CHAPTER TWENTY-SEVEN –
ALORA ASHTON

The pilots are alive. Something about it sends tendrils of relief through me.

I needed something to lift my spirits because seeing Scotty so angry made me break into a million pieces. How can I put a smile back on his face without hurting him?

Seems like all I do is hurt him.

Disappoint him, too, when all he wants is me.

Someone wants to be with me and I won't let it happen.

What the fuck is wrong with me that I can't let him in?

Finding my way back to the wreck, Kelvin is sitting with Corey, Brett is pacing by the fire, and Annie is sitting on the last step of the plane, while the rest of the guys are scattered. She looks up at me, regret forming on her face. "Alora, I—"

I put my hand up and clear my throat. "I don't wanna hear it, Annie. That was not your fucking news to share."

"Why didn't you tell me it was Scotty's?" she asks, tears spilling over.

I sniff, shaking my head. "Because, clearly, you can't keep your mouth shut about anything. You fucked someone else and suddenly it's my fault because I like to sleep around? Because I slept with Scotty before you warned me not to? I helped all these fucking people and what do I get for it? Humiliation? Betrayal from someone who's supposed to be my best friend? Fuck that—and fuck you, Annie. This is a low blow."

She opens her mouth to speak but I walk away, being the bigger person before I tear her head off. "Hey!" I call out to everyone. "I found the pilots!"

Coach comes thundering my way with Gregory by his side. "Where?"

"One is in and out of consciousness and I think the other broke his back. We should move our camp there to keep him safe. I don't want to risk moving him," I answer, looking around at the eager eyes staring at me.

"Move? Well, no, the fire is here, our supplies are here. We're walking distance from the water—"

"He can't move, and it's not smart to leave him out there like that another night," I interrupt Coach. "Christ, we're a group of people with a fire and wolves still came to us."

"Alora," Sophia says, touching my arm. "What if we make a stretcher and carry him over here?"

I pinch the bridge of my nose, shaking my head. "He can't—" I scoff, looking at the trees I just traveled through. These people don't understand and I'm not in the right mind to explain it to them. Maybe if I get them there, Scotty will be able to. "Yeah…sure."

Annie makes her way over, and her hand slides into mine, squeezing it slightly. But there will be no forgiving her right now. I can let go of all the times I took the fall for her drunken stupidity as teenagers but outing me in front of everyone? Telling Scotty about the baby is something I cannot forgive. That was not her place.

I yank my hand from her grip and head for the supplies. Two water bottles and two bags of nuts. No one moves after the decision to make a gurney like it's not important to get this guy to safety. All selfish fucks. Bunch of fucking animals.

Gosh, I'm so livid, I'm on the verge of walking into the forest solo and letting the wilderness guide me to safety or to the trenches of what the bush can hold.

Right as I start making my way to Scotty and the pilots, helicopters can be heard in the distance. Some of the guys gasp, looking around to see if anyone else can hear it, too.

"Holy shit," Corey exclaims through a wince as he tries to get up.

"To the water, we'll wave them down with the fire," Coach says, grabbing all the firewood we collected and tossing it into the fire, building its flames.

Brett and Marshall jump to their feet and grab a couple of their jerseys to wave in the air. There's a spark igniting in me, that sensation of happiness spilling free and soaking into my skin. It spreads this smile on my face. The terrors we endured are over. They're finally over.

"I'll go tell Scotty," I say, smiling as Corey nods at me. "I told you I'd get you home to your girl and your kid."

He winks. "Yeah, thanks, doc."

Sophia and Gregory are hugging each other, smiling with relief that they get to go home to their children. Annie is sobbing, holding onto her belly as Kelvin gives her a lopsided grin.

And me? I'm making my way back to Scotty to tell him the good news.

But getting out of here just means I have to face reality head-on. And I don't think I'm ready for that. Not yet, at least.

CHAPTER TWENTY-EIGHT – SCOTT WESLEY

I can't stop watching the trees, waiting for her beautiful face to emerge.

One minute I'm livid with her, regretting ever falling for her. The next, I can't wait to hold her and kiss her and tell her how I feel.

But I don't think she'll accept me. She's set in her ways, believing love isn't real. But it is, it's what we have. Our love is different, unique. Something that's once in a lifetime.

"She your girlfriend?" Nathan asks, sliding his hand under his cheek.

I sigh, wiping a hand down my face. "It's complicated."

He smirks, groaning softly as he adjusts his head. "My wife and I were complicated at the beginning of our relationship. She hated me, I was annoyed with her, and then one day we just clicked. Been going twenty-two years strong. Mind you, it took us six weeks before I grew a pair and realized my annoyance with her was the fact that I liked her crazy ass."

I chuckle softly, looking off at the trees again in hopes of seeing Alora. "What made her realize it?"

"If she didn't show interest, I'd have moved to Europe. I told her that the same day I told her I liked her, and she told me she wouldn't be able to live without me." He shakes his head. "Woman was obsessed with me, only hated me because we were twenty and she didn't want to settle down just yet. But she settled down, all right. Popped out three babies within eight years of that night we got together. You'll see, Scotty. She'll be your little dove soon enough."

Laughing softly, Alora's gorgeous face flashes through my head. *My little dove.* I can get used to her being mine. "If only she weren't so fucking stubborn, we'd have been happier than pigs in shit over eight weeks ago." I sigh, nibbling the inside of my cheek. The entire team knows our secret, so why not pour my heart out to a stranger? "She's pregnant. Literally just found out. But—"

A great pang grips my heart at the thought that if we didn't crash, then we'd still be playing the same game and she'd have killed our baby alone. She'd have to suffer through all that alone. That upsets me more than the discovery of our little one.

Nathan smiles, reaches a hand out, and taps my leg. "Congrats, man. Kids are a handful, but they're the best thing you'll ever do."

I sniff, wiping my cheek on my shoulder. He doesn't know. How could he? News like this is supposed to be happy. Based on the friends I have, news like this is shared fairly often. But this news isn't happy news, is it? The woman of my dreams is ripping it away from me.

And I'm all for women's rights. This is her decision.

She can keep it or she can get rid of it. And I understand her reasoning. She's still in school. She wants to graduate and find a job, but what she doesn't realize is we can still do that with a baby. She can go to school, she can work, she can do whatever it is she has to, as long as it's with me and our little one.

I clear my throat, too defeated to explain our situation. "Yeah. Yeah, thanks."

"How far along is—"

Nathan is cut off by the sound of helicopters in the distance. I jump to my feet and stare up at the sky; the trees eating up most of it. "Do you hear that?"

"I told you I sent out a Mayday before we crashed." He laughs, crying softly. "We're gonna make it."

A wave of anxiety bolts through me when I stare out at the forest. Alora should've been back by now. What if she didn't get to the team? What if she's lost?

Fucking Christ, what if she's hurt?

I nod, looking at the trees in front of us. "Fuck, I should've gone back to everyone."

My heart's beating out of my chest the longer my eyes strain to see through the dense forest.

She's taking too long. Something's wrong. I can feel it.

"Go find her, as long as you come back," Nathan says, tapping my foot like he can read my fucking thoughts. "I'd be running out there, too, if it was my wife."

Nodding quickly, I don't bother looking down at him. I just head straight for the bushes and trees. I'm off to find my dream and make an honest woman out of her.

CHAPTER TWENTY-NINE – ALORA ASHTON

The sound of the helicopter is getting louder, closer. We're saved. Holy shit, we're saved!

And yet, as much as the relief has sent goosebumps traveling over my entire body, I don't want to be saved. I want away from my life. Away from the ruin I've caused, the deception and lies. I want away from the debauchery. Away from my wicked ways.

I want a new life.

Glancing around, there's nothing but thick trees around me. Am I even going the right way?

I step forward, then stop and turn back only to realize I have no idea which way I came from, let alone which way I'm going.

"Shit," I growl out, running my fingers through my hair. "Motherfucking idiot!"

Closing my eyes, I take a hot, impatient breath, my overthinking mind is ready to consume me. It's just a forest. People are everywhere around me. All I have to do is yell and someone will come running, won't they?

No, probably not. After everything I've done for them, they'll still view me as this petty tramp who opens her legs on the weekends and studies on the weekdays.

If only I could erase my history.

I release another breath, deciding to follow the sound of the helicopter and backtrack once I find the group.

Scotty's face moves through my thoughts. How sad I made him. How much he's wanted to try things with me, be with me. Getting rid of this baby will permanently end any chance of us. And as much as it's killing me, it's better this way. Better for everybody if we cut ties and pretend none of it ever happened. He'll go back to hockey; I'll go back to school. We'll never see or speak to each other again.

He'll be like every other guy in my life. A tool I used to get off. Nothing more.

I whimper as a great sense of dread sweeps through me, sucking the last bit of hope with it. He's more than anything I've ever wanted in life. More than my dream of being a doctor. More than my dream of being happy. He's my dream. He's my happy ending.

I grit my teeth and stop, glaring at the sky that can barely be seen between the swaying trees. "You love him, Alora. Just fucking admit it to yourself. You're in love with him but refuse to let yourself be happy. Just fucking admit it."

I'm sobbing, alone in a forest, that murky dull feeling taking over because I hate how much I'm right. I do. I love him and I want to spend my life coming home to him, cheering him on at games, making memories with him. The best memories I never had.

Starting to walk again, I step over a fallen tree, when my foot sinks into the pile of leaves and I'm falling into a hole in the ground. This deep-rooted sinkhole hole was probably caused by a thick fallen tree. I let out a yelp, my hands trying to grip the sides of the dirt, but I grab onto nothing but roots that tumble down with me.

Before I know it, my ankle twists upon the landing and I yell again, falling back as dirt and wet leaves surround me.

Panic sets in like thin tendrils of vines coursing through my veins.

I've fallen into a hole in the middle of this dense forest. And no one's going to find me.

No one's going to save me.

No one's going to care that I'm gone.

I can't let the fear take hold, I have to burrow through the opening and call for help, even if no one finds me. I have to try.

Pushing myself up, I wince, keeping my weight off my ankle. Another sob chokes me and I place a hand on my stomach. I have to get out of here before this becomes a problem.

Gripping the edges of the opening, I wrap the long roots around my wrists and pull myself up enough so I can grab onto the ground.

I pull, reaching a hand out, and whimper. I'm too weak. Too fucking weak to save myself let alone the baby in my belly.

Maybe I deserved to fall in here for all the naughtiness and sins I've committed. Maybe I deserved this downfall because of the hurt I'm putting Scotty through.

God, Scotty. Just thinking of how he would react if he can't find me. If they left the forest without me. Just thinking about the reality that he might just leave me. He might forget about me because I've pushed him away so many times.

I deserve this. All of it.

I look out the hole and cry. There's nothing else for me to do but give in to the weakness.

Give in to my fate.

CHAPTER THIRTY – SCOTT WESLEY

I make it back to camp and the guys are cheering, hugging each other, and laughing. So much fucking laughter.

"Scotty!" Gregory yells, embracing me. "We're saved, we're fucking saved."

Coach comes out of the bushes that lead to the water and makes his way to Corey. "All right, team, the chopper can only hold four at a time. Sophia, Annie, Corey, and Alora will get on first—"

I glance around quickly, unable to spot her. "Where's Alora? Is she already on the helicopter?"

Gregory glances back at his wife, then Annie, his gaze coming back to me. "No, she went to get you."

As if my heart couldn't break anymore, my breathing hitches and I take a step back. "No, no, I would've seen her— no, she's…"

A haunted look paints Annie's face, stopping Kelvin from collecting the food. "Alora's missing."

He rises, not an ounce of worry on his face while my entire body goes numb.

"She couldn't have gone far," Corey says, taking in the likes of my panic and grabbing my hand. "Hey, Scotty. We'll find her."

Kelvin frowns, looking behind me at the forest. "You're sure you didn't see her? Maybe she's back with the pilot?"

I huff and nod quickly, hoping she is. Hoping my dream is sitting with him and letting him know we're saved.

Rushing back into the bush, Kelvin and Gregory are right behind me. I can hear Annie calling out her name, but I doubt she'll follow us in. It's much too dangerous for a pregnant woman.

A pregnant woman!

My fucking woman is pregnant with my kid and I let her go alone into this treacherous terrain. Some fucking guy I am.

What would Frannie think of me? What would my mom think of me? How could I be so stupid?

Goddammit.

We make it to Nathan and he adjusts himself on his elbows, looking at me. "Hey."

"There's a chopper here," Gregory explains, taking in his back injury. "We're having the women escorted out of here first, then they'll come back with the proper stuff to help you."

I glance around, going into the plane and heading to the other pilot whose head is back against the boulder. He's breathing shallowly.

She's not here.

She's not fucking here!

The worst case scenario is running through my mind.

The wolves attacked her.

She fell and hit her head.

She's lost.

Fuck, what if she's hurt?!

I head back to Nathan and find Kelvin crouched beside him, offering him some water. "Did Alora come back?" My words come out as a shout, but it's not my intention. My panic is taking over the volume of my voice.

Wiping sweat from my brow, Kelvin looks around, gaze falling back on me. "Hey, we'll find her, all right?" he says soothingly.

"She couldn't have gone far," Gregory adds, looking in the direction we came from. "Maybe she headed to the water instead of camp."

I'm hyperventilating, gripping my knees with my head between them. Dread crawls up my spine, prickling my skin as my heart goes into overdrive. Something's fucking wrong.

"Scotty, there's no need to panic. I'm sure you'll find her," Nathan says, wiping water from his chin.

Their words are swimming around me. Suffocating me in a way that's making me want to scream. They don't know if we'll find her. They don't know if she's okay.

They don't fucking know.

Releasing a breath, I start walking for the trees, remembering the exact one she walked by because I couldn't stop staring at it after she left.

"Gregory, stay here. If we don't come back in ten, go get help," Kelvin says, jogging after me.

I'm huffing, breathing deep, slow breaths. A panic attack is tumbling in. I haven't had one of these since I watched them bury my mother. The casket lowered into the ground. The dirt piled on top of her. All that went through my mind was, what if she's still alive? What if they're burying her and she's trying to get out of there? What if she's screaming and we can't hear her? Frannie squeezed my hand and breathed with me. Told me to relax when all I wanted to do was stop it. She was so calm that day. Much calmer than I was. Lowering our mother to the ground sealed her fate. Her final resting place. A hole in the ground for someone who meant everything to me.

Alora means everything to me. This fucking nightmare will not be her final resting place.

"Hey, man. Hey." Kelvin grabs my arm, stopping me completely so we're face to face. "Why didn't you tell me you hooked up with Alora?"

I sniff, just taking in the reality that I'm crying at the thought of losing her. She's torn me open and wrapped her delicate hands around my heart, owning it. "I didn't know who she was until the gender reveal."

Kelvin raises his eyebrows. "She's the girl you met that night?"

I nod, glancing around quickly. Everything is so dense, so…full of trees. I have no idea where to start. For all I know, I already walked past her. She could be fucking anywhere.

"But she's—" He sighs, folding his arms. "She's a whore like my wife. Who says this baby is even yours?"

I thunder toward him, slamming my chest into his. "She is *not* a whore! I'm the last person she's been with in months. Me! Just because she sleeps around, it doesn't make her a whore. Fuck, if she were a dude, things would be fine, wouldn't they? No one would judge her. But no, all you fuckheads judge her because she's a party girl. You don't take into consideration that she's a fucking med student! That if it wasn't for her, half of us would be bleeding out—or your fucking wife would've been mauled by a wolf." I growl, repeating myself and shoving him back a step. "Alora is nothing but nice to every single one of you fucks, but you judge her based on her track record. Why don't you look in the fucking mirror, Kelvin? You slept with anything that breathed before you met Annie, remember? So, watch your fucking mouth around my girl, do you understand?"

He huffs, nodding slowly with a clenched jaw. "You could've just told me."

"You warned us like we were children not to sleep with each other. And she tried so hard to stay away from me. So fucking hard because she hates herself more than anything when people judge her. But I never did. And look where it got us!" I wipe the spittle from my mouth. "She's pregnant, lost, and almost had an abortion to guarantee we don't work out. She would be doing this all alone when you know for a damn fact she would never have to lift a finger with me. So, fuck you, Kelvin. You've really opened my eyes to see what kind of asshole you are to people who are so fucking loyal to you and your family."

I scoff and walk off; I don't need to hear whatever he has to say. He's the type of guy that will argue even when he's wrong. He waits for you to finish ranting so he can say his piece because he always has to be the last person to speak.

Asshole. I think this friendship is fucking over.

I sniff again and stop walking, letting the silence take over. There's a slight ringing in my ears, but I close my eyes and listen. Fate brought us together, now it's going to help me find her.

I can faintly hear Annie calling for Alora, and a few of the guys are calling her name, too. Kelvin's footfalls crunch leaves as he makes his way to me, but I can't hear *her*. I can't hear much other than noise. Goddamn birds, insects, my fucking ragged breaths.

Where is she?

I run my fingers through my hair, my gaze getting lost in the multiple trees surrounding me. Everything looks the same. Everything is closing in on me. Everything is not okay.

Kelvin puts a hand on my shoulder, squeezing slightly. "We're going to find her, even if it means staying behind."

I sniff, wiping my nose on my hand. "What if we can't find her?" I let the words escape my mouth. My biggest fear coming to life.

"Then we bring in as much manpower as we can until we do," he says, dropping his hand. "Alora!" he calls, nudging me to do the same. He starts walking back to everyone else, calling her name over and over.

But I can't move.

All I see is her lying somewhere hurt. Alone. Sad. Thinking we left without her. Thinking no one cares about her. But I do.

So fucking much.

With one last deep exhale, I continue straight,

screaming her name over and over until my voice cracks. I'll burn this entire forest down until I find her.

And I will fucking find her.

CHAPTER THIRTY-ONE – ALORA ASHTON

With a groan, I touch my ankle. It's swelling up, which does not bode well for me. I don't know how I'm getting out of here. I don't know if anyone even notices I'm gone.

Why would they, anyway? I'm just the friend they make fun of and then beg on their hands and knees for help when they need me most.

And I know once we're back in the real world, everything will go back to normal. They'll look down on me for sleeping with Scotty and getting pregnant. While he'll get high fives from them for scoring. Back in the real world, I'll—

Back in the real world.

Oh, God, what if I don't make it back to the real world?

A sob chokes me at the thought of never seeing Scotty again. What if he moves on? Finds someone new? Loves someone new?

Would he even remember me? Talk about me and the baby? Would he still care?

He would. He'd care until his dying day, knowing I was the girl who stole his heart and made a baby with him.

A baby we will love and cherish so much.

A baby who will learn to skate before they can walk.

Scotty and I are doing this. I'm opening my heart,

letting my walls down, and allowing him to envelop me the way he's been trying to since we met.

I knew we were meant to be the second we locked eyes. A sensation sparked inside me.

A blooming of love and lust.

A forever.

We were idiots to think this wasn't going to be more than a one-night stand.

Placing a hand on my stomach, I wince. "I'm so sorry for almost taking you away, little one. You're not some *thing*, you're mine and Daddy's. Our perfect disaster." I sniff, furrowing my brows. "I'm just scared. I don't want to ruin you like my parents ruined me. You deserve the world." A sob breaks out and I bring a hand to my mouth. "I'm sorry, I'm so fucking sorry."

Imagine Scotty and I as parents, raising our baby in my apartment with all the love we have to give. A new emotion that's overtaking my entire being. But it's worth it. It's so fucking worth it.

But now is not the time to break down. It's time to get out of here.

Groaning, I force myself to stand in this narrow hole. I'm getting out of here. I'm getting out of here and things are changing. I never noticed how stale and unhappy my life was. That's why I filled my void with men. But when I found the one that didn't need to be replaced, my insides came to life and it had meaning.

Scotty gave my life meaning—more than studying and partying.

He gave me hope.

Gripping the hanging root again, I hop on one foot. "Fuck," I growl, looking through the opening that's less than two feet from me.

I can do this.

Pulling myself up, the root is slipping free of whatever it's attached to but I tug harder, praying it'll hold. I reach out, hand grazing the wet ground when the root snaps and I tumble back, hitting my head against the dirt with a thunk.

Stars cloud my vision for a second, but I blink rapidly and look up, hearing the helicopter taking flight. The sound of its propellers disappearing the farther away it goes.

They've left without me.

They've left without trying to look for me.

They've forgotten about me.

Weeping softly, I look down at my dirty hands in my lap and wonder what I ever did to deserve this. What wrong have I done in life to be left behind? Would Scotty really do this to me? My hands rest on my stomach and hold on a moment longer, but the deafening silence of the forest takes hold.

Right as I'm about to throw in the towel, I hear it. Shouts and panting. *They didn't leave without me!*

I force myself upright, hopping on one leg and standing right under the opening. I can hear my name. I can hear him shouting my name.

"Alora!" Scotty yells, out of breath. "Fuck! Alora, where are you? Alora!"

I whimper, reaching a hand out but there's nothing to

grab onto. "Scotty? Scotty!"

It's silent.

Did I imagine it? Did I hit my head hard enough that I'm hearing things?

Leaves crunch and squish, and I hear panting again. "Alora!"

"Scotty! Scotty, I'm down here—" A sob rises in my throat as I hear the panic in his voice as he calls my name again.

"Alora!"

"Scotty."

His footsteps come closer and then they stop, but I can hear his heavy breaths. Then I see him, those green eyes so big and frightened. He saved me. He came to take me home. "Alora? Baby. Oh, Jesus Christ. Hey, hey, you're okay."

I reach my hand out to him again, sobbing. "Scotty, I'm sorry. I shouldn't have snapped at you and I should've told you about the baby—"

He reaches down and grabs my hand, straining as the cords in his neck bulge, shoulder muscles flexing. "Now's not the time, okay?"

He pulls me out of the hole, nearly slipping in with me as parts of the ground beneath him start to give out. But I'm out, I'm in his arms and laughing as I cry.

We're doing this.

He squeezes me, hands touching my head, and my back, then wrapping around my waist as my face is buried in his neck. "Are you hurt? Let me see you."

"I'm okay," I say, my voice muffled by him. "I'm

okay."

I need to hold him. To know he's real.

Not having him near me makes me feel uneasy. When he's around, life is good. It's happy. Shit, it's so much better.

But I kept pushing him away because I was scared. Commitment is terrifying, yet Scotty will make it that much easier.

He makes everything easier.

"Look at me, Alora," he says, kissing my neck.

I sniff, lifting my head and staring into those beautiful eyes that stole my heart the moment I saw them. "Let's do this," I whisper, smiling. "Me and you."

He smirks, bopping his nose on mine. "And?"

I nod, smiling largely. "The baby, too."

My name is called again; it's Kelvin's voice this time. Leaves crunch nearby and then pounding footfalls make their way to us. "You found her! Alora? Holy shit, are you okay? Are you hurt?" He's out of breath, sweating almost as much as Scotty. "The baby?"

I sniff, keeping my eyes locked with Scotty's. "We're okay."

As if Scotty can read my mind, he pulls me into a hug, kissing my neck repeatedly. "We're doing this?"

I nod, my chin hitting his shoulder. "Bear with me."

"Until the end of time," he whispers, taking my head off his shoulder and planting a desperate kiss on me.

Kelvin chuckles, taking a step back. "All right, c'mon lovebirds, let's get out of here."

Scotty helps me stand, but I limp with the first step we

take. I don't even have to ask, he already has me in his arms and leads us back to everyone.

Studying him, sweat beads roll down the sides of his face and get lost in that playoff beard. I was an idiot to think I didn't want this. An idiot to let him go.

I wipe the sweat from his face, smiling. "I'm in love with you, shithead."

He chuckles, stepping over some bushes as we enter the clearing again, and Annie waddles to us. "I love you, too, baby." Those succulent lips press onto mine, taking all the chaos away. Giving my heart a one-two jolt at this new journey we're embarking on.

My moment of panic opened my eyes and showed me that life has meaning if you look hard enough. People don't always die of a broken heart. Not couples who are meant to be.

And as far as we knew, Scotty and I are that rare one in a million.

EPILOGUE – ONE YEAR LATER –
SCOTT WESLEY

Since the plane crash, things have been hectic back home. Playoffs were postponed until a bunch of us were able to play. Coach wanted us to forfeit, take some time to process what happened, and mourn those we lost. But no, we wanted back on the ice to show the world we were fighters. Survivors. Nothing could stand in our way.

And it didn't. We won the fucking championship that year for the four team members we lost, honoring them with our victory.

And you know what I got to do when we won? I got to kiss my pregnant wife on the ice in front of millions of people.

Yeah, my fucking *wife*.

The moment we left that godforsaken forest, we were brought to the closest hospital. Alora had a fractured ankle, needed stitches and shots for the wolf bite, and an ultrasound for the baby. Shit, I don't think I cried that much in my entire life. After everything I'd been through, I was given this gift. This beautiful baby from the most stunning, stubborn human. I'm one lucky fuck.

I asked her to marry me on the flight home. She laughed, shoved my face away from her, and said *slow your roll, shithead.*

Two months later, we got married in Corey's backyard with a few close friends and family. Frannie insisted on being my best woman, and I don't think I'd have it any other way. However, our best friends weren't there. Alora couldn't stomach having Annie there after the betrayal she endured. And who could blame her? I'd hate my best friend, too, if they exposed my biggest secret to get the attention off me. And my friendship with Kelvin dwindled, too. I didn't appreciate how he viewed my wife, how he spoke about her still haunts me. I don't need him, not until he fixes his drama. We've gotten closer with Corey and Steph. Our friendship grew since the crash. And seeing my wife tease him like a big sister reminds me of Frannie.

And I love my sister to death.

Five months after our wedding, Alora gave birth to our son, Lockland—a Scottish name meaning "land of lakes" because that's where my woman came to her senses and realized she loved me. Right there on the horizon in that nightmare of a forest.

My son is all chubby cheeks and long legs, looking mostly like his mother, but when he smiles, the kid is all me down to the dimple on his cheek.

Four months after his birth, Alora and I finally moved in together. We tried to manage being at my condo, then at her apartment. But when push came to shove, I got tired of the flip-flopping from one place to the next and told her to choose one place and that would be our home until we found ourselves our forever home.

Well, we're all crammed into her apartment because she hates the city.

Her pregnancy was fairly easy, to say the least. My woman is a badass bitch who powered through her schooling and residency with her big ole belly. I'm so fucking proud of her.

The crowd is going wild tonight, hearing the announcer introduce our team. My heart's dancing like crazy, pumped for an important game that will reveal if we've made the playoffs this season. We're down several guys, and it's hard connecting with these new players. We're not undefeated, but we're still the best team in the league. And I plan on having my son sit inside the trophy this year while I kiss my wife. A perfect picture-taking moment I plan to have every single year with her. We'll fill our walls with them. Just like we started with last year's picture.

I follow the guys onto the ice, kissing the wedding ring around my finger.

Alora wears my mother's necklace. She doesn't take it off. No matter what, that belongs to her. She's my little moon, my forever.

I get into position, catching her eye in the crowd, and blow her a kiss. Lockland is in her arms, big noise-canceling headphones on his head as she points me out on the ice. Little shit isn't even looking at me, he's too busy staring at the flashing lights. But this moment here is all I ever wanted.

My love.

My happiness.

My everything standing right there, smiling at me.

I love you, I mouth, smirking when she scrunches her nose.

Fuck you, she mouths back, sticking her tongue between her teeth.

She knows she's going to pay for that later.

I wink at her, biting my lower lip at the thought of taking my wife to the locker rooms. We've done it before. Right after a game, I'm still on that adrenaline high and I use her, pounding her like I'm possessed by the fucking devil until she can barely walk. I hate leaving her sore like that, but fuck, does she ever go wild when I do.

I love you, I mouth again, making her smile.

I love you, baby, she mouths, blowing me a kiss.

Those kisses have become my good luck charm before every home game.

She's my good luck charm. Always has been, I just didn't know it until I found her.

My pain in the ass has a title now. My wife. Mother to my son.

She's branded on my skin, too—a rose tattoo on my neck with her name. Our son's name is imprinted on my chest. I belong to them. My woman, my queen. And our little moon.

And as life continues, we'll create more titles. More memories. Just us. Our family. My beautiful family.

Lockland's gaze turns to the ice when the ref blows the whistle. He finds me and smiles. Kicking his legs with excitement as Alora kisses his cheek.

My son.

My Alora.

I never thought I'd be here. I never thought I'd make my mother proud even though she can't see me. I know she's proud. I'm her little moon and I've given her an even more perfect one with the most amazing woman this world has ever seen.

It took us a while to get into the swing of things, and now that we're here, I couldn't see my life playing out any other way.

Alora smiles at me, biting her bottom lip as the crowd starts to cheer.

"Here we go, baby!" I yell at my teammates as they get into position.

My heart's already beating quickly, and I know, we're going to fucking kill it.

Life is bliss.

It's mental, but holy shit, we made it.

We fucking made it!

Character art by Stephanie Henigin (@stephsbooktherapy)

264

BONUS SCENE – ALORA ASHTON

I've fixed my shirt at least seventeen times from the parking lot to the arena. Now I'm shifting in my seat as Annie, Sophia, and I wait for the practice to be over. A few of the other wives and their kids are running around the arena—Frannie is here, too, taking pictures on Snapchat with Clara and Sammy. It's odd sitting here with the rest of the hockey wives. No, not odd. New.

I never come to these practices, not since the crash. Anything surrounding hockey makes me anxious. But Scotty says we have to overcome the tragedy and see it for what it was for us; our beginning.

But all I can see is the blood and the loss so many of his friends endured.

However, I'm here today because Frannie came to visit, and she insisted I join her. And I can't say no to my sister-in-law. Oh, God, I'm a wife. How freaking weird is that?

I'm also almost seven months pregnant—which is even weirder for me. But something about Scotty being by my side through this entire endeavor makes everything that much easier.

Everything with Scotty has always been so effortless, hasn't it?

Except for this pregnancy—it's a son of a bitch. I'm tired all the time, my back hurts, I pee every ten minutes, and the food! I can't seem to stay satisfied no matter how much I eat.

Oh, and the sex. Poor Scotty. I think for the first time in our relationship, I saw him whimper out of fatigue when I hit on him after yesterday's training. I'm wearing him out, but it's what Mama needs. And being the beautiful man that he is—one I surely don't deserve—he always aims to please.

I'm not going to lie, it's still taking me time to adjust to the idea of being in a relationship. It's all new. Holding hands is new, kissing in front of our friends is new, sitting on his lap, and coming home to him. It's all new.

And truthfully, I love it.

Insert "I told you so" here.

I didn't believe in love because it was something I viewed as fake. Something that was conjured up. But would you look at me now? I'm in love with the sexiest man on the ice, who's lifting his jersey to wipe sweat from his face and showing off those abs. Fucking tease.

Maybe I was an idiot at the beginning. I saw him. I saw his beauty and love for me. And yet, my overthinking mind refused him. Pushed him away because that's all I knew. My father always warned me not to sleep with someone more than three times.

Three times, he said. *After that, they'll develop feelings. You don't want to end up like your mother. Three times, Alora. Remember that.*

But Scotty was my diamond in the rough. I developed feelings for him long before my brain could snap out of it. My brain needed to speak with my heart so they'd agree. Scotty and I would've been in bliss if I wasn't so damn stubborn.

I pushed him away for so long until I opened my eyes and the thought of never having him in my life hurt more than being alone. And when our little man started growing in my belly, I knew he was right. Fate brought us together that night. It opened my eyes to Scotty so that I could see there is love in the world. There is happiness beyond messed-up sheets and drunken nights.

I have the best love a girl could ever ask for—even though it took me a minute to wake the fuck up and realize it.

Of course, we argued—holy crap, those first few weeks were ultimate torture—but he believed in us. And so did I. We always pulled through because of the most understanding man I call my husband.

Closing my textbook, I catch Scotty's eye as he skates to the net, blowing him a kiss. He winks, sticking his tongue out and pumping his legs as the guys practice drills skating back and forth. Corey's on the ice again. He's been anxious about getting back out there for a few weeks, but his doctor said it's good to start skating again. Although, my opinion is the only one he trusts lately—even if I'm not a doctor yet—and it's a pain in the ass. But he's been our rock throughout this pregnancy. I hate to love the asshole.

I tug my shirt again, fixing my jacket with a groan. Sophia laughs, hooking her arm in mine. "Babe, you're pregnant. There's no hiding it or zipping up that coat anytime soon."

I drop my head back. "I'm so fat."

Annie laughs, bobbing the baby in her arms. "It's about time your perfect body has some flaws."

"Fuck off," I blurt out.

Annie and I aren't as close as we used to be. It saddens me in a way, but a loyal friend wouldn't out me like that. No, a loyal friend would back me up and admit her faults instead of revealing my secrets.

My thighs clench together, watching Scotty skate to the other end of the rink and spray ice onto the boards. The way the hockey gear makes him appear bigger than he is. Skates that make him so much taller, too. And as if he knows I'm watching, he keeps lifting his shirt and wiping sweat from his face. The man is killing me.

Coach blows the whistle, ending practice a few minutes early. A few of the guys pick up sticks and move some pucks around, but not Scotty. He comes to me with a smirk on his face.

God, he's fucking handsome.

He tosses his gloves on the ground as soon as he pushes the door open and steps off the ice. Losing his helmet next and showing off that wet, messy brown hair, he hasn't tamed since the crash. I kind of like how wild it gets sometimes.

"Hey, baby," he says, out of breath, leaning down to kiss me. "You gonna join us?"

I raise my eyebrows, letting out a chuckle. "Join you where?"

Sophia gets up, tossing her scarf over her shoulder. "On the ice, silly. We're having a family skate day. Even my kids are getting on the ice."

Gregory slaps his stick on the ice, sticking his tongue out as his wife plops down on the bench in front of the boards and opens a bag with her figure skates inside. Clara and Sammy run over with smiles on their faces as Gregory gets off the ice to help them with their skates.

"Oh, no, Scotty. I don't know how to skate." I swallow thickly. "Plus, I'm pregnant. There's no way you're going to let your pregnant wife on the ice, is there?"

He smirks, tilting my chin up and capturing my lips in a delicate kiss. "Oh, yes, I am."

"What're you nuts?" But he already has me in his arms as he walks like a penguin in his ridiculous skates to the bottom row where everyone else is lacing up. How did I not know it was family skate day?

Groaning, I drop my head back. "You're all sweaty and smell like balls that haven't been washed in weeks."

He laughs, setting me down beside Sophia, who already has one of her skates on. "Isn't my smell your favorite?"

"Only when you use that aftershave. Not when you smell like—"

"Your adorable husband who has been skating his ass off all morning?" He winks, getting on his knees in front of me. "I gotta teach you how to skate before I teach the baby."

I smooth a hand over my stomach. "Whatever we're having, better be nice to my body when they come out."

Sophia rolls her eyes. "If I hear you complain one more time about what you look like now compared to before, I'll flick you."

"She's sexy all the time. I couldn't care less what you look like as long as you're mine." He smiles, slipping off my shoe.

A few of the guys *aww* behind him, hands on their hearts. I flip them all off and narrow my eyes at Scotty. "I will walk out of this arena if you continue with this sappy crap — stopping to pee before I do, though." I groan. "I always have to pee."

He chuckles softly, taking a men's skate from under the bench and helping me put my foot in. I can't help but notice mine don't look at all like the cute dainty ones Sophia's wearing as she walks to the ice.

"Why do I have boy skates?" I ask Scotty as he tightens the laces on the skate.

A smirk grows on his beautiful face, and he looks up at me, tugging the laces. "Better for your ankles."

I puff out my bottom lip as he takes off my other shoe. "Big boy cares about little ole me?"

He kisses my knee. "I've cared about you for a while, sweetheart. Not my fault you were too stubborn to notice."

Scowling, I fix my shirt around my stomach again. "Don't call me sweetheart." Getting to his feet, he helps me to a standing position and I shriek, putting my arms out. "This is ridiculous. What are these fucking things?"

Frannie laughs, walking past us with skates on. "There's nothing to it, Alora. If I can do it, so can you."

"See," Scotty says, pointing a thumb at her.

"I've seen you run in eight-inch stilettos, doc. You can walk in skates," Corey yells, laughing as I try to balance on these things.

I grumble, fixing my shirt again because I feel like my stomach is hanging out, which it probably isn't, but I'm not used to having an enormous belly like this.

Scotty kisses my knuckles and guides me to the opening. "You can do it, baby."

Corey's stretching, taking it as easy as he can, but the position he's in looks like he's humping the floor. I let out a laugh, scrunching my nose. "What is he doing?"

"Stretching out his groin," Scotty says, stepping onto the ice. "The groin frog stretch."

"That's the position you use while doing doggy, isn't it?" I stick my tongue between my teeth. "Y'know, when I'm lying on my stomach and you just have at it."

Gregory laughs loudly, poking Corey's padded butt. "Apparently, that's the position Scotty does. You better stop before they end up fucking on the ice."

Corey groans, sitting back on his ass and stretching his legs out in front of him. "Great, now I'm envisioning them having sex." He looks back at me. "Thanks for that, Alora."

"Oh, you're welcome. I always aim to please, plus we've already filmed each other fucking six times. I think we're due for a live audience." Shimmying my shoulder, I scrunch my nose as Corey groans, dropping his head back in annoyance.

"A live audience *again*, you mean? They've caught us twice before," Scotty adds, laughing softly as Frannie skates by him and punches him in the arm.

A giggle leaves me, but as soon as I meet Scotty's eyes, the realization that I'm about to skate washes over me. There isn't a reason as to why I never learned to skate other than I've always been scared of getting injured. My mom didn't know how to skate, and let's face it, if there wasn't a bottle in front of her, she wasn't leaving the house. And my father didn't have the time.

Shit, I don't even know how to ride a bike.

When Annie started dating Kelvin, he taught her how to skate almost immediately. I always made fun of her for it, too. We used to laugh when we were kids as we watched couples skating on the rink at Rockefeller Center, saying it was corny. Anything to do with couples I was against. Now look at me, married to a hockey player and pregnant with his baby—and I'm about to get on the ice. Oh, have things ever changed?

Swallowing the lump in my throat, I look at Sophia and a few of the other girlfriends and wives skating around the ice. Even some kids are out and about. Clara smiles her toothless grin at me, skating so flawlessly as Gregory hands her a hockey stick.

Scotty turns my chin to face him. "Do you trust me?"

"Loaded question, shithead," I tease, exhaling a breath.

He tilts his head. "Seriously, baby. Do you trust me?"

"Of course, I trust you. We wouldn't be where we are if I didn't," I say, arching an eyebrow when he sticks his tongue out and lifts me onto the ice. "Oh, my God, Scotty!"

My heart is in my throat, my entire being shaking at the thought of falling and harming my child. But Scotty stands behind me, hands on my hips. "I got you, baby."

He leaves a kiss on my neck and guides us around the ice. I'm squeezing his wrists until my knuckles turn white, but he doesn't tell me to stop. We round the corner, gliding through the ice. He lets go of me and starts skating backward, leaving me for a fraction of a second without his support.

"Scotty," I gasp, panicked.

He takes my hands with a laugh, looking behind him as we turn past the net. "You're good, you're good. Now bend your knees and push off the ice."

"I'm not doing anything of the sort. I'll stand like a statue and you can pull me wherever you want us to go." Looking down at the ice marks from their skates decorating the ice, I gulp. "This is fucking terrifying."

"So when our baby gets on skates, you're just going to watch us from the stands?" He looks behind him as Corey helps his wife on the ice and takes their son from her arms. "Tsk, tsk, tsk. You gotta be a decent skater by the time the baby's in skates."

"You forget how stubborn I can be, Mr. Wesley." I squeeze his hands as we make another turn. I still don't understand how he's doing this backward. It's ridiculous.

He twists his hips again, turning us to the center of the rink. "And you seem to forget how persistent I can be, Mrs. Wesley."

"Shut up."

He does a sharp turn and spins me, pulling my back against his front. "Tell me, baby. How much do you love me?" His arms wrap around my waist and I grip them immediately.

"I swear, I will kill you if I fall."

He kisses my cheek. "I'd never let you fall. And if you fall around me, you know you'd have my body to cushion your fall."

I snort, bending my knees slightly as we make the letter S around other people. "You're harder than concrete, Scotty. I'd be better off falling on ice than your muscled body."

He spins us slightly and stops in the middle of the rink. "You didn't answer my question."

Groaning, dropping my head back onto his padded shoulder. "No, I hate your sexy face."

He laughs, biting my neck. "Tell me you love me."

Holding onto him in a death grip, I turn to face him. "I love you, Scotty. You crazy man."

He captures my lips, smiling against them. "Now remember how much I also love you, and how much you mean to me, and how you're the air I breathe, and all that sappy crap you hate because I have something to tell you."

My brain always goes to the negative and unfortunately, it immediately goes to something he did to ruin us. Because even though my views on relationships and love have started to change, there will always be that voice at the back of my head saying this won't last.

Tears well in my eyes, and my face drops, releasing him. "What did you do?"

He takes in the redness of my face, fear licking up my spine that my happiest moment is over. "What? No, no, no. Whatever you're thinking, rethink it. You're my one and only, I swear it. Okay?" He cradles my head, wiping his thumbs under my eyes. "I love you to death, Alora. I would never jeopardize this." He kisses my lips, but I don't kiss back until he spits out what the hell he's talking about. "I have a surprise for you. It's something that will make you smile and erase the overthinking you're doing."

Tendrils of relief sweep through me, releasing a shallow breath as I rest my head on his chest. "Fuck you."

His deep laugh fills me with even more calm than I thought I needed. I don't know what I would do if Scotty weren't a loyal and caring man. "I'd never leave you, baby. You're stuck with me." He lifts his neck, turning it to the side to show the tattoo he got two months ago. A red rose with *Alora* underneath it. I nearly smacked him when I came home from class one day and saw him with a bandage on his neck. But holy crap, is that not the most romantic thing I've ever seen?

"You're inked into my skin. My Alora forever." His hands meet my hips and he glances behind me before meeting my gaze. "Can I show you my surprise?"

I smirk, sniffling. "The last time you said that, we got caught in the locker room."

A growl rumbles through him, kissing the tip of my nose. "Don't make me carry you back there."

Biting my lower lip, I waggle my eyebrows. "It would be kinda kinky with these skates on."

Another growl seeps from his lips, bringing the memory of the last time we fooled around in the locker room to the surface. He just finished practice and pulled me to the locker room with him, hoisting me up against the side of the lockers and ramming me no matter who walked in—until the entire team did, laughing about it. Sex with Scotty is always intense and beautiful. We may fuck, but it's so much deeper than that. Our souls united, intertwining from the moment we met. I was just too much of an idiot to notice.

He licks up the side of my neck and nibbles on my chin. "Fuck, you're killing me."

"Surprise!" Everyone around us screams, making me jump and slip, nearly falling, but Scotty has me. He'll always have me. And as scary as that is, it's the only reassurance I need.

I look around at everyone holding pink and blue balloons, a banner dropping against the glass that reads: *Boy or Girl?*

Scotty's lips meet my forehead, making tears blur my vision. "I know you said you didn't want to know the gender of the baby—and if you did, we'd do it just us. And you also said you didn't want a baby shower because they're tacky, but you deserve the world. So I set this up."

Meeting those green eyes, I shake my head with a teary-eyed smile. Selfless and thoughtless, as always. I didn't want him to make a big deal about this. Christ, we don't even live together yet. We spend one week at his condo, then another at mine. I didn't want a baby shower because then our relationship would grow even quicker than it has. I'm still terrified about everything. Still getting used to the flow of things. I know I'm pregnant—I can't even tie my shoes anymore—but having a baby shower and building a crib makes things…permanent.

I have no choice but to be ready for it, but I don't know that I'm mentally prepared yet. Thus, the no baby shower.

Yet as I look around at all our friends smiling, I realize it's okay to be happy and do things that other people do. I don't have to live by any stupid rules my father bestowed on me as a teenager. I make my own damn rules.

"We don't even know what we're having yet," I say, smiling as Leila waves from the stands with more balloons and gift bags surrounding her. My father salutes me from behind the glass.

Scotty jerks his head at Corey, who skates over and purposely sprays ice at me. "I had Corey call the doctor and ask."

Corey tosses a puck in the air with a smirk. "And right in here, doc, is the answer to a question we're all dying to know. You just have to let your hubby go for a sec so he can whack this at the net."

Taking the puck from his hands, I shake it. "What's inside it?"

"Blue or pink powder," Scotty replies, waggling his eyebrows, then tilting my chin up. "Get mad at me all you want. I want this to be perfect."

The little fighter in me wants to shake him, but this is truly a thoughtful surprise. No wonder everyone was insisting I come to this practice.

Releasing a deep breath, I meet Scotty's eyes again. That little voice is rising, telling me to run for the hills. But there goes my heart, settling that stubborn bitch down. "Do you want to wait or find out what we're having?"

Scotty captures my lips. "I have the patience of a God, and you're an indecisive little shit—"

"Hey!"

He chuckles, turning me and skating us to the net. "I wanna do this."

If he does, then I do, too. We're a unit now and I'm learning to grow as a couple. I'll always be an independent woman, but I have the most adoring man cheering me on as I grow on my own as well.

I smile, scrunching my nose in agreement and he spins me to Corey, making me yelp and grip onto Corey's jersey. "Don't do that, shithead!"

Scotty's deep laugh echoes through the arena and he takes the puck from me, skating to the bench for a stick. Corey takes my hand with another on my hip, helping me move closer to Scotty as he places the puck on the ice.

Annie isn't on the ice, but she's behind the glass with her phone recording. Sophia and Clara have smiles on their faces, taking pictures of us. My father is recording, too, smiling from ear to ear. Frannie is squealing softly, standing by Scotty. So many smiling faces over a relationship I kept trying to push away.

And now—even on my doubtful days—I can't see my life any other way.

Corey places both hands on my hips. "You've made him a very happy man, doc. Don't think I've ever seen him so alive before."

I nudge him and grin as Scotty moves the puck slightly. "Don't get all mushy on me."

Corey snickers, winking at his wife who's sitting on the ice with their on son her lap. "It's just so easy to tease you about this mushy-gushy stuff."

"Shut up."

Scotty whistles, nodding his head at me. "Ready when you are, baby."

I nod, biting my bottom lip, and he doesn't wait. He winds up and slaps the puck toward the net, exploding blue powder everywhere. My heart leaps from my chest, exploding just like the puck did.

We're having a baby boy!

Scotty's face lights up, arms shooting in the air as if he just scored a winning goal.

Corey whistles loudly and hugs me from behind.

"It's a boy!" Frannie cheers, jumping up and down.

Scotty boots it toward us and lifts me with a spin, kissing my face repeatedly.

I cradle his smooth face in my hands, pressing our foreheads together as I wrap my legs around his waist. "We're having a boy."

"I love you," he says, blinking tears back.

Smoothing out his cheeks, that dimple makes my smile grow. We've come a long way—shit, I've come a long way from the whore people labeled me as.

I once believed love was a construct.

Now, I believe my love story just hadn't found me until that night when a green-eyed hockey player smiled at me from across a bar.

Character art by Alyssa Milani

Character art by Alyssa Milani

Character art by Alyssa Milani

Character art by Alyssa Milani

Character art by Paige Moreland (@LPM_DRAWS)

ABOUT THE AUTHOR

I'm an award-winning Canadian mom of two who studied at
Concordia University obtaining a Major in Creative Writing and a
Minor in English Literature. I independently published my first novel
in 2014 of all the works that I wrote during my years at university. I
now have twenty-five independently published novels under my belt,
many of which are award-winners.
For more information on upcoming releases and events, follow me
on Instagram: @alyssamilani

Other Works By Alyssa Milani

- What Is and What Once Was (an anthology)

- Lylie

- A Truth Be Told

- Arcane

- The Decision (novella)

- Jayme

- Asylum Of Diction (an anthology)

- Dire Road

- Him & I (parts 1 – 3)

- Was This The End? (A.M. Pickford)

- Labeled: Miss Popular

- Breaking Through To You

- Horrorscope Volume 4 (anthology) (short story contribution)

- Tell Me You Do (novella)

- The Stowaway Series (Books 1-3)

- As Far As We Knew (novella)

- Meeting You

- Until Adeligh

- Strangest Fiction Vol. 2 (anthology) (short story contribution)

- Deception

- Seeking Me Through You

www.ingramcontent.com/pod-product-compliance
Lightning Source LLC
Chambersburg PA
CBHW070438170726
48291CB00002B/561